CW01513236

O, Deadly

Night

Also by Vicki Delany

O, Deadly Night

Night

A YEAR-ROUND CHRISTMAS MYSTERY

Vicki Delany

NEW YORK

Published in the United States by Crooked Lane Books, an imprint of The Quick Brown Fox & Company LLC.

Crooked Lane Books and its logo are trademarks of The Quick Brown Fox & Company LLC.

Library of Congress Catalog-in-Publication data available upon request.

ISBN (hardcover): 979-8-89242-187-4
ISBN (ebook): 979-8-89242-188-1

Cover design by Elsa Kerls

Printed in the United States.

www.crookedlanebooks.com

Crooked Lane Books
34 West 27th St., 10th Floor
New York, NY 10001

First Edition: October 2025

10 9 8 7 6 5 4 3 2 1

To Gail Cargo, my mom.
One hundred years strong.

Chapter One

Is there anything in this world more guaranteed to bring joy to the hearts of both children and adults than a Santa Claus parade?

Waking up early Christmas morning and slipping downstairs in the dark to see a lit and fully decorated tree, stacks of brightly wrapped packages underneath, is a strong contender. But I still maintain that the parade is the top of the list, provided the day is cool and crisp, but not too cold, and a light snow, not too much to impede traffic or visibility, is falling; certainly no icy rain, as can sometimes happen in Upstate New York in early December.

This year, the weather was as perfect as though it had been organized by Santa Claus himself. Thinking of Santa, I took a quick look around the parade assembly grounds. There he was, Old Saint Nick himself, dressed in his full uniform of red jacket with white trim and wide white belt, red pants, white cuffs and upturned hem, wide black belt, jaunty red hat with a white pom-pom bouncing gaily at the end. All-white beard, mass of curly white hair, glasses, rosy-red cheeks, sparkling blue eyes.

My father, Noel Wilkinson. I know Dad isn't Santa Claus, but sometimes I do wonder. Particularly on a day like today, as I watched him climb onto the Santa's castle float and make his way past the smiling elves to take his place on the high throne. He saw me watching and gave me a wave.

Santa's head toymaker, in position next to the throne, also waved at me. In contrast to his parade appearance, Alan Anderson was not in his nineties, and he didn't normally have bushy sideburns and an enormous gray mustache spreading out from his cheeks as though he were about to use them to take flight. He wore a wool topcoat, green breeches over green stockings, and black shoes with shiny gold buckles. He carried a feather-topped pen and a long paper scroll, on which he would write down children's gift wishes.

"Listen up, everyone!" the parade marshal bellowed into his megaphone. "Time to get this show on the road. We move in five minutes, be ready. No stragglers."

A member of the band from Rudolph High blew a note on her trumpet. Costumed children giggled nervously in excitement and anticipation. A few of the costumed adults giggled also. It's always difficult to tell who's more excited: the children or their parents.

"Are we ready, George?" I asked. George Mann would be pulling my flatbed with the help of his World War II–era tractor, as he did every year.

"She's not here." He peered intently into the crowd. "She said she'd be here. She knows what time we start."

"Perhaps something unexpected came up. We can't wait. I refuse to be disqualified, *again*."

"We'll have to go when they get underway," he said. "She was so looking forward to it. Let me try and call her.

She might be on her way and forgot downtown streets are closed to traffic." He pushed a few buttons, and I didn't need to see the expression on the craggy, windblown, permanently tanned face to know he got voice mail. "No answer. Okay, Merry. Let's go." He climbed into the seat of his tractor, and I ran around to the back of the float to check everything and everyone was in place.

The theme of Mrs. Claus's Treasures float this year was The Elves' Workshop. Not terribly original, and I'd done something like that before, but it was getting increasingly difficult to come up with a new idea. My boyfriend, Alan Anderson, aka Santa's head toymaker, had outfitted the flatbed with a high wooden table, which he covered with various pieces of discarded woodworking equipment and hunks of wood that hadn't made the final cut in his woodworking business. Semiconstructed toys, rejects from his own exacting standards, were on the benches as though in the process of being assembled. I wore my regular Mrs. Claus costume of mobcap with attached curly gray wig, fake spectacles, floor-length dress over substantial padding, and gingham apron.

My landlady, Mabel D'Angelo, was supposed to be helping me, and it was she who had failed to put in an appearance. She'd been pleased and excited when I asked her to be the elves' foreman today and had consulted in great deal with me about her costume.

I needed another adult on my float to help supervise the kids who made up my elves, caps bobbing with enthusiasm, winter coats peeking out from under homemade green and turquoise tunics, as they banged away with toy hammers on old pieces of wood. I'd borrowed children from my friend Vicky's vast collection of relatives to be my elves. They stood at the bench now, bubbling with excitement, hammers in hand, and looked mighty cute.

"Ready to go, kids?" I asked.

"Ready!" they shouted with such enthusiasm the pom-poms on their hats shook. A girl clapped her hands. My dog, Matterhorn, sat at her feet, a matching turquoise ribbon tied around his neck. Even Mattie looked excited, although it could be hard to tell sometimes.

I was in need of another adult because this year my mother, Aline Steiner, decided at the last minute she'd have a float of her own rather than ride on mine as she'd always done before. Her float was done up like an opera stage, which would promote her vocal classes.

Needless to say, Mom's float looked more like what one might find in one of the great opera houses of Europe than a small-town Santa Claus parade. Mom had been a soloist with the Metropolitan Opera for many years, and she'd sung at many of those great opera houses. She was not, shall we say, inclined to cut corners when it came to appearances. Unfortunately, Mom having her own float meant I didn't get the time and attention I needed from Dad and Alan to get mine ready. I had little, as in no, hope of winning the best-of-parade trophy this year.

Her float would follow mine, with some of her littlest students seated on the flatbed next to her, while the older children, as well as several adults up to and including retirement age, marched behind singing carols. The parades (plural: in the town of Rudolph, we also have one in July) were the highlights of the season for Mom's highly-sought-after singing classes.

The float in front of mine was from Victoria's Bake Shoppe. This year Vicky Casey was featuring The Elves' Christmas Eve Party. From what I could see, their festivities involved a lot of eating. Some of the helpers carried trays of tiny gingerbread cookies to hand out along the route. I suspected Vicky would have hot chocolate, maybe laced with something to "keep the chill away," and full-sized cookies for the panel of esteemed judges. Vicky usually won the best-in-parade trophy every year. Twice.

My sister, Eve, ran through the crowd, waving at me. She was supposed to walk in front of Santa's float, handing out candy canes, and looked lovely in a knee-length black cape lined with fake white fur and a matching hat borrowed from our mother. Her black boots with sky-high heels were more suitable for clubbing with celebrities in LA than marching in a parade, but to Eve, appearances were everything. She was a struggling actress trying to make it in Hollywood, home for the holidays as she had "a temporary gap in her calendar."

She grabbed the back of my flatbed, and I reached out my hand to give her a good yank up. "Got a text from Dad, who got a text from George. Your helper hasn't shown up, so I've been volunteered. You can't manage all these kids as well as that dog on your own."

"What about candy cane duty?"

She held out her basket. "Want one?"

Horns tooted, trumpets trumpeted, kids cheered, adults cheered, my mom sounded a note, her children broke into an enthusiastic round of "We Wish you a Merry Christmas," and the annual holiday season Rudolph, New York, Santa Claus parade began.

Without the participation of Mabel D'Angelo.

Chapter Two

"D id you see Mrs. D'Angelo earlier?" I asked Wendy as children were being helped off floats, tools and instruments packed away, and flatbeds towed to their resting places until they'd be needed again seven months from now.

"You mean today?" Wendy said. "No, I didn't. I know she was super excited about being on your float." Wendy and her husband, Steve, and their daughter, Tina, were my neighbors in the second-floor apartments we rented in Mrs. D'Angelo's once-grand and still-huge Victorian house.

"She didn't show," I said.

"Was that a problem?"

"Not really. We had no emergencies such as kids getting sick and throwing up all over Mattie in their excitement or trying to jump off the float when they saw a friend. So I managed with the help of my sister, Eve."

"The actress? I heard she's in town. I'd love to talk to her about all the famous people she's met."

"Famous people she's seen across a set or leaving a restaurant, most likely."

"Now, now, Merry. Don't be catty."

"Was I? I didn't mean to." And I hadn't. Eve kept up a brave front when she talked about her career, and she was eternally optimistic (probably a requirement in that business), but she couldn't help occasionally let it slip that things were not progressing as she'd so desperately hoped. She was thirty now, getting late to make it as a woman in Hollywood.

"There's no more difficult career to take on than being an actress," Wendy reminded me. "As for today, wasn't Jackie available to be with you?" Wendy was referring to my shop assistant, Jackie O'Reilly.

"Jackie, the traitor, apologized profusely and falsely. She said she didn't realize I'd need her, as I have every year since I opened the store, and she volunteered to be on the *Gazette* float. I got a glimpse of her in her elf costume, and I'm pretty sure she's hoping to be the front-page picture in the paper tomorrow. I'm also pretty sure the real Santa wouldn't want his elves showing that much cleavage at work, but never mind." My other assistant, Melissa, had been needed on her father's fire department float.

Finding help on Santa Claus parade day can be a heck of a challenge in a town where everyone is involved in one way or another.

"Mrs. D'Angelo could get distracted by a squirrel," Wendy said. That, I knew, was true enough. "Have you tried calling her?"

"I didn't want to once the parade started. George is doing that now."

At that moment, the old farmer came around the flat-bed, holding his phone. "I finally got her. She's hoping to make it to the after-party if you still need her."

Mattie sat quietly by my side, exhausted from the excitement of being admired by people all along the parade route. I tucked my plain glass spectacles into my apron pocket, pulled off my cap, and gave the top of my head a good rub. That cap itched. "I don't need her, as I have no specific duties at the party, but if she wants to come in costume, that's fine."

No duties other than to put my cap and glasses back on and make friendly as Mrs. Claus. The town always sponsored a children's party in the community center after the parade. Santa would greet children while his head toymaker recorded their requests. The staff at Vicky's bakery had been frantically busy over the past week, preparing all sorts of lovely little holiday baked goods to be on offer along with hot chocolate and warm apple juice for the kids and mulled cider for the older partygoers.

The best-in-parade winner would be announced at the party. No doubt Vicky would make sure the judges had full mugs of spiked cider as they made their deliberations.

"Did she say what happened to cause her to miss the parade?" I asked George.

"New neighbors moved in across the street. Highly inconvenient of them to come today of all days, she says. Their truck pulled up just as Mabel was about to leave the house. They didn't have much in the way of goods, so she thinks they're finished now, and she can come down. Did you happen to hear a lot of phones going off as the parade was happening, Merry?"

"I couldn't hear anything, but I did see people checking their screens, yes. Both parade participants and those watching from the sidelines."

Wendy, George, and I exchanged exasperated looks. Mabel D'Angelo is the gossip queen of Rudolph. She lurks at the heart of a vast web spread throughout our town and beyond. Little happens in Rudolph or environs Mrs. D'Angelo doesn't know about. If she doesn't witness the event herself, one of her network of contacts does. And if they don't—then she makes it up.

Yup, new people on our street meant phone lines in Rudolph were as busy as at FBI headquarters. I sometimes thought Mrs. D'Angelo should be put on the payroll at the FBI or CIA. Except, of course, for her tendency to exaggerate in order to make her information sound more important than it was.

"One crisis averted," Wendy said. "I'd better find Steve and make sure he hasn't let Tina overdose on parade candy." As an employee of the town, Wendy walked the parade route handing out candy canes.

"Too late!" I called after her. "Come on, Mattie. I'll take you to the store for a while. Party time is not for you."

* * *

"It seems to be a single man, Merry," Mrs. D'Angelo said to me. "Most unusual on our street, I'm sure you'll agree. He didn't have many possessions, hardly any furniture—just one bed, a couple of chairs, a small table, and a lot of boxes. He didn't have a moving company, just a rental truck and one man, a friend likely, to help lift the heavier things."

"Two men," I said. "Maybe they'll live there together."

She ignored that point. "A single man, living in a house that size. And so little furniture? I don't know what to make of it."

"Make nothing of it," I said. "Maybe he moved from another country, didn't bring many possessions, and is starting over. Maybe he doesn't need much. Maybe his family is still to follow. If he doesn't have a family, that doesn't mean anything either. Plenty of single men live in houses. Even big ones. Like Alan." Alan has a rambling old stone farmhouse in the woods about ten miles outside of town. Not only does he need a big place for his woodworking shop and storage areas, but he forages on his own property for treefall and follows the county's maintenance trucks as they tidy up the woods and clear growth near the roads. Along with toys and home decor items, even hugely popular necklaces and earrings made of concentric wooden rings, much of which I stock in my own shop, he makes beautiful handcrafted furniture that sells well all over Upstate New York.

"Alan Anderson's different," she said. "He's a Rudolphite, through and through."

"Did I hear my name?" Alan put his arm around my shoulders. "Hi, Mrs. D. Did you enjoy the parade?"

"Unfortunately, I was delayed. I wasn't able to get away until the party started. Something of perhaps vital importance to the town came up."

George Mann joined our group. "Mabel. At last. Did you run into a problem earlier?"

"Duty, George, duty."

He smiled at her. "Don't let your duty to the town take the place of enjoying yourself."

She giggled, putting me in mind of a high school girl when the captain of the football team happened to look her way.

George turned to Alan and me, and his face became serious. "I had a call just now from my friend Bob. Bob Gravel. Lives in New York City now, although he's an old Rudolph boy."

"Gravel. Robert." Mrs. D'Angelo flipped quickly through her memory banks. "Don't know that name."

"He moved to the Big Apple," George explained. "Must be forty or more years ago now. Him and his wife, uh . . . sorry, forgot her name. Anyway, she died recently."

"I'm sorry to hear that," Alan said.

"Yeah. He took it hard. I hadn't heard from him in donkey's years, but notice of his wife's passing was posted in the *Gazette*, so I gave him a call. Like I said, they didn't have any children and he had a hard time dealing with her death, but he's starting to come back."

"Back?" Mrs. D'Angelo asked. "He's moving back to Rudolph? Can't be him I saw this morning. Those were younger men."

"Don't know about him moving," George said. "I meant back to himself. Starting to get interested in life again . . ." His voice trailed off.

"But?" Alan prompted.

"He's met a lady."

"Isn't that good?" I asked.

"I don't know. I'm telling you this, Merry, because I don't know how to handle it. Don't know if I should handle it. You see, he met her online. They talk on FaceTime and send texts. He's never actually met this woman in person. She says she lives in Kansas City."

"'Says she lives.' You don't think that's true?"

"She asked him for money so she can come and visit him in New York."

I raised my right hand high in the air. "Red flag!"

"Merry's right," Alan said. "If she can't afford the trip, why doesn't he go to Kansas City?"

"He says she's never been to New York and has always wanted to see it."

"I assume you're telling us because you're worried about your friend," Alan said.

"Yeah. I am. He's not short of funds—he did well in his life—but . . . I wouldn't want to see him cheated."

"Hard thing to deal with," I said. "Have you told him about your concerns?"

"I tried to. He laughed it off and said I was jealous. He offered to ask his new girlfriend to find one for me."

"I hope you said no!" Mrs. D'Angelo said. "What's the world coming to when people think they have a relationship with someone they've never even been in the same room as? The idea's preposterous. I notice not many cookies are left. I haven't had any yet." She grabbed George's arm and dragged him away.

Alan and I exchanged looks, and then we both laughed. Mrs. D'Angelo would ensure George didn't stray into an online scam. I felt sorry for his friend, though.

The post-parade party was winding down. Exhausted, overstimulated, oversugared children were being gathered up and stuffed into winter coats; townspeople heading off to get ready for another busy holiday week; catering staff cleaning up the few leftovers and packing away dishes.

My mom and her classes had sung a couple of carols to get the party started, and then Mom slipped away. Dad was still *ho-ho-ho*-ing to the last of the children and a few teen-agers who pretended to still believe, but Alan had folded up his scroll, tucked away his pen, and peeled off his mustache and sideburns with a sigh of relief.

The restaurants and bars in town would be packed tonight, so we decided to order pizza and watch a movie at my place. Vicky Casey, despite being my bitter rival for the best-in-parade trophy, and her husband, Mark Grosse, were going to join us.

Victoria's Bake Shoppe's float was, to absolutely no one's surprise, announced as the winner of the trophy. Blushing and giggling and telling everyone how shocked and delighted she was, Vicky accepted the big statue. Which would now be returned to its regular place at the top shelf of the bakery, where it would remain for another year.

I tried not to be too bitter about that. It was, truth be told, a good float. Mark, head chef at the best restaurant in town, had gone all out to help Vicky put it together, and he'd dressed in his chef's whites, making a show of serv-ing the holiday meal to the preteen children of her staff, who played the elves. The kids themselves had a blast, dressed in their fathers' old suits or mothers' cocktail dresses, pretending to be drinking wine and engaging in fine dining as they waved to their proud, beaming parents and grandparents.

"I'll check if Vicky needs a hand cleaning up," I said to Alan. "Then I have to pop into the shop for Mattie."

"See you in about an hour," he said. He was going home first to get out of his toymaker getup and to collect Ranger, his Jack Russell terrier, who, if left at home overnight, would tear the softer parts of the furniture to shreds. As well as put a few bite marks into the harder parts of the furniture.

I went into the community center kitchen, where I found everything, as expected, under control. Vicky was packing mugs into a plastic tub. I tried not to look at the trophy sitting on the counter, ready to be transported to the bakery.

"You win again," I said.

Vicky turned to me with an enormous grin. "Yet another triumph. And I mean more than my gingerbread. Help yourself."

I already had, and I was biting the head off a lady cookie. Vicky's gingerbread is a Rudolph tradition and justifiably famous throughout New York State and beyond. "Do you need any help here?"

"No, thanks. We're almost finished."

"I can take all this back to the bakery," Mark said. "And then go to the house, if you want to go straight to Merry's. One of us has to check on Sandbanks; no point in us both doing it." Sandbanks was their geriatric golden Lab.

"Good idea," Vicky said. "Merry and I are long overdue for a solid girlfriends gossip session before you and Alan show up and ruin it."

"I hate to think," Mark said.

Vicky wrapped me in a spontaneous hug. "I love parade day!"

I hugged her back and said, "So do I." Vicky and I have been best friends since the first day of school. I'd been shy, timid, terrified of the new environment in which I found myself. Vicky'd been confident, brave, excited about the new environment in which she found herself.

I can still be timid, although I hope I'm no longer shy, and Vicky is still confident and brave. And, always, fun to be with and a fiercely loyal friend.

Except when it came to the Santa Claus parade trophy. Which I'd forget about until time to get ready for the next event in July.

"I had a peek over my shoulder a couple of times to check on you," Vicky said. "I can't believe that tractor of George's keeps chugging along. It'll outlive us all. I thought Mrs. D'Angelo was going to be on your float? I didn't see her."

"New neighbors moved in, and she had to be at her post." I snapped to attention and saluted sharply.

Vicky laughed. "Poor things. They have no idea what they're in for. I could have leant you Aunt Marjorie if you needed help."

"Eve came with me, and we were fine. If you're ready, then, let's go."

Chapter Three

The main shopping street of our town was renamed Jingle Bell Lane when Dad and the town council hit on the Christmas Town idea. Past the bandstand and the town's lakeside park, it returns to its original boring name of Broad Street.

In the spring and summer, our house has the most beautifully maintained front garden on Broad Street. In the autumn, every leaf is raked up moments after it decides to fall; in the winter, the sidewalk is shoveled before the town can even get to it, the front path scraped down to the cement, and a thick layer of deicer applied. Over the holiday season hundreds, maybe thousands, of tiny colored lights illuminate the bushes and lower branches of the trees.

Not necessarily because Mrs. D'Angelo is all that house proud but because she's always outside, watching the activity on the street. Ever-present cell phone in its sparkly pink case clipped to her belt, earbuds firmly in her ears. Most of the year, she spends her non-gardening/raking/shoveling time sitting on her wide front porch. She keeps a pair of high-quality binoculars on the small table by the door, ready to spring into action at all times. In the coldest days of winter, even she can't sit out for too long, so she lurks at her living room window, watching for passersby.

Today, the front door was open and Mrs. D'Angelo on the porch before Vicky, Mattie, and I so much as turned into the driveway. Holiday lights were on, as were the lamps above the porch and over the front door. "Merry Wilkinson! And Vicky Casey, how nice! Do you have time for tea?"

"No," I called back. "Sorry, we don't. Alan and Mark will be here soon."

"You don't need to stay for long. Tea's ready." She held a dog biscuit in one hand and waved it in the air. "Mattie. Here, Mattie."

Matterhorn is a Saint Bernard. One hundred and seventy pounds of slow, lumbering canine with a mind of his own. He's well trained, as a dog of that size has to be if we're to have a happy relationship, but sometimes he forgets that. Such as when a dog biscuit appears out of nowhere.

He took off across the snowy lawn, dragging me behind, and loped up the steps. I stumbled up after him, barely able to keep myself erect.

Mrs. D'Angelo gave me a self-satisfied smile and Mattie the biscuit. "How nice. You and Vicky take seats, dear, and I'll get the tea. I have a fresh batch of my special molasses spice cookies ready, and I know how much you like them. I'll be right out." She bustled off.

"About the last thing I need right now is a cookie," I said. "Another cookie."

"We're here now," my friend said, and we sat down at the small round table. Dry cushions were on the chairs and thick fluffy blankets placed over the backs in case we got cold. Mrs. D'Angelo knew to be prepared.

The house was a grand old Victorian, all wraparound porch, gingerbread trim, turrets, and dormer windows, as were many of the houses on this street not far from the center of town. In its heyday, Rudolph had been an important Great Lakes shipping port, and shipowners and businessmen built impressive houses on substantial lots for their large families and numerous servants. In the years of the town's decline, many of those houses had been torn down, converted to offices or divided, like ours, into apartments. Now the town was prosperous again. Largely through the vision and leadership of my father, Rudolph had been revitalized by taking advantage of the town's name and marketing itself as "Your Year-Round Christmas Destination."

I tugged a blanket free and put it across my lap. The daytime temperature had been perfect for the parade at just under the freezing point, keeping the snow clean and fresh and parade-goers from freezing along with it. But it was dropping rapidly now the sun had gone down and the wind come up. Up and down the street, colorful lights broke the gloom of the early winter night.

"We'll stay a couple of minutes to be polite," I said to Vicky, "and then we have to go. Never mind the boys, it's cold."

"Have you ever been inside this house?" She kept her voice low.

"Once or twice. Let's just say she spends more time on the yard than the interior. I don't think the furniture or the appliances have been updated since Mr. D'Angelo was around. And that was long before my time."

Mrs. D'Angelo came out, carrying a tray containing a jug full of ice, three glasses, a plate of homemade cookies, and another dog biscuit. "I hope you girls don't mind having iced tea. I made it nice and sweet to keep the chill off."

I shuddered at the thought of the icy liquid running down my throat.

"I love a nice glass of iced tea on a cold day while sitting outside being cold," Vicky said.

Mrs. D'Angelo put the tray down, took a seat, handed Mattie the dog treat, and then poured the tea. She still wore her costume of a long brown dress under a full white apron adorned with hand-embroidered pink flowers and a lace-trimmed bonnet. "I made these cookies specially to welcome the new neighbors. I find people appreciate a nice friendly gesture such as this as an introduction to their new home. In her day, my mother would always make one of her famous tuna fish casseroles to take over, but these days people usually order pizza or go out for fast food on moving day, don't they?"

"Sometimes," I said.

"Speaking of new neighbors, Vicky dear, how are you and Chef Grosse getting on in your place?"

Vicky and Mark had married and bought a small 1970s-era house the previous spring. "We love it," she said.

That wasn't entirely true. Vicky didn't "love" the house. She and Mark bought the best place they could afford in town, close enough for Vicky to walk to work, which was important to her. The house was small and dark, nothing but a stopgap until they could afford something better. But Vicky was in love with Mark, and she loved being married to him, and they were excited about the future they were building together.

Mrs. D'Angelo smiled at her. "And how are you finding your neighbors, dear?"

"Nice." Vicky sipped her tea. She smiled back, clearly having no intention of allowing herself to be drawn into a discussion of the proclivities of her new neighbors.

"And the book? When will I be able to get my hands on a copy?"

Vicky's face fell. "We've run into some . . . glitches."

"You have not," I said. "That's how publishing works. The editor suggests a few changes. If you like her suggestions, you accept them. If you don't, you explain why you don't and go from there."

"I've done that. But she keeps insisting." Vicky threw up her hands. She hadn't taken a cookie. "I don't know why I bothered. It's all just too much work. Too much stress. Too much time. Too much . . . everything."

Over the spring and summer, Vicky had written a cookbook. I was wildly excited about it—*Holiday Recipes From America's Christmas Town*. Between Vicky's skill and reputation and the Rudolph name, the book had such promise she'd easily landed a contract with a major publisher and received a hefty advance. Now, as she and her editor worked on refining and perfecting the book, nerves and doubts were kicking in.

"You're almost there," I said. "And then all that'll be left is basking in the glory."

"And promotion. They want me to go on a book tour. I can't take time off from the bakery. Why did I think I could do this?"

"Because you can," I said. Normally my friend was the most confident of women. She worked hard; she'd made a huge success of her bakery. She loved deeply, and her husband loved her just as much in return. No one could ask for a better friend. All she needed, I knew, was the occasional word of encouragement in this new endeavor. No one who knew her doubted the book would be a huge success. (Subject to the whims of the baking and publishing worlds, but I wasn't going to think about that now.)

"I, for one, am looking forward to it," Mrs. D'Angelo said. "Please, dear, do have a cookie. I've had the recipe for decades. It was my mother's before me."

"They look good," Vicky said. "Nice color. But not right now, thank you."

"I made this batch for the new neighbors, but I didn't get a chance to go over in person and introduce myself."

"Why not?" Vicky asked.

"They seem to have left right after dropping off their things."

We all looked at the house across the street. It was, like this one, large and ornate and very Victorian, also with a wraparound porch and gable windows. It had been a rental property since the death of the owner, one Dorothy Johannesen, about ten years or so ago. Dorothy left the house to her niece, Beth Torrone. I'd known the Torrones' daughter, Raquel, in school, but not well, as she was younger than I was. As I remembered, the family moved away from Rudolph before Dorothy died. When they inherited, they hadn't wanted to come back to Rudolph or to sell the house, so they rented it out.

The previous tenants had lived there for most of the time since, until the last of their six children was off to college, and then they relocated to an apartment in New York

City. Why anyone would exchange a house and garden on Broad Street for an apartment in Manhattan was the topic of much town gossip for a long time. Turned out nothing was at all nefarious about it. The wife told Mrs. D'Angelo they loved good restaurants and musical theatre; they both had work-from-home jobs and were looking forward to no longer being responsible for teenagers' sports activities, school clubs and plays, and everything else that goes with a large, highly active family.

"If the new people only moved in earlier today," Vicky said, "isn't it natural they'd be going out for dinner? Maybe they have more stuff to bring tomorrow."

Mrs. D'Angelo leaned toward us. Instinctively, Vicky and I leaned toward her. Having had his treat, Mattie was resting on the edge of the porch, his chin on his paws, watching the traffic pass. "I see no sign of a *they*. Just two men. One man drove a car, and another followed with a small truck. They unloaded the truck, and I have to say, I didn't see many signs of normal furniture."

"Normal?" Vicky asked.

"Like a sofa and chairs. Dining room table. Instead, all they had was a few chairs and a small table. Only one bed. That and a lot of big boxes. The man who came in the truck drove away, and not long after the other one left in his car. He has not been back."

"He might have come back while you were at the party," Vicky said.

Mrs. D'Angelo pointed. "It continued snowing while I was out, yet there are no fresh tracks in the snow."

The lamp over the front door was on; otherwise, the house was wrapped in darkness. Unlike every other house on this street and in most of Rudolph, it displayed no holiday lights.

"That's not at all abnormal," I said. "Single men do live in houses. They have to live somewhere. If it is a single man. They have friends who help them move. He might not even be single; perhaps his partner and any children they have stayed behind for a while. So the kids could finish the school year."

"I didn't see a woman viewing the house, Merry. Nancy—that would be the previous tenant," she explained to Vicky, "told me they were donating most of their excess furniture to a secondhand charity shop, because it would be far too much for their new place in Manhattan. I myself saw the charity truck arrive last week and take away a great deal. Then, the next day, the moving truck came. Nancy told me they were leaving the light fittings and the rugs and drapes in the house." She sat back with a self-satisfied expression.

Despite myself, I glanced once again across the street. At that moment a man stopped to look at the house. He stood on the sidewalk, next to a huge old blue spruce laden with pine cones. I could only see him from the back, heavily wrapped in a winter coat and scarf with a hat pulled over his ears. Hard to tell it even was a man except for the six-foot height and the bulk beneath his coat. He pulled his collar up, tucked his chin down, and walked rapidly away.

"Who was that?" I asked.

"Who?" Vicky said.

"That man? He was looking at the house. Seems to have disappeared."

Vicky shrugged. She hadn't noticed anyone. "I didn't recognize him," Mrs. D'Angelo said. "All these winter clothes can be as effective as a disguise sometimes. Likely a curious neighbor—people sometimes don't know when to mind their own business."

As well as the man, I'd noticed the drapes were closed. "Does it matter that rugs and drapes were left for the new people?"

"It matters enormously, Merry. What woman would want to live in a house with someone else's choice of drapery?"

"Will you look at the time." Vicky stood up. "Thanks for the tea, Mrs. D'Angelo, but we have to be off. Mark and Alan will be here soon. The new people are taking their time moving their things in, that's all."

My landlady looked at the plate of cookies. "What am I to do with these if he doesn't come back soon?"

"You could freeze them," Vicky said.

"Yes, I suppose I could." Mrs. D'Angelo glanced at the house across the street. "I do want to be welcoming."

I called to Mattie, and Vicky and I made our escape.

"Must be a slow news day in Rudolph," Vicky said as we rounded the house, heading for the stairs to my apartment. "Talk about trying to make something out of nothing."

Chapter Four

The November/December parade marks the official start of the holiday season in Rudolph, and I had little time over the next week to worry about my new neighbor(s) or to stop and chat with Mrs. D'Angelo, much as she tried to flag me down to update me on the happenings, or lack thereof, across the street.

In the morning when I left for the store, or in the evening when I arrived home, I often saw her at her living room window, trying to conceal herself behind the curtains as she peered across the street through her binoculars. All I saw of the residents of the house under observation was tire tracks in the snow on the driveway leading from the street to the closed door of the double garage and back again. No footprints marked the driveway, lawn, or front walk, so I assumed the garage opened directly into the house.

I then chastised myself for being as bad as Mrs. D'Angelo. If the new resident(s) wanted to stay out of the cold as they came and went, it was absolutely none of my business.

Friday afternoon, I had an unexpected visitor at the store. We were in the midst of a busy day, which is always good. The holiday season was in full swing, everyone looking for that perfect gift or the perfect items to add to their own holiday decor.

Melissa was behind the counter, ringing up purchases, while Jackie helped an elderly gentleman choose a gift for his wife. Jackie might be exasperating sometimes (okay, much of the time), but as a salesclerk she couldn't be faulted. She flirted lightly with the man and ensured he knew he could take his time making this important decision. She tried on jewelry and posed for him, her eyes sparking and smile bright. Eventually he settled on a necklace and earing set, largely because Jackie told him it had been made by a local woman.

The customer I'd been helping finally decided on a table runner and matching linen napkins with a nutcracker theme, and she took her selection to the counter.

The chimes over the door tinkled, and Mabel D'Angelo came in. I couldn't recall her ever being in my store before, and today I instantly concluded she wasn't here to embark on a shopping spree. Her face was set into serious lines, and rather than admiring the goods, her eyes darted around the shop, searching for something.

They found it. Me. She spotted me and hurried over. "Merry, there you are. I need to talk to you."

"Can it wait? I'm rather busy." Two women had followed Mrs. D'Angelo in, and they had the look of serious shoppers about them. Having finally selected his wife's gift, the older man asked Jackie for recommendations for his preschool grandchildren. She steered him to our selection of toys, specifically the train set handmade by Alan Anderson.

Other customers browsed, but none of them seemed to need my attention at the moment, so I said, "Is it important? We're open late tonight, but we usually have a lull around six."

"Very important. Perhaps vitally important, Merry." Mrs. D'Angelo's eyes pleaded with me.

I gave in. "Okay. Let's go into my office, but I have to warn you, I can't stay long." I called to Jackie and Melissa to tell them I was taking a break and led the way through the curtain into the back passage.

Mattie lifted his head when he heard the office door open. He saw who I was with and lumbered to his feet, tongue lolling, dripping drool, obviously hoping she'd stopped by to bring him a dog biscuit. Instead, Mrs. D'Angelo ignored him. Which isn't easy, as my office is small and my dog is big.

"The man across the street. The new renter in the Johannesen house," she began. I mentally groaned. Not this again. She'd stopped me at least twice this week on my way home after work to ask if I'd seen the new neighbor. I had not. "He was in the house earlier," she said now. "Shortly after two, the car drove up, the garage door opened automatically, and he went in. The doors closed without him emerging. I realized this was my chance to dash over with my cookies and introduce myself."

"You didn't go before this?" I asked despite myself.

She shifted uncomfortably. "I was hoping to see him outside, shoveling the walk perhaps, or bringing in the groceries. But no. I haven't set eyes on anyone since the day he moved in. Very strange, wouldn't you agree? I wouldn't want him to think I've been spying on him, tracking his movements."

"Goodness no, you wouldn't want that."

"Today, I decided it was time. I let him settle in for about fifteen minutes, and then I carried my cookies over and rang the bell." Dramatic pause. "No one answered. Not a sound came from within. It was so quiet it was uncanny, Merry. Thinking perhaps the bell wasn't working, although if such was the case it would be unlike Nancy to not have had it fixed before moving out, I knocked. Several times. To which I got no reply."

"You keep saying he, but you haven't seen this person since the first day."

"I've seen a shape in the car, Merry. When it pulls slowly into the driveway and waits for the garage door to open. Always one person only. The driver. I can't say for sure it's a man, but this person has broad shoulders and short hair. As did the man I saw carrying boxes and furniture in on moving day. He wore a ball cap at least once. You don't suppose another person was lying on the back seat for some reason? Or," she gasped, "hiding in the trunk?"

I struggled with what to say. If this new neighbor didn't want to make friendly with Mrs. D'Angelo, that was clearly the business of no one but him. Unless he did have someone trussed up, gagged, and stuffed into the trunk, but we could probably dismiss that idea for now.

He, or she, or they, might have been warned their across-the-street neighbor was a notorious busybody and gossip. It didn't seem to have occurred to Mrs. D'Angelo there might be two men living in the house and they went out separately. "It's a double garage," I said. "Do they have two cars?"

I'd only seen the one set of car tracks, but I didn't want her to know I'd also been curious.

"Just the one. A big black SUV. The other half of the garage is piled high with boxes. He must have moved those in while I was at the parade after-party, as I didn't see them arrive."

"Maybe he works shifts," I said. "And thus he comes and goes at different hours than the rest of us." He might also be a vampire, moving stealthily by night, avoiding the sunlight. I didn't mention that.

"That still doesn't explain why he didn't answer the door to me, Merry. I didn't give him time to go to bed."

"Have you asked any of your ... uh ... friends if they've met him?"

"I put the word out. No one knows. Which I consider to be strange in itself. Donalda—you know Donalda, of course, Merry." I didn't, but that didn't matter. Mrs. D'Angelo was acquainted with an entire underworld of people I'd never heard of. "Donalda stopped by with a casserole. No one answered the door to her either. She left it on the front porch, with a nice little handmade card welcoming them to the neighborhood. Of course, she called me the moment she got home to tell me. I was in the kitchen, making a fresh batch of cookies, when she called, and when I looked outside only moments later"— *drumroll*—"the casserole dish was gone!"

"Did Donalda go back for the dish?" I asked, again despite myself.

"Unfortunately, no. She put it in a disposable aluminum tray, and her note said not to worry about returning it. A serious oversight on her part, wouldn't you agree, Merry?"

"Mrs. D'Angelo, I don't know what you want me to do. I don't know what you can do. If this person, or persons, doesn't want to answer the door to someone they don't know, isn't that entirely up to them?"

"But, Merry, suppose something is wrong! It's the responsibility of good small-town neighbors to watch out for each other. To care for each other. Suppose there's a medical emergency at that house and no one knows about it."

"I assume they have a phone," I said.

"But I don't have the number, Merry. I don't even have a name." That wasn't what I meant, but a sudden idea occurred to Mrs. D'Angelo. "Beth and Richard Torrone should have the name of the person they rented the house to. I haven't spoken to them in years, not since they left Rudolph, but someone should still have their number. Good idea, Merry. I can start there. I do hope it's not something like John Smith."

"Great. Glad to be of help." I edged toward the door, trying to edge Mrs. D'Angelo along with me. She would not be edged. Disappointed, Mattie had gone back to sleep.

"Was there something else?" I asked.

"I did have a reason for discussing this with you, Merry. As you know, I'm not one to interfere in people's private affairs." I refrained from laughing out loud. "But I am wondering if we need to alert the police."

"The police? About what?"

"About the new neighbor. Let the police know something seems to be . . . off over there. As you are such close friends with Diane Simmonds, I thought you might be willing to take that task on." She smiled at me.

"First, I'm not friends with Detective Simmonds. I've had some contact with her in the past, but only because of . . . things that happened."

"My point precisely. You and she have a professional understanding."

"We do not."

I might as well not have spoken. "Therefore, I thought, who better to bring the matter to the authorities."

I shook my head. "I won't do that. I have no reason whatsoever to bring this person, or persons, to the attention of the police. Mrs. D'Angelo, if you want my advice, let it go. Leave them alone."

Her face pinched in disapproval. "That wouldn't be at all neighborly of me, Merry."

"It would be very neighborly, if it's what they want."

"I . . . suppose . . ."

"I can do one thing," I said. "I'll speak to my dad. If the town has any concerns, Dad will know."

"Thank you, Merry. As well as Noel, perhaps—"

"Great. I'm glad we've sorted that out." I leaned around her and opened the door. "If you have any gift shopping to get caught up on, don't forget Midnight Madness is tomorrow. We'll be open until midnight for all of your holiday shopping needs."

Chapter Five

Midnight Madness is appropriately named. People come from all over the eastern United States and parts of southern Canada to engage in an orgy of shopping in America's Christmas Town.

The night air was cold and crisp, light snow falling. Absolutely perfect. This year the weather seemed to be working in our favor. We can keep the Christmas spirit going through thunderstorms and torrential downpours if we have to, but it's never easy.

Once again, the town and the business district association had gone all out to charm our visitors (and get them to open their wallets). The annual snow sculpture contest in the town park was well underway, and visitors were invited to cast their votes for the creation they liked best. The Yuletide Inn, where Mark Grosse is head chef, provided a sleigh pulled by two high-stepping, gaily-adorned horses to ferry shoppers from one end of Jingle Bell Lane to the other, including a stop at the park. A grill outside the butcher provided hot dogs and hamburgers, the candy store served hot chocolate piled high with their homemade marshmallows, and Vicky's bakery was open and doing a roaring trade in mince tarts and gingerbread. My mother led her adult students through town singing carols, all of them dressed in Charles Dickens–era–appropriate suits or capes, long dresses, and elaborate hats, reading from paper song sheets.

Dad as Santa walked through town, followed by two high school students dressed as elves, popping in and out of shops, spreading holiday cheer everywhere he went.

I'd managed to convince Alan to wear his toymaker costume and sit on the bench outside my shop, whittling on a piece of wood. He soon came inside, complaining his hands were getting cold and his mustache was itchy. Whereupon he called Santa Claus and suggested a stop at the bar at A Touch of Holly.

"He'll meet me here first." Alan put his phone away. "He wants to talk to you."

"No time for talking," Jackie said before turning to a new customer with a welcoming smile.

"We're almost out of the train sets," I told Alan. "We had a rush on them this week. I don't suppose you can make more before Christmas Eve?"

He shook his head. Too busy over the holiday season to get his hair cut, the blond locks were starting to get into his eyes and curls touching the back of his neck. Alan was not classically handsome, but his tender smile, expressive blue eyes under long, dark lashes, and gentle laugh made him handsome to me. I'm five foot four, and Alan towers over me at a long, lean six feet. We'd been in school together, even casually dated a few times, but I hadn't known until a couple of years ago that Alan, shy, bashful Alan, had long adored me from afar. On graduation, I headed for college to take art and design and then secured a job at a national lifestyle magazine with offices in Manhattan. Alan stayed behind in Rudoph, building his woodworking business. When I came home at last, he was waiting for me.

"Sorry, Merry. You're not my only customer, you know," he said now. "The toy shop in Rochester put in a rush order for them, and I have a backlog of nutcracker solders to fill."

Jackie whipped around. "I've just had the most brilliant idea! You could hire Kyle to give you a hand, Alan. He's short of work at the moment and needing some extra cash."

The smile froze on Alan's face. Kyle Lambert was Jackie's boyfriend. Hard to think of a less promising employee.

"Sorry," Alan said quickly. "I don't have time to teach anyone the ropes, not this late in the season. I saw Kyle earlier. He's manning the grill at the butcher shop. I thought he didn't want to do that anymore."

"Yeah, that. He hasn't been getting much work at the paper lately. When the butcher offered him the job, he wasn't keen on doing it again, but I asked him, 'How many times does a grill explode anyway?' I mean, they got a new one after what happened to the last one. Right?"

"Totally," Alan said.

His dreamed-of career as an avant-garde artist having failed (due to lack of ambition, drive, and talent), Kyle now wanted to make his name and fortune as a professional photographer. He took the odd picture that he sold to the *Rudolph Gazette*: the girls' high school basketball team after a win over Muddle Harbor High; spring flowers bursting to life at the Yuletide Inn; participants in the bridge tournament at the seniors' residence. He hadn't yet captured the Pulitzer Prize–winning shot of a firefighter fleeing a burning building with a kitten nested in his protective arms, or Detective Diane Simmonds bringing down a murderer in a blaze of gunfire, which he so hoped for.

His shots of the Santa Claus parade didn't even make the cut. Instead of using his photos of Jackie in all her seductive elven glory, the paper went with a group of little singers from my mom's float clutching their sheet music, mouths open in song, eyes bright with the joy of it, fat snowflakes falling on their tiny shoulders. My mom had taken that picture with her phone and didn't charge the paper for it. Not as long as the copy mentioned the children were enrolled in her vocal classes.

"Ho, ho, ho," a deep voice boomed as Dad came into the shop along with Eve. At this time of night, my customers were all adults, but they pretended to be thrilled at meeting the big man himself. Judging by the expression on many of their faces, maybe they weren't pretending. Pictures were taken of them posing with Dad, something to impress children and grandchildren.

Eve leaned against the sales counter, trying to keep up the pretext of big-city girl *soooo* bored at being stuck in her hometown for the holidays. Jackie abandoned her current customer in midsentence and rushed over to interrogate Eve about the famous people she'd met and what her next movie would be. "Things are slow over the holidays," Eve drawled, "even in Hollywood, so I grabbed the opportunity to come home. I'm expecting a callback for a major role in—" She named one of the biggest shows currently streaming.

Jackie gasped. "Oh my gosh. I love that show. The clothes alone are enough to keep me watching."

Photo opportunity over, Dad jerked his head at me. The customers returned to their browsing, and Jackie continued peppering Eve with questions. My sister's oh-so-bored facade cracked, just a little, as she reveled in the attention.

I followed Dad to a momentarily quiet corner next to the holiday tree. I keep a real, fully decorated tree up all year and replace it about once a month. This month it was a Fraser fir, plump and reaching to the ceiling. Strings of lights were tucked between the branches, and small glass decorations glimmered. Those same decorations were displayed for sale on the table next to the tree, with more by the front door to greet shoppers as they entered. "Your phone call yesterday wasn't the first I've heard concerning apparently strange happenings on Broad Street," Dad said.

I was shocked. "You mean there's something to it?"

"Absolutely and totally not. Mabel D'Angelo has her network of gossips in an uproar over nothing. A new resident or residents have moved in and they are not wanting to make friends, which is entirely their prerogative. To be honest, honeybunch, if they'd been warned about Mabel, I'm not entirely surprised they're keeping a low profile. It's also quite possible they're moving in slowly and have not yet taken residence. You haven't seen any children around?"

"No. Nor any signs of them. If there were kids, I'd expect marks in the snow at least."

"Right. Meaning there's nothing for Mabel to see because there's nothing to see. If they don't want her cookies, that is also entirely up to them. Maybe they're vegan or have allergies."

"They took Donalda's casserole in. Do you know someone named Donalda?"

"Yes. If a meal containing meat was left on my porch, I'd take it in, even if I had no intention of eating it. I don't want small animals mistaking my house for a self-serve restaurant. I might have to suggest Sue-Anne have a talk with Mabel. No one less than the mayor herself needs to tell her she's in danger of having a complaint made against her. Everyone in Rudolph is entitled to their privacy."

"Somehow, I'm not."

He ruffled my curls. "Mabel might be the gossip queen, and she might well have an excessive interest in things that are none of her business, but she's only curious. She never uses what she knows for her own advantage, other than gaining prestige amongst her gossiping peers. These last years anyway."

"What does that mean? Did something happen years ago?"

My Dad eyed me. "Did you ever wonder why there is no Mr. D'Angelo?"

"Not really. I assumed they got divorced. I also wondered if the *Mrs.* is nothing but an old-fashioned courtesy title. She never talks about him, so she's unlikely to be widowed."

"Once upon a time there was a Mr. Mabel D'Angelo."

"And?"

"And? What happened to him, no one knows. Have a nice evening, honeybunch. Good evening, madam. May I say, that sweater is a particularly nice color on you. I believe this shop has some silk scarves in the exact same shade."

The customer squealed. "Oh, thank you, Santa. I'd love to see them."

"This lady will assist you. Now, I must be off. If I'm away from the workshop for too long, some of those naughty elves have been known to take advantage of my absence and slack off."

* * *

Monday morning, I was rearranging the shelves in an attempt to cover up the empty spots. The weekend had been an exceptionally good one saleswise.

Precisely at opening time, none other than George Mann came into Mrs. Claus's Treasures. Like Mrs. D'Angelo, he hadn't ever been in my shop before as I recalled, and I greeted him warmly. "Good morning, George. Looks like it's going to be another nice day." Temperatures had begun rising yesterday, and all our lovely snow was rapidly melting. When I walked past the park on the way to work, the snow sculptures had been looking somewhat limp and soggy.

He pulled off his farm-equipment-store ball cap and mumbled something noncommittal about the weather. His gray-and-black hair stood on end, and he looked as though he hadn't taken time to shave this morning, but his jacket and boots were clean, and the bright baby-blue scarf wrapped around his neck gave him a jaunty pop of color.

"Is everything okay?" I asked.

"Not sure. Have you heard from Mabel over the last couple days?"

"She was in here on . . ." I tried to remember. "Friday afternoon. I invited her to come back for Midnight Madness on Saturday. I don't think I've seen her since."

"She didn't come Saturday night?"

"No. Why are you asking, George?"

"I thought it might be nice to go out to dinner last night." Embarrassed, he studied the floor and shifted his feet. George and Mrs. D'Angelo "dated" occasionally, meaning they sometimes went together to town functions. "I called her around noon, left a message, but she didn't return my call."

Come to think of it, I hadn't seen my landlady over the weekend either. Not standing at her post in the window with her binoculars or out on the porch wired into her network with her cell phone and earbuds. Snow was melting, but a fresh layer of deicer hadn't been spread on the sidewalk or driveway at our house. "Perhaps she's gone away. She visits her sister occasionally."

"Still no reason not to answer her phone. I tried again last night and then this morning. Went to voice mail."

My landlady lived by her phone. It was possible she'd gone to visit her sister and had lost the phone. I mentioned such to George, but he didn't look convinced. "Do you know her sister's number?"

"I don't even know her sister's name," I said. "Wendy might, in case of a problem at the house that needs to be seen to immediately when she's away. Let's try Wendy." I phoned my neighbor, and she did have the number of Mrs. D'Angelo's sister.

"Before I call her," I said, "have you seen Mrs. D since Friday afternoon?"

"She was shoveling the front walk when I got home from work on Friday. Tina was bellowing that she needed to pee, right now, and I didn't stop to talk. We were away over the weekend, visiting Steve's parents, only got back late last night."

"Thanks, Wendy. I'll give her sister a call now."

I did so. The sister, whose name was Iris Murdoch, answered. She hadn't heard from Mabel for about a week. "No reason I should. We don't talk all that much, not if we don't have anything to talk about. Do you think something's wrong?"

"No, nothing like that. I wanted to talk to her about . . . something. That's all. It'll wait."

I studied George's craggy, worried face. "Why don't I try Mabel myself. Maybe she's, uh . . . not answering you for some reason." Had Mrs. D'Angelo ghosted George? That was a thought. I made the call. Voice mail informed me the message box was full.

One shouldn't read too much into a woman of late middle age not answering her phone for a couple of days. But she did live alone, and accidents did happen.

"Why don't we go over there?" I suggested. "She might have lost her phone and is waiting for a replacement."

"Good idea. Truck's outside."

I flipped the sign on the door to *On coffee run, back soon*, locked the door, and followed George to his truck. At this time of morning, he'd been able to park directly outside my store. The truck was roughly the same age as his tractor, meaning probably older than my dad. Good thing I was wearing pants today, I thought as I hoisted myself into the passenger seat. It might be an old vehicle, but it was immaculately clean. A lot cleaner than my car, at any rate.

George threw it into gear, the engine sputtered and coughed, and we lumbered into Jingle Bell Lane and headed to Broad Steet. The sun was up in a cloudless sky, and the lights of the town's Christmas tree were off as we passed the park. A real tree occupies the covered bandstand all year round, replaced every month with a fresh one. It's always decorated seasonally appropriately: red hearts and red and white lights in February; eggs and bunnies and pink and blue lights at Easter; miniature flags and lots of red, white, and blue bunting in July; pumpkin-shaped balls and orange lights in October; turkey and cornucopia decorations in November; and then the all-out December display to mark the highlight of the year. In the rare month that doesn't have an occasion worth celebrating, the tree is lit anyway, with soft white fairy lights.

Less than a mile after the park and the bandstand, we pulled up in front of my house, and George and I got out. We climbed the steps to the porch. The cushions were still on the chairs. George pressed the bell. We could hear the faint sound echoing throughout the house. George knocked. We listened. George knocked again.

No answer.

We looked at each other. "Should we call the police for a wellness check?" George asked.

"Give me a minute," I said. "She's sure to have a spare key hidden somewhere."

Like most law-abiding people of her age, Mrs. D'Angelo never considered that any prospective thief would immediately be able to figure out where she left her spare key, so I found it after a few seconds of searching. Not that I'm a prospective thief, just a concerned friend.

It was in a small metal box attached to the underside of the porch's wrought iron tea table by a magnet. I freed the key and held it up to show George. He nodded and knocked again, loud enough to have the house shaking.

When once again we got no answer, I used the key to slowly open the door. We peered in.

"Mabel," George called. "It's George and Merry. Are you here?"

"Sorry to bother you, Mrs. D'Angelo," I said, "but we're worried about you."

All was quiet. All the lights were off.

The house was badly dated in terms of furnishings and decor but clean and uncluttered.

I called my landlady's number again, and we listened for the sound of ringing echoing through the house, but we heard nothing. I was once again informed the voice mailbox was full.

"If her phone's not here," I said, "she's unlikely to be."

"Better check. She might have put it on silent or the battery ran down," George said. He went left, to the living room, dining room, and kitchen, and I went right, to the bathrooms and bedrooms.

The ceilings were high, the plasterwork ornate, the baseboards tall, and the interior doors thick.

Once, this house would have had a den, perhaps a library and a morning room. Likely a scullery and a pantry also. In the 1960s when the second floor was converted to apartments and the third floor, the servants' level, enclosed, excess space on the ground floor had been converted to bedrooms and washrooms. I walked down the dark hallway slowly, my heart pounding in fear of what I might find. All the doors leading off the hall were open. I stepped into each room but didn't go any farther. I didn't need to search. Mrs. D'Angelo would be unlikely to have concealed herself beneath the bed and now be unable to get herself out.

To my intense relief, I saw no signs of my landlady. The two smallest bedrooms were empty of all but a minimal amount of furniture, not even a blanket or duvet on the beds or cases on the pillows. In the larger room at the back of the house, the bed was made, pillows fluffed, a book resting on the night table, the door to what was presumably the closet closed. A pink dressing gown was tossed over a chair and fluffy pink slippers lined up beneath. I recognized that dressing down and those slippers.

I met up with George by the front door.

"No sign of her," he said.

"That's good," I said. "She's not here. Nothing appears to have been disturbed. Did you find anything in the kitchen?"

"All looks normal to me. Nothin' on the table, no dishes in the sink."

"Let's go," I said.

Back outside, I returned the key to its hiding place.

"Better have a peek in the garage," I said. "Just to be sure."

I have a clicker to open the double garage doors attached to my key and did so now. All that was inside was my car and Wendy and Steve's van. Mrs. D'Angelo didn't own a car. She sold hers a while ago, saying she so rarely used it, it wasn't worth what it was costing her. She still had a driver's license, and on the rare occasion she had a big shopping trip to embark upon and no friend available to go with her or she went out of town, she rented a vehicle.

George rubbed at his face as the garage doors slid closed once again. "What do we do now, Merry?"

"Nothing we can do," I said. "It seems unlikely, highly unlikely, but she might have gone on a spontaneous vacation and simply turned off her phone. Maybe she went to Canada and didn't get a data plan that works there."

George didn't look all that reassured.

"All the police can do is what we did," I said. "A quick look around the house to make sure she isn't . . . in distress. I saw her Friday afternoon. It's now Monday morning. Let's give it another day or two."

He shrugged. "I'll drive by every now and then, check if the lights have been turned on."

"If I hear anything from my place upstairs, I'll give you a call," I said.

We got into the old truck, and George backed out of the driveway. I couldn't help but take a glance at the house across the street. The lights over the front door and the garage were on, but no car was parked outside and nothing moved behind the windows.

Chapter Six

When I locked up the shop and got ready to leave that evening, it was late. Well into December, taking advantage of tourists here for Saturday's Midnight Madness, the shops on Jingle Bell lane stayed open until eight. I'd tried Mrs. D'Angelo's number once again. The voice mailbox had not been emptied.

Mattie and I walked down Jingle Bell Lane heading home, past the brightly lit shops and the bustling restaurants. The lights of the town Christmas tree, accompanied by the glow of decorations from the houses, illuminated the dark midwinter's night. At our house, the holiday light display, flashing blubs of alternate blue, red, and green, were on, but that didn't mean Mrs. D'Angelo had been home: They were controlled by a timer. Lights glowed behind curtains in Wendy and Steve's apartment next to mine, but downstairs, the interior of the house was dark. The weekend's snow had completely melted, so I couldn't even check for footprints on the path leading to Mrs. D'Angelo's porch.

Mattie and I went around the back and climbed the stairs to the second floor. As I fitted the key into the lock on my door, I could hear the low buzz of high-pitched cartoon voices coming from the other apartment. I let Mattie and me in and pulled off my boots with a welcome sigh. Holiday season was great. Until it wasn't. Mattie ran for his bowls, and I went to the front windows, intending to pull the curtains closed. Instead I stood there for a long time, looking out.

Cars drove slowly down the street, a few dog walkers were enjoying a post-dinner stroll, two women jogged past.

The house across the street had put up no holiday display; plain white bulbs glowed above the garage and front door. The same lights had been on in the middle of the day.

I tried to remember if that house kept their outdoor lights on all the time. I was pretty sure they hadn't been on other days, but anyone could forget to turn them off in the daytime.

Which meant absolutely nothing, if the residents had gone away for a few days and wanted the lights kept on to deter burglars.

Perhaps it was time to contact the police about Mrs. D'Angelo's sudden absence. I took my phone out of my pocket and twisted it between my fingers. Mattie gave me a nudge to remind me it was past his dinnertime. It was past my dinnertime too. I put the phone away and went into the kitchen. I served up Mattie's dinner, and while he inhaled it, I studied the meager contents of my fridge. I'd been so busy this past week, I hadn't had time to go grocery shopping.

I returned to the front window and studied the Johannesen house. I pulled my phone out once again and made a call. "Feel like going out for pizza?"

"No," Vicky said. "I do not. I've had dinner, and it's after nine. I'm getting ready for bed. Such is the exciting life of a baker at Christmastime."

"Is Mark home?"

"Still at work. His life is as exciting as mine is these days. You know that, Merry. Why are you calling? Is something the matter?"

I hadn't called Vicky hoping she'd be up for pizza. I didn't feel much like pizza myself. "Sort of. I'm not sure."

"Spill."

I told her my worries about Mrs. D'Angelo. "George and I checked the house this morning, and nothing appears to have been disturbed. Her phone isn't ringing in the house, which means either it's run out of power or it isn't there, and I didn't see it."

"She's a grown woman, Merry. She's allowed to come and go without checking in with you."

"I know all that, but . . . it's so uncharacteristic of her, and I am worried. She occasionally visits her sister, but her sister hasn't heard from her lately either."

A long silence came down the line.

"What do you want to do?" Vicky asked. "I'll go to the police with you, if you need company."

"I might go to the police in the morning. They, at least, could find out if she rented a car. They likely won't tell me what they learn, but if they don't follow up, then I'll know she's safe. But . . . I want to check something first. Can you come over? If it's not too much trouble."

"You know you only have to ask. Check what?"

"Mrs. D'Angelo's been extremely interested in the goings-on of the new people, or person, who moved in across the street to the place she still calls the Johannesen house. She considers their behavior to be suspicious, although I think they're nothing but people wanting their privacy. I'm wondering if it's possible she started peeking in windows and maybe had a fall or something."

"Or something."

"No one seems to be home. The lot's a big one and deep. If Mrs. D'Angelo is calling for help from the back, she might not be heard from the street."

"Has Mattie reacted? Like tried to check out that house or anything?"

"No." If he did hear someone calling for help, I liked to think my dog would try to investigate. But if the woman was lying unconscious in the dark? Perhaps not, not if his mind was focused on dinnertime. Although his breed originated to assist people lost in winter storms on the treacherous paths through the Swiss Alps, Mattie himself was most definitely not a search-and-rescue dog.

"I'm sure you're worrying about nothing, but to put your mind at rest, I'm on my way. Ten minutes."

"Thanks."

Mattie and I were standing on the sidewalk nine minutes later when Vicky drove up in her sporty little Miata. She didn't get the convertible out much in the wintertime, but tonight she didn't want to take the time to walk over to my place.

Together we studied the building across the street. "It's a lovely old house," Vicky said, "and nicely maintained, but there's something about houses that age that give off a spooky feeling in the right light. Might be all that gingerbread, the ornate trim, the deep, dark recesses. That, plus it's the only place on the street without Christmas lights. Some of the houses in Rudolph are so well lit they might be signaling to space aliens. Lead on."

No traffic was coming, and we ran across the street. I watched Mattie carefully but saw no unusual signs of alarm or alertness. He simply trotted happily at my side, out for our regular postprandial stroll.

We stepped off the sidewalk and walked boldly up the driveway and down the walk. As we reached the front steps, Mattie started sniffing at the ground.

"He senses something," Vicky said.

"Just unexplored territory. He's never been here before."

We climbed the steps. I rang the bell and heard the faint echoes of the sound bouncing around inside. In case someone was home, I intended to ask permission before poking around the property.

We waited. I did not hear footsteps approaching.

"Do these people have a dog?" Vicky asked.

"Not that I've seen any evidence of."

Vicky pointed down. Mattie's ears were up, the long hairs on his neck standing on end. He let out a low whine, crouched low, and scratched rapidly at the door with both front paws.

"Might be a mouse," I said.

"Might be. Might not be. Shush."

I shushed.

I heard a creak. Might be a floorboard. Might be an old house shifting and settling, although the night was calm and no wind blew.

And then I heard something else, something sounding like a muffled cry. Mattie barked and began scratching at the door with renewed enthusiasm.

"That's no mouse." Vicky hammered at the door. "Hello! Hello! Is anyone in there? We're calling the police."

I grabbed my phone and dialed 911. I identified myself, gave my address, and gasped out that I needed help. Someone might be trapped.

"Is this person in immediate danger?"

"I don't think so, but . . . I don't know."

"I'll send someone as soon as I can, Merry," the dispatcher said. "But there's been a major incident in a neighboring town, and all available units have been dispatched."

"What sort of incident?" Vicky asked.

"Turn on the news," she said. "Meanwhile, you keep this line open and tell me if the situation escalates."

"Get someone here as soon as you can. We'll call you back." Vicky plucked my phone out of my hand and hung up.

"What'd you do that for?" I asked.

"I'm not waiting around." She hit the door again with her fist. "The police have been notified! We're coming in!"

She twisted the door handle. Nothing happened. She threw herself against the door. Nothing happened to the door, but Vicky said, "Oof," pulled a face, and rubbed her shoulder. Mattie barked.

We looked at each other. And then, between the barks, we heard it again.

"Shush, Mattie, shush." I grabbed his muzzle and tried to keep it closed. I wasn't entirely successful, but it gave us enough of a quiet break that this time the sound came clear and distinct.

Definitely a human cry and definitely coming from inside this house. Mattie barked all the louder.

"Might be easier access around the back," Vicky called as she ran down the steps. "You stay here and wait for the police."

"I'm not too stupid to live," I said, "even if you are. I'm coming too." I set the flashlight on my phone, and Mattie and I followed Vicky through a gate at the side of the house.

The property was nicely maintained. A brick path weaved between trees pruned back and bushes wrapped tightly in burlap. Fall leaves were raked and flower beds turned over.

The lights at the back of the house were off, but my beam of light shone on a wide wooden deck, now empty of furniture and flowerpots, stretching out from the back of the house. Sliding glass doors opened onto it. Vicky had climbed the steps, and she was attempting to peer into the house with the help of her own phone. I could see a kitchen, thoroughly modernized, looking never to have been used. Only two objects lay on the large center island. One was a cell phone. I knew that sparkly pink case. I also recognized the tin cookie container, the top with a painted scene of a horse and carriage prancing through the snowy woods.

The cry came again, and this time I could make out the word. "Help!"

"Someone's trapped in there. We have to get inside," Vicky said.

If the residents of the house hadn't heard us knocking, they couldn't miss Mattie's barking. It was getting frantic now. On the other side of the long wooden fence surrounding the property, a light came on.

Over all the years we'd been best friends, Vicky had been the brave one, the bold one, the one rushing into things. I'd been the timid one, the one checking the situation out first. Obviously nothing had changed. "We can't just break in," I said.

"Sure we can. I don't suppose you have a hammer handy."

"No, I do not have a hammer handy."

She swept the weak beam of light across the empty deck and onto the lawn. Something glittered as the light hit it, and Vicky let out a cry of triumph.

A bird feeder lay on the brown grass. The metal post had rusted and collapsed. Vicky leapt down the steps, crossed the lawn, and grabbed it. Then she was back, yelling, "Get Mattie out of the way, Merry."

I grabbed the increasingly frantic dog by the collar and attempted to pull him away. When Mattie didn't want to move, he didn't move. "Wait!" I screamed. I tore off my coat and threw it over the dog's head, hoping to at least protect his eyes if shards of broken glass flew. Then I turned, bent my head, and wrapped my arms around my neck.

Vicky hit the door. Once, twice. On the third blow I heard glass shattering and falling to the deck.

"What's going on over there!" a man called from the neighboring house. "I'm calling the police."

"Please, do," Vicky yelled back.

"It's Merry Wilkinson," I shouted. "Someone's in trouble over here."

I straightened up and turned around. One pane of glass was completely shattered, glistening shards scattered across the deck. Mattie was trying to toss the coat away while

Vicky pulled her own coat off and wrapped it around her right arm. "Stand back," she said to me as she used the protected arm to sweep broken glass from the doorframe.

"In here! I'm in here!" a weak voice called.

Vicky, followed by Mattie and then me, stepped over the doorframe and into the house.

The kitchen was large and totally modern, with granite countertops, glistening steel appliances, an induction stove, pale hardwood floors, marble-topped island. Interior walls had been ripped out, opening the space to the living and dining areas.

New residents moved in here more than a week ago, but it looked as though they hadn't taken advantage of the amenities. The trash can was full of pizza boxes, crumpled paper napkins, and takeout coffee cups. Pop cans and beer bottles crowded the countertop next to the sink. No toaster or coffeepot on the counter, no kettle on the stove. No canisters of sugar and flour. No washed coffee mugs or wineglasses on the drying rack. Not even a drying rack, or dish towels tossed over the handle of the oven.

A closed door was on the other side of the island, and something larger than a mouse was thumping inside it.

Vicky ran around the island and wrenched open the door while I fumbled for a light switch, found it, and threw it on. The pantry shelves were empty of tins and jars or wintering fruits and vegetables; no boxes were on the floor. The only thing in the room was Mabel D'Angelo, crouched in a corner, feet bound, hands tied in front of her and fastened by a long rope to a shelf attached to the wall. Her eyes were wide, her hair disheveled, her wrists torn and bleeding. A rough cloth was wrapped around her chin. I guessed it had been used to gag her, but she'd managed to work it out.

For the briefest of moments, Vicky and I simply stood there, staring. And then we both leapt forward.

"Knife," Vicky yelled. "Find a knife."

I ran back to the kitchen and pulled open drawers. All were empty.

"It's okay, it's okay," Vicky said. "The police are coming. Merry, if you can't find a knife, run home and get one."

"Where's Mattie?" The big dog hadn't rushed to Mrs. D'Angelo's side. He wasn't attempting to comfort her or sniffing around for dog biscuits, and he wasn't getting in Vicky's way.

Instead he was in the dining room, standing at an old door on the far side of the room from the kitchen, leading to what was likely the cellar. The only furniture was a couple of straight-backed chairs and a small folding card table. A group of cardboard boxes were stacked against the walls.

I stepped cautiously forward, and even more cautiously twisted the handle and eased open the cellar door. I peered down into the darkness, and then I found the light switch on the wall. The stairs were steep, the light poor, and the scent of damp walls and decades of mold rose up.

Mattie got past me before I could stop him and hurtled down the stairs, still barking.

Above the damp and the mold, I caught the smell of something strong and unpleasant. I started cautiously down the steps, taking care to watch my footing.

Unlike the rest of the house, the cellar had not been updated. The steps were steep, narrow, and rickety. The walls were stone, and the beams holding up the ceiling were formed from whole tree trunks. The furnace hummed softly.

The space was crammed full of modern equipment and stacks of cardboard boxes. The glow of small green and yellow lights indicated the equipment was switched on. I couldn't identify most of it, but I didn't worry about that now.

Mattie's barks had turned to a low whine. He stood above an unmoving shape on the concrete floor. I took another cautious step down. Mattie turned his head to look at me. The shape did not move.

It was a woman. She wore tight jeans, a baggy sweater, and sneakers. She lay on the concrete floor, face down, arms thrown out to the sides, a river of sleek blond hair spread out around her like a halo. The weak light from the single bulb in the ceiling glistened off a pool of dried blood beneath her.

Chapter Seven

I took a cautious step down and then another. Mattie nudged the woman with his nose. She didn't react.

"For heaven's sake, Merry, what are you doing?" Vicky called. "I need a knife here."

I hesitated, and then I decided Mrs. D'Angelo was more in need of help right now than this unmoving woman. I summoned Mattie, and he eventually, reluctantly, came. We climbed back up the steps. I left the light on and the cellar door open.

"Merry, what's happening?" Doug Kincaid, who lived next to this house, stepped through the broken glass door into the kitchen. "I called the police. Do you need help?"

"Yes, yes, we do," Vicky said. "I need a knife."

"What for? Oh my gosh," he said. "Mabel, what are you doing in there?"

I came into the kitchen to see him pulling a penknife out of his pocket and joining Vicky in the pantry. Mrs. D'Angelo's sobs filled the kitchen.

A moment later, Vicky emerged, and then Doug half carrying Mrs. D'Angelo. He was not a young man, and he was clearly struggling, but my landlady's legs were all rubber. Vicky slipped one of her arms over her shoulders and looked around the kitchen, searching for someplace to put her.

"Hi, Merry," Doug said, as though this were a normal neighborly encounter.

"Chairs in the dining room," I said. "She needs to sit down."

A weeping Mrs. D'Angelo was helped into a chair. Vicky crouched next to her and rubbed at her feet. Her hands were torn and bleeding. Doug hovered nearby, wanting to help but unsure of what he could do.

I kept my voice low and half turned from my landlady. I didn't know if she was capable of understanding, but I didn't want to add to her distress. "Someone's in the cellar. A woman. Dead, by the look of it."

Vicky pushed herself to her feet. She and Doug stared at me open-mouthed.

"You two stay here. I'll go down and have a quick check." At that moment, we heard the sound of sirens approaching, and I let out an enormous sigh of relief.

"I'll wave them down and let them in." Doug ran for the front door, and moments later medics and police flooded into the house.

"The cellar," I said. "Someone . . . something's down there. You need to check it out. Right away." I pointed to the old door now standing open. "Careful. The steps are steep, and it's dark."

"I'm on it," an officer said as he turned. He called over his shoulder, "Campbell, you stay with these people. No one's to leave until we've checked all this out."

Vicky and I went into the kitchen. We huddled close together against the far counter. We stood there, watching.

I kept a firm hand on Mattie's collar. His entire body quivered, but he stayed by my side. The police would not thank us for getting dog hair and drool in all the forensic evidence they'd be searching for.

"What on earth has been going on here?" Officer Candice Campbell said to us as she came into the kitchen. Past her, I could see medics giving Mrs. D'Angelo a quick check over and then helping her onto a stretcher. I was pleased to see that although she was wobbly, she was able to stand with minimal assistance. Doug remained in the background, pressed up against a far wall, watching. Mrs. D'Angelo was wheeled away, past more uniformed police flooding into the house as word spread they were needed.

From the cellar, a man yelled, "Get medics down here. ASAP."

"I have absolutely no idea," I said in answer to Candy's question. "Your colleague in the cellar might need some help. We'll stay here. Promise."

I smiled my most innocent smile, and she gave me a stern look in response before going to help her partner. Candy and I, as well as Vicky, had been in the same class all through school. She and I had never been friends, and all these years later I still sometimes thought she was hoping to catch me getting myself into trouble.

"You found a body down there?" Vicky whispered to me.

"Yes. I'm pretty sure she was dead."

"An old one? Like, bones and stuff?"

"No. Recent enough the blood was still wet." I swallowed heavily. "Looked that way, anyway. I didn't get close. The light wasn't good."

"Geez," Vicky said.

Mattie let out a low whine and pressed himself into my leg. I ran my shaking fingers through the long thick hair on his head, seeking, and finding, comfort there.

"You don't think? Mrs. D?" Vicky asked in a whisper.

"I can't see her killing her kidnapper and then tying herself up in the pantry for us to find."

"No," Vicky agreed.

Candy came up from the cellar, shouting into her radio that the second ambulance didn't need to hurry. Another officer was talking to Doug. All Doug was doing was shaking his head.

Mattie let out a low whimper, and when I looked down at him, he was licking his right front foot. On the kitchen floor, a few drops of blood marked his passage through the house.

"Hey there." I couched down next to him. "Let me have a look." I lifted the paw and studied it. He licked my face. "He's stepped in some glass. The foot's cut."

"Let's wait outside. No one said we had to stay right here," Vicky said. "You take one end, and I'll take the other. We don't want him walking through any more glass." Between us, grunting and groaning, we managed to wrestle the dog through the broken door without him touching ground. "He needs to go on a diet," Vicky panted when we were on the deck, I was crouched beside him, and Mattie was licking his sore foot.

"He is what he is." I took the foot gently in my hand. "As I recall, I wanted a small dog. A Pekingese, maybe, or a fluffy little bichon frise. But no, you needed homes for your cousin's unwanted Saint Bernard puppies."

"Can you say you've ever been sorry?"

"Can't say that, no."

At that moment, Mattie forgot his injury, pulled his foot out of my hands, and leapt to attention. His liquid brown eyes sparkled, his ears stood up, his tail wagged furiously. His idol had arrived.

Detective Diane Simmonds walked into the kitchen and stepped through the shattered door to join us on the deck. "Matterhorn, sit," she commanded. "This is not a social call." Mattie sat.

"First things first," she said to me. "Don't let him put any weight on that foot. If a piece of glass is embedded, we don't want it getting pushed in further. If it's worse later or doesn't stop bleeding soon, take him to the vet. In other matters, Mabel's been taken to the hospital. The medics say she's severely dehydrated and has some bad cuts and chafing but otherwise appears to be unharmed. Physically, at any rate. Your neighbor Mr. Kincaid says he heard you two yelling; he came to investigate and found Mabel tied up in the pantry."

Vicky and I nodded.

"Not to mention a dead woman in the cellar. Recently dead, by the looks of it. Very recently."

I nodded again. "Mattie found her. I mean, Mattie indicated something was down there, so I opened the door. I saw a lot of equipment; do you know what it is?"

"I do," she said, without offering an explanation. "Did you touch the body, Merry? You or Matterhorn?"

"I didn't go all the way down the stairs, but Mattie did. He sniffed at the . . . at it. I can't say for sure if he touched it or not. I was more concerned about Mrs. D'Angelo, so I didn't investigate."

"Did you recognize her?"

I swallowed. "She was lying on her front, head turned away from me so I couldn't see the face. But nothing seemed familiar, no."

"Who lives here?" Simmonds glanced over her shoulder into the kitchen. "The place doesn't exactly look lived in. Not much furniture at all. Unpacked boxes."

"We don't know," I said. "The current owners don't live in Rudolph, so they rent out the house. New people, or a new person, moved in a little over a week ago, but they've kept themselves to themselves."

"A heck of a lot seems to be going on here, and I have a long night ahead of me, but before that, I need a quick overview about what brought you two breaking the door down tonight. And I do mean make it quick."

I tried to be as succinct as possible. Vicky nodded along, and when I finished, she said, "What Merry said."

"I have to get to the hospital and talk to Mabel once the doctors say she's able to speak to me. You two go home. I'll be around soon as I can to take your statements." Simmonds looked at the adoring dog sitting quietly between us. "And watch that foot. Clean it up and probe gently for any glass that might still be in it. The bleeding seems to have stopped, but don't hesitate to go to the emergency vet if it starts bleeding again or he seems to be in pain."

*　*　*

Mattie favored his foot as we crossed the backyard, but he wasn't completely avoiding putting any weight on it, which I considered to be a good sign. We went through the gate and rounded the house and stepped into a blaze of light and activity. Police cars and ambulances were parked every which way. Red, blue, and white flashing lights overwhelmed the holiday decorations. Just about every one of the residents of the street was on their porch or gathered on the sidewalk, many in varying degrees of nightwear. Several had fortified themselves with mugs of steaming liquid, and a few carried beer bottles or wineglasses. Phones were in hand, and more than a few flashed as pictures were taken.

"Never a dull moment in Rudolph, New York," Vicky mumbled.

"There they are!" someone shouted.

"Merry, what's going on?"

"They say someone's dead. Is that true?"

"Who is it?"

"Where's Mabel?"

"I have been assigned to escort you to your door." Candy Campbell approached us. "Hopefully this will mark the nadir of my career."

"Never thought I'd see the day," Vicky said.

We walked down the driveway. Kyle Lambert lifted his camera and snapped our picture. I stuck out my tongue.

"A statement for the press?" Russ Durham fell into step beside us.

"No," Vicky said.

"These ladies are under police orders not to discuss the situation until they've spoken to the detective," Candy said.

"Not even with me?" Russ drawled in his slow, sexy Louisiana accent. He gave her a grin and a broad wink, and Candy flushed a most un-police-like red. She and Russ, the editor in chief (and sole remaining full-time employee) of the *Rudolph Gazette*, dated for a short while, but it hadn't worked out. For reasons I didn't know.

"No comment," Vicky said. "I've always wanted to say that. Sounds so nice, I'll say it again. I have no comment for the press at this time."

Deep in my pocket my phone was vibrating as though to announce an incoming hurricane. I heard the faint tones of Vicky's phone ringing. Word was spreading. And fast.

Russ pointed to the porch of my house. "Rumor says Mabel D'Angelo was kidnapped by the Sicilian mob and only freed after payment of a multimillion-dollar ransom, facilitated by none other than Vicky Casey and Merry Wilkinson. I'd be inclined to dismiss that, except for the fact that quite noticeably she is not standing on her front porch, relating the biggest story of the year—so far—to all and sundry."

"No comment," Vicky said, and we continued walking.

When we reached the bottom of my steps, Vicky said, "We can manage from here, Officer Campbell. You may return to your duties. I think the street needs watching."

"Don't push your luck," Candy muttered. "I for one haven't forgotten you two were the first people I encountered, after Doug Kincaid, at the scene of the crime. I'll dismiss him as a suspect because he plays on the old guys' baseball team with my dad."

I was too tired, and too overwhelmed by the events of this evening, to come up with a snappy retort. We climbed the stairs. I was pleased to see that although Mattie stepped gingerly on his sore foot, it didn't seem to be worrying him overmuch.

My parents have a spare key to my apartment, so I wasn't entirely surprised to see them waiting for me. Mom was on the couch, flicking through her phone, and Dad stood at the front window, peering out at the activity, while white, red, and blue lights flashed across his face. I gave them a wry grin and checked my own phone. Unasked, Dad headed for the fridge and got out a wine bottle.

I ignored most of the texts and voice mail messages and returned Alan's call first.

"Merry? What's happening?"

"Nothing good. I'm okay. Vicky's okay. Mattie's okay. That's all I want to say over the phone."

"Do you want me to come?"

"Yes," I said.

"Mark's on his way," Vicky said to me.

Dad handed us each a glass of wine. Vicky dropped onto the couch. Mattie went into the kitchen to see if he'd overlooked any part of his dinner. My mom said, "Anything we need to be concerned about, dear?"

I followed Mattie. I soaked a clean dishcloth in water, sat on the floor, and called the dog. When he'd given his empty bowl a disapproving lick, he came to me. He handed me his paw. I washed it gently, pleased to see a minimal amount of dried blood transferring to the cloth. He whimpered slightly when I touched the cut, but he didn't pull away. I talked as I worked. "Nothing for you to worry about. Not even Mattie here. He stepped on a shard of broken glass, but it looks like it didn't get stuck in the paw."

"Need we know why Mattie was walking on glass?" Dad asked.

"You'll hear all about it in the fullness of time," I replied. "Mrs. D'Angelo has been taken to the hospital, but she'll be fine. She was right about strange things going on at that house across the street, and it would appear her nosiness almost got her killed."

"All I saw was not much in the way of furniture or people's things," Vicky said, "but you asked Diane about some equipment. What's that about?"

"The cellar was full of machinery. I have absolutely no idea what it might be used for. As for what else was in the cellar . . . you'll be hearing about it soon enough. A dead body."

"Goodness," Mom said.

"Who?" Dad asked.

"I have not the slightest idea. All I saw was a young woman with long blond hair. I didn't investigate further."

"Which is something to be thankful for," my mother said.

I gave Mattie a few hearty thumps to tell him he was a good boy and stood up. "I'd better call George Mann. It was him who first alerted me that something might be wrong."

I made the call, and a sleepy voice answered. "George, Merry here. Have you heard the news?"

"News? What news? I haven't had the TV on."

Despite the seriousness of the situation, I smiled to myself. Imagine, someone in this day and age who relied on television for breaking local news.

"Mabel's fine. She's unharmed but has been admitted to Rudolph General for observation. I thought you'd want to know."

"What happened?"

"It's a long story. I'll let her tell you all about it herself."

"Is she taking calls tonight?"

"I doubt it," I said. "She's probably been given something to put her to sleep. We'll talk in the morning, George. Good night."

Mom stood up. She came to me and gave me a tight hug. A comforting wave of her familiar perfume washed over me. When she pulled away, her eyes were wet. "The things you get up to. Alan and Mark are coming, and you two are obviously fine, although perhaps a bit shook up. Your father and I will be going. If you need anything, call us."

I hugged her back. "I will."

"You should get yourself to bed," Dad said.

I shook my head. "Detective Simmonds needs to talk to us once she's been to the hospital."

Dad gave me a quick kiss on the top of my head, and then he and Mom left.

Mark was next to arrive, followed almost immediately by Alan and Ranger, his Jack Russell terrier. Mark said little more to me than hi before he bundled Vicky out the door. Alan and I settled onto the couch to watch a movie while we waited for the good detective. Mattie curled up on the floor at our feet and promptly fell asleep. He had definitely had more than enough excitement for one day. Ranger, who never has enough excitement in his life, bounced from one apartment window to the other, keeping a keen eye on the activity on the street. I didn't close the curtain, and red and blue lights lit up the inside of my apartment for many long hours.

Chapter Eight

One of the many texts I'd received last night was from Jackie. I replied to her as soon as I woke after a restless and troubled sleep.

Me: *Busy night. Be late to work. Can you open?*
Jackie: *Only if you promise to tell me everything!!!!!*
Me: *Promise. Thx.*

Okay, so I lied. But it was the holiday season and I did have a business to run, and I needed the store to open on time.

Diane Simmonds had called to tell me she was on her way to my place shortly after midnight. Alan put a pot of coffee on for her and fixed mugs of hot chocolate for himself and for me.

"How'd you hear I was involved in the goings-on anyway?" I asked Alan, never one to spend much time on social media, as he served the drinks.

"Russ Durham called. I phoned Mark at the inn."

"That was nice of Russ," I said.

Once she'd greeted Mattie, taken a seat on the couch, and accepted the offered coffee, Detective Simmonds asked me what made Vicky and me want to check out the house across the street. I told her what little I'd observed, explained Mrs. D'Angelo's suspicions and curiosity about the new neighbors and my increasing worry at not only her disappearance but her failure to answer her phone. "Not for a minute," I said at last, "did I suspect she'd be tied up in the pantry. I thought she might have been prowling around the yard, on the pretext of delivering her homemade cookies, when she fell and wasn't able to call for help."

"In some of that, you're right." Simmonds sipped her coffee. Mattie sat proudly at her side. Before getting down to the matter of kidnapping, confinement, and murder, the detective checked the dog's paw. "It looks clean, but at any signs of swelling or renewed bleeding or indications he's having pain, call the vet."

"I will."

That matter attended to, she said, "Mabel D'Angelo should be able to have visitors tomorrow. The doctor wants to keep her for a few days, as she's severely dehydrated and in some considerable shock, but nothing appears to be more serious than that. No other injuries."

"How long was she in there?" Alan asked.

"Two days, at least," Simmonds said.

"Meaning since sometime Saturday," I said.

"So it would appear."

"Did she tell you anything?"

Simmonds lifted her hand. "I'm not here to answer questions, Merry, but to ask them."

"Okay, but one thing before we continue. When Doug called 911, he was told the police might be delayed in getting to us, as they were responding to a major incident. Anything to do with what happened to us? To Mrs. D'Angelo?"

"No. A child had gone missing. Walked out of her house in nothing but her diaper and a T-shirt into the snow. I'm happy to report she was found in the neighbor's doghouse. Being kept warm by the dog." Detective Simmonds gave Mattie a fond smile.

"Good animals, dogs," Alan said.

"Yes." She cleared her throat. "At any time, Merry, did you see the people who moved in across the street well enough to identify them?"

"Never. I wasn't home when they initially moved in, and after that, they, or he or she, drove into the garage, and the doors shut behind them. I only know that based on tire tracks on the driveway and lack of footprints outside. Once or twice I saw someone lingering outside the house, as though they were watching it, but they didn't stay long, and I simply assumed they were just curious. In the same way Mrs. D'Angelo was."

"Anything noticeable about these observers?"

I shook my head. "It's wintertime, and everyone is well bundled up. I might have seen a man once, maybe slightly on the bulky side, but I didn't notice anything you'd call identifying about him. Might even have been a tall, overweight woman in a big coat. I have no reason to believe he wasn't enjoying a breath of fresh night air." I shrugged. "It's December in Rudolph. I don't have enough time in a day to attend to my own business, much less pay attention to anyone else's. For more on the comings and goings on the street, you'll have to ask Mrs. D'Angelo."

"Rest assured, I will. Alan, anything to add?"

"No. I never saw anyone going into the house, coming out of it, or even standing outside. Like Merry says, it's December in Rudolph."

"So everyone keeps telling me. I'm going to show you a picture of the person Merry found in the cellar. Are you ready?"

Alan put his hand on my shoulder. I nodded. Simmonds handed me a photograph, and I shared it with Alan. The picture showed the face of a white woman in her late twenties, early thirties maybe. Her expression was calm, her eyes closed. Thin face, slight cleft in the chin. She would have been pretty in life, I thought. Pretty, but not beautiful. Long golden hair spread out around her head, falling past her shoulders. Silver hoops ran through her ears. To my considerable surprise, something tugged at the back of my mind, and I realized I dimly recognized that face.

"Alan?" I asked.

"Yeah. I think I know her." He snapped his fingers. "Her, or someone who looks like her. From years back. Name's not coming to me."

"You know her?" Simmonds sounded surprised. "From where? Did you see her in town or at Merry's store?"

"Not recently. Long time ago." I dug frantically through my memory banks. Judging by the look on Alan's face, he was doing the same.

"Rachel . . . something. No, not Rachel. Raquel."

"The face is vaguely familiar," Alan said, "but I can't place her."

"Raquel Thornton," I said. "No, Torrone. Raquel Torrone. I remember that hair in particular. She had hair like out of a movie, the envy of every girl, including me, at Rudolph High. I haven't seen her since we graduated high school."

"You're saying she was a student at your high school?" Simmonds asked.

"Yes. I'm positive. She was a couple of years younger than us, which is why Alan probably doesn't remember. She was friends with my youngest sister, Eve, as I recall. I'm pretty sure she's the daughter of Beth and Robert Torrone, who own that house. The Johannesen house. Mrs. D'Angelo mentioned them the other day, when she was trying to find out about the rental people. Or person."

Simmonds kept her face impassive, but her eyes flared with interest. "You're sure of this, Merry?"

"I am. Unless this is a sister or close relative of the woman I'm thinking of. I don't remember Raquel having a sister, although I might not have known if she did. You can ask Eve. She's here for the holidays."

"I'll do that." Simmonds put the picture away. "You say you haven't seen this woman since high school?"

"Nope. Never gave her a thought either. I might not have recognized her now except for the hair."

"Same with me," Alan said. "No reason I should know whatever she was up to these days. Like Merry said, it's only that her hair was so individual, and spectacular, I even remember her."

"Imagine being known only because of your hair," I said.

Simmonds stood up. "Thank you for your time. I'll be in touch if I need anything more. And I'm sure I will."

"What was she doing down there?" I asked. "In that cellar? What was all that equipment?"

"Like I said, I'll be in touch. No, Matterhorn, you cannot come with me. You stay here with Merry."

Mattie's head had dipped in disappointment as the detective showed herself out.

"Should we take flowers to the hospital?" Alan asked me now.

"We probably should. I'll phone and ask if Mrs. D'Angelo can have visitors."

The hospital informed me the patient was awake and able to see well-wishers, so Alan and I swallowed a quick breakfast of coffee and cereal and headed out. In Rudolph in December, it's hard to find flowers in colors other than red and white, but we managed to get a nice assortment of yellow roses at the florist across from Vicky's bakery. As the clerk wrapped the stems in cellophane and ribbon, she asked, "Dropping in to see Mabel, are you, Merry?"

No point in denying it. My only worry in attempting to see Mrs. D'Angelo was that the hospital would be forced to put a limit on the crowds of visitors.

"Do you particularly want me to come with you?" Alan asked me once we were out on the sidewalk.

"No need, if you don't want to."

"I've got unfinished work sitting on the bench. Stuff I'd planned on getting done last night. I have demanding customers, you know." He gave me a wink. "And, by the way, I did manage to fit in a couple of train sets."

I thanked him, he handed me the bouquet, and we went our separate ways. I glanced across the street. The line at Victoria's Bake Shoppe stretched out the door as far as the sidewalk. I called my dad. "Feel like a visit to the hospital?"

"To see Mabel? Good idea. As you can imagine, honey-bunch, rumors are running wild. Last I heard, her Sicilian relatives tracked her down, seeking revenge on her branch of the family for some ancient slight which no one can explain. Are you at the store?"

"I'm standing outside the florist."

"I'm at town hall, leaving now. Meet you in the parking lot."

I waited for the light to change and dashed across the street. In the summer the brick walkway between the bakery and the town complex is planted with beds of bright annuals. In the winter, strings of fairy lights are strung between the buildings. As I reached the parking lot, Dad was coming down the steps. We met at his car. He was in his "civilian" clothes today. Brown corduroy pants, winter jacket, scarf and gloves. No matter how he dresses, he always manages to look like Santa Claus trying to be incognito. At Vicky's wedding in the spring, he looked like Santa Claus as a wedding guest.

"Diane came around to the house first thing this morning," he said once we were in the car and waiting for a break in the traffic on Jingle Bell Lane.

"To see Eve?" I asked. "To ask her about the woman who died? I seem to remember they'd been friends at school."

"You know about her?"

"Detective Simonds showed us a picture last night. Do you remember her, Raquel Torrone?"

"Her specifically, no I don't. Your mother doesn't either. I know—knew, rather—the family vaguely. They moved away a number of years ago; I don't know where they ended up. Dorothy Johannesen, who owned the house where all this happened, died shortly thereafter and left the house to Beth Torrone, Raquel's mother, who was her niece. Sister's daughter, if memory serves. The Torrones didn't come back to take possession of the property; they rented it out."

"What did Eve have to say?"

"She told Diane she hadn't seen or heard from Raquel since school. According to Eve, the girl had a bad reputation, even back then."

"Bad reputation? What for exactly?"

"She and Eve weren't friends for long, which sounds like it was a good thing. According to what Eve told Diane, Raquel was in and out of trouble. Always trouble of her own choosing. She hung around with a bad crowd and was plausibly accused of breaking into school lockers and taking stuff. Eve said Raquel dropped out of school in their senior year, before graduating, and she left town. That's all she knew. Never heard a word from or about her since, and forgot all about her."

"I don't suppose Diane Simmonds filled you in on what Raquel's been up to since or why she found herself back in Rudolph only to end up dead in a cellar on Broad Street?"

"She did not."

Chapter Nine

Dad and I found Mrs. D'Angelo awake and propped up on a pile of pillows. An IV was in her left hand, both wrists heavily bandaged, her eyes sunken pools in a stark-white face. A small cut, rapidly healing over, marked her chin, and blue and black bruises were on her right cheekbone and beneath the eye, likely where she'd bumped her head when dragged into the pantry. She gave us a weak smile when we came in and thanked me for the flowers.

The curtain around the bed next to hers was pulled closed, and steady snoring came from behind.

I searched for a place to put the flowers. The narrow windowsill overlooking the parking garage and every other available surface was covered in cards and vases overflowing with blooms.

"Looks like you've had a lot of company already, Mabel." Dad settled into one of the visitors' chairs, and I took the other.

She shook her head. Her neatly coiffed gray hair was no longer neatly coiffed but plastered to her head in greasy strands. She clutched the bedsheets to her chest. "I don't want to see anyone. I told people not to come."

Dad half rose. "I'm sorry. We should have called ahead."

"Sit down, sit down." She struggled to sit upright. "You and Merry are welcome. Detective Simmonds tells me it was Merry and Vicky Casey who saved me."

"I wouldn't put it like that," I said.

"I would. Heaven knows how long I might have been down there before I was found. Or"—she shuddered—"not found."

"No need to think about that anymore, Mabel," Dad said cheerfully. "You'll be back on your feet in no time."

A phone, not in a pink case, sat on the table behind me. It rang, and I half turned to reach for it, intending to hand it to her. "Leave it," Mrs. D'Angelo said sharply. "If it's important, it will go to voice mail."

"Yesterday when I tried to get you, the voice mailbox was full."

She shrugged, not much caring. "The police took my phone into evidence and brought me a temporary one. Doesn't matter. I don't feel like talking to anyone. All they're after is the salacious details." She sighed and closed her eyes.

Dad and I exchanged worried glances.

"When you're released, do you have someone who can stay with you for a few days?" Dad asked. "In case you need help?"

"Iris, my sister, is coming."

"That's good."

"As long as she doesn't plan on staying too long. A couple of days of Iris is quite enough for me."

"Rather than thanking Vicky and me," I said. "You should be thanking George Mann. He noticed you were missing first, and it was only then he alerted me."

A small smile touched the edges of her pale lips. "Dear George. A truly good man. If only we'd met many long years ago." She opened her eyes. "No doubt you're wondering what happened?"

"Yes, but if you're not up to talking about it, that's okay," I said.

"I told Detective Simmonds everything I could remember, and she didn't tell me to keep it to myself. As you know, Merry, I was getting concerned when the new neighbors didn't respond to my many overtures of friendship. I had another batch of my molasses spice cookies ready to go when I saw her in front of the house. A bunch of advertising material had been stuffed into everyone's mailbox that morning. Darn nuisance all that rubbish is, and even worse when the carrier doesn't put it properly into the mailbox but leaves it to scatter to the winds. Which is what happened across the street. I was considering going out myself and picking the unsightly mess up from their yard when her car drove up. It went into the garage, as usual, but instead of going directly into the house from the garage entrance, a woman got out and collected the papers. She tucked them under her arm and went into the garage, and the doors shut behind her. I realized it was the perfect opportunity to deliver my cookies, so I hurried over as soon as I could. Unfortunately, I wasn't yet dressed for the day, so I had to take time to do that, and then I couldn't find my boots, so I was delayed once again." She paused and took a breath. "Merry, would you be a dear and pass me that glass of water."

I hurried to do so and held it while she sipped through the straw provided.

Snores continued from the next bed, increasing in intensity. People came and went in the corridor outside. A woman laughed and a man yelled. A nurse spoke to another. A porter pushed an empty stretcher down the hall.

"Thank you," Mrs. D'Angelo said when she'd had a sip of water. "Finally, I was ready to go, and so I went across the street with my tin of cookies and rang the bell. No one answered. I knew she was at home: I'd seen her moments before. I thought maybe she was in the back. It was cold, but the sun was out, so perhaps she was relaxing on the deck."

Dad and I said nothing. Anyone else would call that snooping.

"I scarcely can credit what happened next. The gate to the backyard was unlocked, so I went in and onto the deck. The blinds were open, and I could see her in the kitchen. Her back was to me. She was at the sink, pouring beer into a glass. I rapped on the door and put on my brightest, most welcoming smile. She turned, and the look she gave me, Merry, would send chills up your spine. It certainly did mine, but before I could make my escape, she opened the door and invited me in. I should have turned and run, but you know me, Noel. Always thinking the best of everyone."

Dad didn't laugh, which I thought showed enormous restraint on his part.

"I held out my cookies, stepped into the house, and . . ." She closed her eyes.

I waited.

"Next thing I knew, I had the most awful headache. I couldn't see a thing, and I was unable to move. It was like something out of a horror movie." She shuddered.

"It's over," Dad said, his voice calm and comforting. "You're safe now, Mabel."

"I don't know how long I was in there. Detective Simmonds said two days. Two days! I might never have been found. If not for Merry. I can't bear to imagine what might have happened to me!"

"And George," I said. "Don't forget George Mann, who first raised the alarm."

The phone rang again. I left it where it was.

"What did she look like?" I asked. "The woman who, presumably, bashed you over the head and stuffed you into the pantry?"

"Young. Quite young. She had exceptionally nice hair. Very long, halfway down her back. Shiny and blond. That's all I had time to notice."

"Had you ever seen her before that day? Before she picked up the flyers?"

"Detective Simmonds asked me that. I'm certain I did not. It was two men who were moving furniture and boxes in the day they arrived. I suppose it might have been her in the car those times I saw someone pulling into the garage, or in the car leaving, if her hair was concealed, but I can't say."

Dad and I sat quietly, letting her gather her thoughts.

"I'm having trouble putting everything in sequence," she said. "I suppose I dozed on and off, although I was so dreadfully uncomfortable, I don't know how I managed that. Some light leaked in under the door, enough that I could see

I was in a small room with empty shelves. I tried yelling for help, but she'd put something into my mouth. I knew she was there, she or someone else. I heard footsteps moving about in the kitchen. And then, for a long time, it was very quiet. The light had changed when I heard voices."

"Changed how?" Dad asked. "Lamps turned on or time passing?"

"Time passing, I believe. Natural light, from the daytime, had gone, and the kitchen lights were on."

"Voices?" I said. "Was it the same woman talking to someone?"

"A young woman, at any rate. She hadn't said a word to me when I showed her my cookies. Not that I can remember. I just don't know what happened . . . then. She was talking to a man. A man, and her, the same young woman, or another. They were in the kitchen, standing close to where I was, arguing."

"Arguing about what?" Dad asked.

"I don't know. She said this, whatever this was, was a bad idea. They needed to cut their losses and get out of here. He refused. Said they'd gone to all this trouble and they weren't leaving now because of a bunch of neighborhood"—she flushed and looked away—"busybodies. She said it wouldn't work without Lou, and he said he'd sort out things with Lou and get everything back on track in no time. But first"—she swallowed heavily—"they had to get rid of the temporary inconvenience she'd caused."

"What do you think that meant?" I asked.

"I took it to mean he wanted to . . . get rid of me. I was the inconvenience."

"Obviously, that did not happen," Dad said. "No need to dwell on it, Mabel. They will not be back."

"Who's Lou?" I asked.

"I've no idea. She said what's done was done, and she was finished. She wanted what she was owed, and he told her not to be in such a rush. They could still make it work."

"Then what happened?" Dad asked.

"The voices moved away. I couldn't hear any more. I . . . I didn't know what to do. I considered trying to make a noise, to attract his attention. Maybe they weren't talking about me, maybe he didn't know I was in there. But I didn't like the sound of that man's voice. He used a lot of bad words when talking to her, and I didn't like that. I decided to trust the woman, to trust she'd eventually realize she'd made a mistake and come back and free me. I mean . . . she could have killed me, Noel, instead of putting me in that room. But then . . ." Her voice trailed off.

Dad patted her hand.

"Detective Simmonds showed me a picture. A picture of a dead woman. It was her, the woman from the kitchen. The one with the blond hair."

"Did you recognize her only from the picture? Had you seen her previously?"

"No. Not that I remember. I can't say what happened after the argument I overhead. The voices left. I heard no more footsteps. Time passed. I must have slept on and off. The light changed; it got fully dark. And then daylight again. I managed to work the rag out of my mouth and call for help. I couldn't get the rope off my hands, though." Her eyes drifted closed.

Dad stood up. "We'll leave you to get some rest, Mabel. Call me, anytime, if you need anything."

"Mabel D'Angelo, there you are." Two women burst into the room. They were of late middle age, carrying spindly bunches of red-and-white carnations. "You are the talk of the town, you are. I've been calling and calling all morning, but your mailbox says it's full. You really should listen to your messages and delete the old ones. Suppose someone's trying to get you in an emergency? I phoned Ellen here, and we decided to pop in for a visit. Did the police confiscate your phone? Do they need it for evidence? Oh, Noel, hello. Don't let us keep you."

"I believe Mabel's ready for a nap," Dad said.

"Nonsense." Ellen gave him a dismissive wave of her hand. "The nurse at the desk told us she's up to accepting visitors. Now, tell us everything." They plonked themselves down on the recently vacated visitors' chairs and assumed the position. Chins in hands, eyes bright, expressions expectant.

Mrs. D'Angelo's neighbor snored on.

"Mabel?" Dad said.

"Thank you for coming, Noel. Merry. I am rather tired, June. I don't feel up to talking."

"Nonsense," June repeated. "I heard from Donalda that she knew something was amiss in that house but no one would believe her."

"I'll ask a nurse to pop in," Dad said. "To help you settle."

"It's worrying," I said as my father and I walked down the long corridor after having a word with the nurses. "She's not on her phone taking advantage of all the attention. Never mind actually discouraging visitors."

"She's had a shock, honeybunch. A bad one. She needs to rest, but I fear her so-called network won't let her. Still, she's capable of telling the nurses no visitors, if that's what she wants." He pushed the button for the elevator. The doors swished open, and none other than Detective Diane Simmonds stepped out.

The doors shut behind her, and the elevator departed without Dad and me.

"Noel, Merry. Not surprised to see you two here," the detective said. "Can I assume you were visiting Mabel D'Angelo?"

"Briefly," Dad said. "She has a couple of friends with her now."

She smiled. "Not a problem. I can chase them away. Before that, if you have a few minutes, I have some information to share with you."

"That's a first," I said.

"By share, I mean inform you of some details of what we've learned in the last fourteen hours so you can in return provide me with further information. Coffee?"

"Sure," I said. Dad pushed the elevator button once again.

Simmonds and I settled ourselves at a big table by the window in the largely empty hospital cafeteria while Dad went for the drinks. It was ten in the morning. Staff grabbing coffee and muffins for breakfast had been and gone, and visitors and mobile patients wanting to chat over lunch had yet to arrive.

"World's worst coffee," Simmonds said to me. "Every hospital is equally bad."

"I suppose you've been in a lot of hospitals."

"More than I like. The deceased woman has been identified, as you suspected, as one Raquel Marie Torrone. She lives in New York City, where she is, as they say, not unknown to the police."

Dad put three mugs on the table. The coffee was a muddy color, not at all appealing. "Not unknown for what?"

"Minor embezzlement, for which she did six months in jail. A couple of fraud cases thrown out of court when the complainants failed to appear. All small-scale stuff, but the NYPD tells me she had some acquaintances they don't consider to be small scale. Also of interest, she has a file with us."

"Us?"

"Rudolph PD. Sealed, as she was a juvenile at the time. The house in question, by way of considerable interest, is owned by Beth and Richard Torrone, previously of Rudolph, currently of Rochester, New York."

"Raquel's parents," Dad said. "I believe they inherited the house from Dorothy Johannesen, Beth's aunt. That was some years ago, and as far as I know, they never attempted to live in it."

"You're right. The Rochester police paid a call on them to deliver the news of their daughter's death. They weren't at home. Fortunately, a neighbor was, and that neighbor has their phone number. I have spoken to them. They're in North Carolina on vacation and will be traveling back today. I have an appointment with them later this afternoon. They tell me they haven't had any personal contact with their daughter in thirteen years. Her choice, not theirs. She walked out of the house one day with a suitcase, when she was a high school senior, and cut them out of her life almost completely. They knew she wasn't dead, because once or twice a year she would send an email asking them for money. They always gave it, always sent it by bank transfer, and then didn't hear until the next request came in. They don't know why she would be in that house, or even in Rudolph. Obviously, we couldn't get into a detailed discussion over the reasons for the estrangement or about the money they sent her over the phone. I hope to learn more when I speak to them in person."

"Sad," Dad said. He looked at me with eyes overflowing with love. "To lose a child, no matter how rarely you see them." I stretched my arm across the table toward him, and he took my hand. He cleared his throat, reclaimed his hand, and said, "The house itself is interesting. Did Raquel rent it under her own name?"

"No. The lease is under the name of Scott McNamara. Do you know anyone by that name?"

"No," Dad and I chorused.

"Seems strange she'd be in a house her own parents own without telling them a friend of hers, if we assume Scott McNamara is at least an acquaintance, is renting it."

"Are the Torrone parents, as you put it, also 'known to the police'?" Dad asked.

"Nothing more than the occasional parking ticket. He's a technician for a phone company; she's a teller in a bank. The family never lived in that house. Beth inherited it from her aunt Dorothy Johannesen, who lived in it for more than forty years before her death."

"Dorothy Johannesen. I remember her," Dad said. "And, in the interest of full honesty, not at all fondly. She was what we at town council call a pest. Garbage wasn't picked up on time. Sidewalk not cleared in a timely manner. Squirrels running rampant through the neighborhood. Racoons over-turning her trash cans. Cars parked on the street. Dog complaints, noise complaints. She died, as I recall, about twelve or thirteen years ago."

"Ten," Detective Simmonds said.

"I won't say the town hall staff celebrated at the news, that wouldn't be correct, but they did let out a sigh of relief."

"She left the house to her niece, her sister's daughter, Beth Torrone. When I spoke to the Torrones earlier, Beth told me they hadn't wanted to return to Rudoph to live in the house and it wasn't a good time to be selling, so they decided to keep it as a rental property. The most recent tenants lived there for eight years. They moved, and the house became available about a month ago, and this Scott McNamara took it. I should mention, by the way, that so far I have not been able to locate Scott McNamara. Might be an alias."

"Which," Dad said, "brings us to the question of why one needs an alias to rent a house, and why a daughter of the town took steps not to be seen."

I'd abandoned my coffee after my first sip, as had Dad. Simmonds was almost finished with hers. I guess, as a busy cop, one takes one's coffee when one can get it. And how one gets it. "That, I assume, has to do with the stuff I saw in the cellar."

Simmonds grinned at me. "Precisely. I have to say, Merry, I'm glad to hear you didn't recognize it. That cellar was set up as a counterfeiting operation."

"Counterfeiting? As in money?"

"As in money."

Chapter Ten

"That would explain why they were being so private and even secretive," Dad said. "If they were intending to use the house as a place to run a criminal operation."

Simmonds shrugged. "Bad idea. All they managed to do was to create interest on the street. Never mind Mrs. D'Angelo and her network; any reasonable neighbors in a town as close-knit as Rudolph would soon start to wonder why they never saw the residents."

"Did Mrs. D'Angelo tell you she overheard Raquel and a man talking about Lou?" I said. "Whoever Lou is, they needed to sort things out, whatever that means, with him or her."

"She did. But I don't have any idea who Lou is." Simmonds drained the last of her coffee and gathered up her bag.

"If you can tell us," I said. "How did Raquel die?"

The detective tossed the bag over her shoulder. "Autopsy hasn't been done yet, but I don't need any official verdict. She was stabbed. One thrust direct to the heart. No defensive wounds on her hands or arms, so she likely didn't see it coming. Evidence indicates she was stabbed in the dining room and then shoved down the cellar stairs, presumably in an attempt to delay the discovery of the body."

"Can you estimate the time?" Dad said.

"The autopsy will be more specific, but as an educated guess, likely late Saturday afternoon."

I let out a long breath. Poor Mrs. D'Angelo, trapped in a house for two and a half days with a dead body. Thank heavens the killer didn't dump Raquel into the pantry.

"Why did they leave Mabel alive, do you think?" Dad asked. "It sounded to Mabel as though they were arguing about killing her."

"I can't say, Noel. Mabel was obviously focused on her own situation. They might well have been arguing about something completely different. At a guess, Raquel Torrone didn't tell her killer she had a neighbor tied up in the pantry. He, if it was the person she was arguing with earlier, killed her and left."

"If they were counterfeiting, did you find funny money?" Dad asked.

"Some, yes. Several bags of it. At first glance, not terribly good-quality stuff, as befits the small-scale operation they seemed to have." She turned to go and then swung back. "I want to follow up with a few more questions about Raquel with your daughter, Eve. I'd like to pay a call on her later. Is she planning to be around?"

"She should be," Dad said.

"Highly unlikely this death has anything to do with Raquel's past here in Rudolph," Simmonds said, "but if Eve can give me some further insights into the woman, even as she was years ago, it might help."

We watched the detective walk out of the cafeteria. Two uniforms were coming in, and they exchanged nods as they passed.

"One good thing in this," I said.

"It has nothing to do with us," Dad said.

"Yup. If Raquel was involved in a counterfeiting ring, clearly she had a falling-out with one of her confederates and they killed her. Looks like they abandoned the operation and fled back from whence they came."

"No reason for you to get involved, honeybunch."

"For which I'm grateful. I'll be busy enough over the next two weeks."

* * *

But not too busy to meet Eve and Vicky for an after-work-drink. The store closed at six today, and after telling Mattie I wouldn't be too long, I locked up and ran across the street to A Touch of Holly, where I found Vicky and Eve settled at a tall table by the window in the comfy wood-lined bar. A fire burned cheerfully in the gas fireplace, and tiny white lights interwoven with lengths of holly lined glass cabinets packed full of bottles and glassware. Small vases of freshly cut holly graced every table, and a larger arrangement sat at both ends of the bar.

I noticed a couple of men eyeing the table. No surprise there; they were two lovely young women. Vicky, tall and lean with her short dramatic hair, sharp cheekbones, and large eyes. Eve, tiny, fine boned, and blond, pretty enough to have a good chance at making it in Hollywood.

I slipped onto an empty stool. Vicky and Eve had their drinks already, and a glass of white wine waited for me. The men turned back to their conversation.

"Cheers." I lifted the glass.

"Cheers."

"Good day?" my sister asked.

"Good as in productive and profitable. Not so good in that I'm absolutely beat."

She sighed dramatically. "It must be *soooo* hard, running a business at *your* advanced age."

I stuck my tongue out at her, and she laughed. Some things never change between sisters.

"Hey there, kiddo," Vicky said. "Don't forget Merry and I are the same age."

"I know," Eve said. "You just seem so much younger."

I rolled my eyes.

"What's happening with the book?" Eve asked. "Merry told me you've written a cookbook and it's going to be published. How fabulous is that!"

"It's mostly out of my control now," Vicky said. "And you know how I hate not being in control."

"You can say that again," I said.

"You know how I hate not being in control," Vicky said again. "The book's finished and handed in to the publisher. It's now in edits, and the editor and I are having a few disagreements."

"Serious disagreements?" Eve asked.

"No," I said. "All totally normal. But the person who hates not to be in control is having trouble dealing with it. I keep telling her the job of an editor is to make a good book better. And this one is great."

"Can't back out now," Vicky said. "The advance has been paid, and already spent."

"Did you get a good advance?" Eve asked.

"My agent said it was very good for a first book by an unknown author in a crowded market. Publication is scheduled for next October, in time for the holiday season. I can't believe I have to wait almost a whole year to find out what the world thinks of it."

"They'll love it." I wasn't just saying that to be polite. I'd done my part by tasting as much as I could of the recipes as Vicky developed them. As well as taking on that important role, I'd been the one who initially put Vicky in touch with an agent and a publisher, so I had a keen interest in the book's success.

"They're keeping my title," Vicky said. "I'm happy about that. *Holiday Favorites From America's Christmas Town.*"

"Next year's gifts," Eve said. "For everyone I know." She lifted her glass in a toast. "To its success."

We clicked glasses.

"Did Detective Simmonds pay a call on you earlier?" I asked Eve.

"She did. She had questions about Raquel, but I didn't have a lot to tell her."

"Spill," Vicky said.

"Not much to spill. Not recent news anyway. She was a handful back in school. We were friends for a while, when we were in tenth grade. She was so pretty I was flattered to be in her group." My sister was no slouch in the looks department either. The two of them together must have really turned heads in our small-town high school. "Mom and Dad didn't like her right from the start, but they were smart enough not to try to order me not to hang around with her. I decided soon enough all on my own Raquel was trouble."

"In what way?" Vicky said.

"Mouthing off to the teachers. 'Accidently' tripping other girls or 'accidently' spilling her drink down their front when they were wearing a new outfit. She 'accidently' dropped her entire tray of lunch—hot soup and all—onto the head of a girl who'd gotten the cheerleading spot Raquel was after." Every time Eve said *accidently*, she made air quotes. "Kids started asking me why I was being friends with her, so I stopped hanging around with her. Raquel was pretty and mildly popular, but the cheerleader was even more popular, and she was dating the captain of the football team, so after the lunch stunt, the in-crowd turned against Raquel. I read the signs on the wall and dropped her. Makes me sound like a sheep, I know—"

"We're all sheep in high school," Vicky said. "Nothing was more important in life than maintaining the goodwill of the in-crowd."

I smiled at my friend. In Vicky's case, that wasn't true. She could have been one of the most popular girls in our year. Instead, she hung around with me.

"Raquel-wise, things began escalating after that. Several times kids' lockers were broken into and stuff stolen. Raquel was accused, but no one could prove it."

"Did she do it?" I asked.

"She pretty much admitted it, and dared the victims to do something about it. She knew to focus on the new kids or those who didn't have influential friends, plus she had a way of tossing all that blond hair and fluttering the lashes over those blue eyes that had the adults thinking she had to be totally innocent."

"How did her parents react to all this?" I asked.

"I can't say. They had two other kids, both boys, who seemed to be okay. Funny how I haven't given her a thought in years, and now it's all coming back. The brothers were quite a bit older than Raquel. Anyway, she didn't graduate. Quit school in the middle of senior year. I heard she had a major blowup with her parents and left town. I never heard from or of her again, until this week."

"She left town, what, thirteen years ago?" I asked.

"Yeah. Our senior year. Detective Simmonds told me her family moved away not long after she left. I didn't know that. No reason I should." Eve sipped her drink. "Sad, really. I wonder what she got up to in the intervening years that someone killed her."

"Counterfeiting, it would appear," I said.

"What!" Vicky and Eve chorused.

"The basement of that house was full of counterfeiting equipment. Simmonds said they found fake money too."

"Is counterfeiting still a thing?" Eve asked. "I would have thought with almost everyone using phones or cards these days for just about everything, certainly anything over a couple of bucks, counterfeit money wouldn't be worth so much. I can't remember the last time I paid cash for anything more expensive than a latte."

"It's still a thing," Vicky said. "At the bakery we get a lot of cash, including the occasional fifty or even hundred-dollar bill. My staff know how to check for fakes, but the technology is changing all the time, trying to keep one step ahead of detection."

"Might still be a lucrative venture in the world of money laundering," I said. "I'm proud to say I know absolutely nothing about money laundering."

"That likely doesn't much matter," Vicky said. "Sounds to me as though this Raquel whatever was a pretty low-level operative."

"Low level in high school," I said. "Doesn't mean she stayed that way. Although Simmonds did say the fake money wasn't of very good quality."

"Not our problem," Vicky said. "On to more important things. Eve, your mom told me you auditioned for a big role in season three of that superhot historical series. Have you heard?"

Eve held up both hands and crossed her fingers. "I was called for a second round of auditions before Thanksgiving, so I have my hopes up. Unlikely I'll hear anything over the holidays. I'll relax and forget about it and enjoy Christmas with my family."

I laughed out loud. Like there was the slightest possibility of that happening.

Chapter Eleven

Mrs. D'Angelo was released from the hospital on Wednesday morning. I was at work, but George Mann informed me he'd pick her up and get her settled at home. Iris, Mrs. D'Angelo's sister, was scheduled to arrive shortly thereafter.

I heard nothing more from the police, and I was confident the investigation had moved on to the underworld of New York City.

"Kyle," Jackie informed me as we prepared to throw open the doors for another day of (hopefully) retail frenzy, "is simply devastated."

"Devastated," I said, not paying much attention. Some degree of drama was always circling around Jackie and Kyle. She made sure of that. "About what? Do you think we should move the nutcracker soldcrs to thc front of the display? They seem a bit lost there in the shadows."

"About Raquel Torrone, of course."

That stopped me in my tracks. Nutcracker soldiers forgotten, I said, "What does Kyle know about it?"

"Imagine, her back in town after all these years, only to end up dead. Of all things."

"Did you know her?"

"By reputation only. She wasn't in my year. But no one could fail to notice all that blond hair she was always tossing about." Jackie tossed her own head in imitation. "Or the *Don't mess with me* looks she gave anyone smaller or weaker than her."

"Was Kyle friends with her?"

"Oh yes, Merry. They dated for a long time. Couple of months at least. Broke his heart, it did, when she left town without a word in the middle of their senior year."

"Did he know where she went?"

"No. He didn't even know she was leaving. He went around to her house after a few days, asked her parents why she wasn't at school. Why she wasn't returning his calls. Her mom told him she'd quit school and gone to New York City. Then she shut the door in his face. Kyle didn't think her parents liked him much."

That didn't come as a surprise to me. "Were you friends with Kyle then?"

"No. We hooked up a few years after we left school." She grinned at me. "Funny how that works out sometimes, isn't it, Merry? Same as you and Alan."

I didn't respond to that. "How did he hear about her death?"

"The police put out her picture. They're asking anyone who'd seen her around recently to get in touch. I sort of thought she didn't look too good. Like the years have been hard on her. But, well, I suppose no one looks good in a mug shot."

"I guess not."

"Can't say I'm surprised Raquel had a mug shot. That must be hideously embarrassing to her family."

"I'm sure embarrassment is not at the top of their emotional load right now, Jackie," I said.

"Whatever. Anyway, Kyle's, like, really upset. He says they had some good times together, he and Raquel. He was super serious about her. He was planning to propose to her at the end of the year when they graduated. My luck that didn't happen, right?"

"If you want to put it like that."

"How about if I take the afternoon off, Merry? With pay, I mean. I need to be with Kyle. In his bereavement."

"It's Christmas season, Jackie, and Melissa isn't scheduled to come in today. You can comfort Kyle in the depths of his grief after your shift."

She pouted, but she wasn't all that upset at me turning her down. She'd known the day off—with pay—was never going to happen.

"Did Kyle mention if he'd seen Raquel over the last couple of weeks? Now she was back in town?"

"No. He says it came as a heck of a shock to him to hear about it. He's wondering why she didn't look him up, give him a call. Suggest they go out for a drink or something. Maybe she didn't have time. Just as well that didn't happen. She might not have understood that Kyle has moved on. That he's with me now."

The first of the day's customers came in, putting an end to that line of conversation. We were steadily busy all day, but as I greeted customers, helped them select gifts, accepted payment, and wrapped their purchases, I couldn't get one thought out of my mind.

Raquel had dumped Kyle without a word, leaving him figurately on bended knee. That had to have been a huge blow to his teenage pride. When she breezed back into town and didn't so much as bother to call him, might that have stirred up old resentments? Had Kyle seen Raquel and her highly distinguishable blond hair driving through Rudolph? Had he followed her to the house on Broad Street, where he confronted her? Had she laughed at him; had she mocked his teenage longings? Had he struck out in anger and killed her? Simmonds said Raquel had not seen the attack coming. She'd done nothing to defend herself. That had to mean, didn't it, she was killed by someone she trusted? Or at least someone whom she had no reason to fear?

I peeked at Jackie, smiling flirtatiously at an older gentleman trying to decide on a gift for his wife. Had Jackie had reason to think Kyle would get back with Raquel and thus dump her?

Had Jackie been the one to follow Raquel to Broad Street, and taken steps to ensure that didn't happen?

Absolute nonsense, I told myself. I had not the slightest reason to think anything of the sort had happened, regarding either Jackie or Kyle.

Raquel had a criminal background, and she was engaged in criminal activity at the time of her death. I need not look at my own circle of acquaintances for her killer.

* * *

My own circle of acquaintances expanded later that day.

George Mann came into the store shortly after Jackie got back from her afternoon break. He brought a friend with him, a man about his age, although better dressed and better groomed.

The shop was momentarily reasonably quiet, a few customers browsing, no one in need of my attention. Jackie gave George a friendly wave as she headed for the linens cabinet to straighten the display rumpled by enthusiastic shoppers.

"Merry," George said. "Meet Bob Gravel, the man I was telling you about."

"Pleased to meet you," I said, although for the moment I couldn't remember George telling me about a friend of his.

"Go ahead, Bob. Don't be shy. Tell Merry what you told me."

Bob thrust out his hand, and I shook it. He didn't look all that shy. He had a neat silver goatee, thick gray hair, heavy black-rimmed eyeglasses. He wore a knee-length camel hair coat, a bright-red woolen scarf around his neck, and immaculate brown leather boots. "I don't know that we need to involve you in my troubles, young lady," he said. "But George here insisted."

"I was telling Merry just the other day I had my concerns about you, Bob. Now, fill her in, and then we can go to the police."

The penny dropped, as they say, and I realized who Bob was. The man George feared was being embezzled by an online scam.

The chimes over the door tinkled, and a group came in. "Would you like to discuss this in private?" I asked. "We could go to my office."

"Good idea," George said, without waiting for Bob to reply.

"I'll be right back," I called to Jackie as I led the way through the curtain to the back rooms. I showed the men into my office. Mattie lumbered to his feet and greeted the visitors with a thorough sniffing. That done to his satisfaction, he allowed George to give him a hearty scratch between the ears.

"Big dog," Bob said.

"That he is," I said. "And a good one. Have a seat."

Bob sat. I only have one visitor's chair, so I gestured to George to take the one behind the desk, but he shook his head and leaned against the wall.

"Okay, let's get straight to the point," Bob said. "As usual, my old pal George is making much ado about nothing. But if it amuses him, I don't mind telling you. I might look like an old geezer to you, but I keep up on the social media thing. I don't even need a lot of help from my grandchildren, not that they're ever around to be much help."

"Get on with it," George grumbled.

"Okay. Okay. I met this . . . lady . . . online. Nice young lady, about your age. Pretty too. I've always had a fancy for long blond hair. I wanted Evelyn—that's my late wife—to dye her hair, but she refused. Said it would make her look like a floozy." Bob winked at me. "Nothing wrong with looking like a floozy, I always said."

I had absolutely no difficulty in guessing where this was going. "I assume this . . . young lady . . . sent you a photograph of herself."

"Better than that, we FaceTimed regularly. Added a bit of spark to my day, it did." He winked at me again.

George caught the wink and rolled his eyes. "Played you for a fool, she did, Bob."

"Rather a fool than a dull old geezer."

"Can I guess this woman was Raquel Torrone?" I asked.

"Such turned out to be her name," Bob said. "Although she told me it was Robyn and she lived in Kansas City."

"How did you . . . uh . . . meet?"

"Online, like I said. I'm fond of the horses, like to place a bet now and again—nothing too large, mind—and I like to chat to the like-minded. Social media is great for expanding one's circle of acquaintances. Robyn, as she called herself, and I started talking as part of an online group, and then she suggested we break away and talk privately." Bob smiled. He didn't seem to be all that distressed at being, presumably, scammed, so I guessed the situation hadn't progressed too far.

"Bob sent me a screenshot a while ago of his new lady friend." George sniffed in disapproval. "And so, when I saw a picture of that very woman, or one much like her, on the local TV news, I called him right away. Told him to get down to Rudolph ASAP."

"Where do you live, Bob?" I asked.

"Manhattan."

"Had you ever met Raquel, this Robyn, in person?"

"Never. She lived in Kansas City, didn't often get a chance to get away. She was a waitress, she told me, in a bar."

I assumed George hadn't brought his friend to meet me to talk about horse racing or his FaceTime conversations, so I dared to ask the pertinent question. "Did she ask you for money?"

"Of course she did."

Mattie and George let out similar sniffs of disapproval. Although in Mattie's case, I assumed it was because no one was paying him any further attention. He returned to his favorite spot under the desk, circled twice, and settled down.

"And?" I prompted.

"And I sent it to her. A hundred here. A couple of hundred there. Not much more than I would have lost on the horses, and nothing I couldn't afford. I'm not a total fool, despite what George here might think."

"How long did this go on?"

"Seven months. I last heard from her about a week ago. I made the mistake of telling George about her, and he figured I was being scammed. Hardly news to me, I told him. I knew all along it was a scam. What on earth does a young girl like that want to be online friends with an old geezer like me for, if not money? My wife's dead. My children have moved away and don't visit often. I've never liked to travel. I play golf in the summer, but the rest of the year . . ." He shrugged. "Winters can get mighty boring in New York." He checked his watch and stood up. "Almost two, George. Time to get going."

I threw a look at George.

"We have an appointment with Detective Simmonds at two. If Bob's friend Robyn is this Raquel Torrone, the police need to know. Not every old geezer still has all his marbles, and for some of them a hundred here and a couple of hundred there is all the money they have in the world."

"George is right about that," Bob said. "For me, it was a lark. FaceTiming with her, listening to her stories about the characters she met at her bar, her hardscrabble upbringing and tough-as-nails working-class family, provided some entertainment in a long, uninteresting day. Like interactive

TV. If she worked so hard as a waitress, I thought but never said, how come she always had evenings free? I was sorry to hear she died, because I did like her, and I enjoyed her online company. But if she was scamming me, she was likely after others as well. And some people aren't as kindly disposed to being fooled as I might be."

Chapter Twelve

It never does a tourist-oriented town any good to be the location of a well-publicized murder, and I knew from Dad that Rudolph's powers that be had been holding their breath, worried about fallout from Raquel's death. So far, that hadn't happened. The police report was as vague as usual, and they asked for anyone who'd seen anything in the area, or who had recent contact with the dead woman, to come forward. But the news stories couldn't help but imply that the deceased had been involved in activities of interest to the police, and thus visitors to the town had no reason to fear they'd be murdered in their comfortable hotel beds.

Talk of the kidnapping of Mrs. D'Angelo was a sensation in Rudolph, even more than the murder, but it didn't get all that much exposure in the outside world.

As Mattie and I walked home at the end of another productive day, I thought about George and Bob's visit. Bob's experience with Raquel was definitely an avenue for the police to explore. Might her death have had nothing to do with the counterfeiting ring? Had an enraged relative of one of Raquel's elderly victims sought revenge? Was Bob himself as blasé about it as he implied? Had he really known all along she was phony and only after whatever she could get from him? Or had the revelation come as a shock and surprise to him?

Bob said he'd last had contact with Raquel a week ago. That would indicate Raquel Torrone didn't confine herself to one criminal operation at a time. How many more scams might she have had on the go? And thus, how many more enemies?

If, as the police were assuming, she'd known her killer enough to invite him (or her—never forget her) into the house and get close to her, could that person have been one of her online lovers? Had she invited Bob, or a man like him, to drop in on her in Rudolph? Maybe he offered to bring her a little (or a large) gift. Jewelry? A car? Expensive clothes? Something that couldn't be mailed or transferred online.

Possible. Bob didn't look to me like a killer, but presumably Raquel's killer hadn't looked like one to her either. Otherwise she wouldn't have let him (or her) get so close. She was a criminal. Surely that meant she had a criminal mind and didn't trust people.

Most of us—me, anyway—tend to think of criminals as people "not like us." I've known people who killed in anger, or because they believed they had a perfectly reasonable reason to want to get rid of someone. But Raquel was different. It would seem, from what Eve said, she'd started her criminal activities when she was still in school. I was interested in how that sort of thing came about, and what it eventually led her to.

I reminded myself Raquel was the victim in this. She'd knocked out Mrs. D'Angelo, tied her up, and left her in the pantry, but she had not killed the older woman. If what Mrs. D'Angelo overheard was correct, Raquel wanted to abandon the operation and simply leave. Perhaps I was naive and wanted to think the best of Raquel, but I believed that once she left, Raquel would have told someone where to find the prisoner.

Mattie and I turned up our driveway, but instead of heading around the back, I climbed the steps to the porch and knocked on the front door.

The door opened almost immediately. I'd never met Mrs. D'Angelo's sister Iris, but I knew instantly this must be her. The same small dark eyes, the same olive skin and pointed chin. Iris was slightly shorter and slightly chubbier. Her thick gray hair was bluntly cut, and she wore no makeup. She was dressed in gray trousers, freshly ironed, and a collared white shirt under a dark-gray pullover. Slippers were on her feet.

"You," she said to me, "are Merry."

"That I am."

"Mabel is resting."

"I am not," came a voice from farther inside the house. "Let her in."

Iris frowned, and then she looked at the dog sitting politely at my feet. "I don't care for large dogs. Dirty creatures. He can stay outside. You can come in, if you must."

I told Mattie to wait for me, wrapped his leash loosely around a railing post, and went into the house. Iris shut the door behind me with a disapproving slam.

"Boots off," she said.

I did as ordered.

"My sister has experienced a considerable shock. She is not in a state to be disturbed. I'll give you five minutes, and then you have to leave."

"She'll stay as long as she wants," the voice shouted. "As long as I want, at any rate."

"Living room," Iris said. "I suppose I have to serve tea. I hope you like tea." She walked away without waiting to find out if I liked tea or not.

This house had never been modernized. Closed doors were off the corridor leading to the kitchen at the back of the house. A staircase with a heavy oak banister curved upward, but it led to nothing, as the upper level had been sealed to create the apartments above.

I peeked through the first door to my right and saw Mrs. D'Angelo waving at me. "Come in. Come in. Don't stand on ceremony, Merry. I'm perfectly capable of greeting visitors myself, but Iris insists on me behaving as though I were an invalid. Thirty years as a United States Army nurse, and she's delighted to get the chance to practice terrorizing her patients once again."

The furniture in this room likely hadn't been updated since Mrs. D'Angelo first moved in. Spindly-legged side tables bearing Dresden shepherdesses and a collection of Wedgwood, orange-and-brown upholstery, cream shag rug, grandfather clock clicking steadily away in a corner. I lowered myself carefully onto a chair next to my landlady. She was stretched out on the couch, propped up on a pile of decorative pink pillows, a homemade afghan in lurid shades of pink and lime green tucked around her legs. The bruises on her face were fading, and fresh bandages were wrapped around her wrists.

"You did suffer a considerable ordeal," I said.

"I'll admit, it could have ended worse than it did."

We said nothing for a few minutes. This was a well-built, solid old house; no sounds of tea being prepared came from the kitchen.

"I've been hearing things about Raquel Torrone," I said at last. "Not exactly an upstanding citizen."

"So it would appear."

I waited for Mrs. D'Angelo to expand on that. When she didn't, I said, "Have you heard anything more from the police?"

"They've come around a couple of times," she said. "I'm afraid I can't think of anything further to tell them. Sometimes I don't even know what I remember or what I dreamt."

"Here we are." Iris came into the room carrying a tray. Teapot under a crocheted cozy, three cups and saucers, small jug of milk and sugar bowl and silver spoon. A side plate held six small brown cookies. She put the tray on the low table in front of the sofa.

"That looks nice," I said.

"I was stationed in England for three years. Learned how to make a decent cup of tea. It's late for tea, but as we have a guest . . . Shall I pour?"

"Please do," Mrs. D'Angelo said.

I looked between the sisters. "Are you two twins? The resemblance is strong."

"I'm five minutes older. And substantially more intelligent." Iris poured the tea; steam rose into the air, hearty and fragrant.

She passed me a cup. "You can talk in front of me. Mabel keeps no secrets from me."

"That you know of," my landlady said.

"Cookie, Merry?" Iris offered me the plate. "I don't bake myself, far too frivolous a hobby for me, but I found these in the freezer."

I accepted one. "Like I said, I've been hearing things about Raquel, which naturally makes me curious as to what went on in that cellar."

"Curiosity killed the cat," Iris said.

"I . . . uh . . . okay. I'm wondering what you know about her and her family. That's all."

"Speculation," Mrs. D'Angelo said, "has been running amok."

"Gossip," Iris said, "never did anyone any good. Neither to the gossiper or the gossipee."

"Isn't it time for my medication, Iris?"

Iris checked her watch. "Ten more minutes."

"This tea is delicious," I said. "If possible, could I have a glass of water?"

Iris frowned at me, and then she got to her feet. "I know when I've been dismissed."

She left the room. Mrs. D'Angelo sighed. "I love my sister dearly, but she can be trying at times."

"I am concerned for your physical well-being, Mabel," Iris shouted from the hallway. "Not to mention mental." Her footsteps faded.

I smiled to myself. Families could be trying indeed, but they were there for us when we needed them.

Mrs. D'Angelo sipped her tea. "Dorothy Johannesen. Raquel's great-aunt. I knew her in passing, living directly across the street and all, but we were not friends. She was generally considered to be what is politely called eccentric and impolitely called a miserable old bat. Always complaining. She had the nerve one winter to complain to the town that she slipped on a patch of ice on the sidewalk in front of my house. As if I would ever let ice gather. As if she would ever walk down the street. She didn't drive, so she took cabs to do her shopping and visit the doctor and the like, but otherwise she rarely went out, and as I recall, she almost never had company. That she had no friends came as no surprise to anyone. This was a few years ago—remember, Merry?—and much has happened since."

"I'm only wanting to get an impression," I said. "She left her house to her niece when she died. Beth Torrone, Raquel's mother."

"That's right. They didn't get on, for all that Beth was the daughter of Dorothy's sister. I don't recall Beth or her husband ever visiting her. But, in the end, she did the right thing and left all she had to her closest relative." Mrs. D'Angelo almost dropped her teacup as a thought came to her. She sat up straighter against her pillows. "Good heavens, Merry, I must be getting forgetful in my old age."

A snort came from the hallway. Iris had returned.

"I totally forgot until now. Yes, that girl. Raquel. I have seen her before, but that was a long time ago, and she was much younger. She called on Dorothy a few times over the years. Not that I ever paid particular attention to whatever Dorothy was up to, mind. But one does see things, doesn't one?"

"Of course," I said. "One does. When was the last time Raquel visited her great-aunt?"

Tea forgotten, Mrs. D'Angelo's face crinkled in thought. "Years ago. Likely when she was still in school. Yes, it's coming back to me now. People talked about the girl. They said she was trouble and her parents were worried about her. She quit school before graduating and left town. Some said she stole a considerable amount of money from her parents before leaving, but I can't say if that's true or not. I don't recall hearing about her ever again. The family moved away, Dorothy died, and new people moved into the house. Cathy might know more. As I recall, Cathy and Beth Torrone were friends."

"Cathy?"

"Cathy Kirkpatrick. You know her, of course. Ted's wife."

I didn't know Cathy or Ted. But that never mattered.

"There was another branch of the family. Let me think." Mrs. D'Angelo thought. "Yes, Dorothy had a brother. Can't remember his name now. Dorothy never married, so his last name should be Johannesen." She snapped her fingers rapidly, trying to remember. The light had leapt back into her eyes. The Mrs. D'Angelo I knew and, although I didn't quite love her, was fond of, was coming back. Nothing Mrs. D'Angelo enjoyed more than working out intricate family relationships. "He, the brother, lived in Muddle Harbor. I believe he had a family of his own, but I don't know anything more about them. I'll ask around, Merry."

"Thanks." I got to my feet. "I'd better be off. Mattie's outside, and he'll be wanting his dinner."

Mrs. D'Angelo frantically patted the pillows and coverings around her. "Where's my phone? Iris! What have you done with my phone!"

"I put it away for your own good," the voice in the hallway said. "You need to rest."

111

"I am resting. I can rest while I talk on the phone." She threw off the afghan and started to stand.

Iris came into the room. "Stay where you are. It's time for your medication." The look on her face would have cowed many a battle-toughened soldier.

It did not cow her sister. "I'll stay here if you bring me my phone. Otherwise, you will force me to go in search of it."

The sisters glared at each other, their expressions identical. Iris gave in first, and with a martyred sigh, she pulled the prized object out of her pocket. She handed it over. Mabel snatched it with a cry of triumph.

I slipped away.

Mattie was sitting contentedly on the porch, watching the world go by. I untied the leash and told him he was a good dog. I couldn't help but take a sideways glance at the Johannesen house. The lamp over the door was on, but all the internal lights were off and the drapes closed. Police crime scene tape was still up, hanging limp in the cold, still air. A man stood on the sidewalk, next to the large blue spruce. His back was to me as he watched the house. He was a big guy, but I couldn't see much of him, as he was largely concealed by the snow-covered needles and heavy branches. He didn't look toward me but abruptly walked quickly away, his hat pulled low. He passed under a streetlight and faded into the night.

A curious neighbor, no doubt. People still gathered outside the house occasionally, perhaps hoping for renewed police activity or for the guilty party to return to the scene of the crime.

I went home.

This case might have nothing to do with me or people I cared about, but I found myself developing an interest in Raquel. Maybe because she was a Rudolph girl, like me, who had turned "bad," unlike me, and I was curious about how that could have happened. Maybe because my sister had been friends with her. Most of all, perhaps, because I'd come across her body, and I wondered how her story had come to its end so prematurely and so tragically.

I didn't care about her family relationships, her cranky great-aunt, or the story of her great-uncle who lived in Muddle Harbor. But Mrs. D'Angelo delighted in the joy of the hunt. I might find her love of gossip excessive and often exasperating, but I was fond of her, and if digging into Raquel's background would help her get herself back to normal, what harm could it do?

Chapter Thirteen

"**A**ny plans for tomorrow morning, honeybunch?" Dad asked me on Saturday shortly before closing.

"I have lots of plans. Sleep in late, drink coffee, eat breakfast. Why are you asking?"

"Big happenings in Muddle Harbor tomorrow. As it's Sunday and you don't open until noon, I thought you might enjoy coming with me to check it out."

"Why are you going to Muddle Harbor, and what are these big happenings?"

I stood on the street outside the shop to take the call from Dad. The ever-changeable Upstate New York weather had changed again: the temperature dropping dramatically, snow starting to fall. We were, so the forecast said, in for a lot of the white stuff overnight. The wind was light, and the flakes drifted gently down, caught in the glow of the street-lights and the holiday decorations before coming to a rest on the scarves and hats of pedestrians or the roofs of cars. The lights in the window of Cranberry Coffee Bar went out. Across the street, a waiter at A Touch of Holly brought out a signboard listing the day's specials. At this time of year, the day's specials were always the eggnog martini, turkey with all the festive trimmings, and rum-soaked holiday pudding.

"You know I've been consulting, undercover so to speak, with Janice Benedict on her mayoral campaign," Dad said.

"I do."

"The powers that be in that town are meeting tomorrow morning. Janice intends to present them with her carefully thought-out proposal."

"And that proposal is?"

"All will be revealed tomorrow, honeybunch."

Over the holiday season, about the only time I get to actually relax is a few precious hours on a Sunday morning. I did not particularly want to go to the neighboring town of Muddle Harbor. I had little interest in what passes for political machinations in that town, but my dad and Janice had worked steadily and secretly over the summer and fall, laying their plans for a rapprochement between the two feuding communities. (In fairness, all the feuding emanated from their end.)

"Will I be back in time for store opening?" I'd nipped out to take the call and was starting to freeze in my simple cardigan and the ballet flats I wear when on my feet all day.

"Why don't we drive separately in case I'm delayed?"

"Okay. I have to admit, I'm interested in how Randy's going to react to a threat to his authority."

"Randy Baumgartner has been mayor of that town for nigh on twenty years. Long in the post, not because he's popular but because no one else wants the job. The only time he was challenged was fifteen years ago, when a previously unknown descendant of a local family wanted to turn Muddle Harbor into America's Circus Town."

I laughed. Muddle Harbor's residents were not known for their sense of humor.

"Randy squeaked out a win with fifty point two percent of the vote. Tomorrow's meeting is at the café. Nine o'clock. Before I go, any further news from the police about the recent incident?"

I hopped up and down, trying to get some warm blood flowing into my feet. I rubbed my arm with my free hand. "Not from my end. George told me Detective Simmonds appeared to find his friend Bob's story interesting indeed. You heard about that?"

"I did. The police issued a statement, without mentioning any names, to elderly people, warning them to be aware of online scammers. The police might not have mentioned names, but George made sure everyone knew they were specifically referring to his friend. And, as for said friend, Bob's not exactly hiding it. He's rather proud of the fact that, according to him, he recognized a scam from the very beginning and played along. In order—again, according to him—to lure the guilty party into a trap."

"Did the police happen to ask Bob where he was on Saturday evening?"

"They did. He was at his bridge club holiday party. He left around seven, not too late to drive to Rudolph, but he is an older man, and he doesn't drive on the highway at night because of his cataracts. According to him."

"Which might or might not be true. Have they dug up any other gentlemen friends of Raquel?"

"If they have, that information has not been shared with me. All I've been telling you, I got from George and Bob."

"I'd ask if any unfamiliar older men have been seen around town recently, particularly in the vicinity of a specific section of Broad Street, but unfortunately, Rudolph in mid-December is full of unfamiliar people."

"Commonly called tourists," Dad said. "And yes, some of them are divorced or widowed men accompanying their families on vacation."

"Doesn't have to be a single man who made so-called friends with Raquel. I wouldn't be surprised if plenty of married men think they're pulling one over on their wives."

Dad chuckled. "Not thinking of anyone in particular, I hope, honeybunch?"

"No, Dad, I am not. The police have been around to talk to Mrs. D'Angelo a couple of times, but she tells me she can't remember anything more." I let out a puff of air and watched the mist form in front of my face. I wiggled my toes to ensure they were still operational.

"How's she doing?" Dad asked.

"Okay, I think. She seems to enjoy sparring with her sister, and she's once again assumed her rightful position as the processing center of all gossip in Upstate New York. Not only is she processing the gossip like some mega computer system, but she herself is the actual center of attention this time."

"I'm glad to hear it. I might admit, if only to you, I find Mabel's insatiable need for gossip to be a mite tiring at times, but it did worry me when she seemed to have lost interest for a while there."

"I haven't seen Detective Simmonds for a couple of days," I said. "Which I take to mean that she and her investigation have moved beyond the town limits of Rudolph."

"Which is most certainly a good thing. See you tomorrow, honeybunch." Dad hung up.

I decided I'd have time to make one more phone call before I permanently froze into a good enough ice sculpture to be erected next to the bandstand, and I made a quick call. Couldn't go to Muddle Harbor without reinforcements.

"Up to a trip to the Heart of Darkness tomorrow morning?" I asked.

"If you mean Muddle Harbor, no," Vicky said. "If you mean someplace else that's known by that sobriquet, sure."

"Great. Muddle Harbor it is. I'll pick you up at the bakery at quarter to nine."

* * *

Like Rudolph, Muddle Harbor in the early and midtwentieth century had been a bustling, thriving center of Great Lakes shipping. But whereas Rudolph had been able to reinvent itself in the twenty-first century as a tourist destination, Muddle Harbor settled into a slow, and then rapid, decline. They could have used their proximity to Rudolph to take advantage of overflow activities and accommodations, but they (largely under the influence of the eternally lazy perennial mayor Randy Baumgartner) stubbornly refused to accept any dependency on what they thought of as their bitter rival. One attempt after another to revitalize the town had failed, and finally, last spring,

Janice Benedict realized that if anyone was ever going to do something about it, it had to be her.

She called my dad, a former mayor of Rudolph, for advice.

I'd have thought two weeks before Christmas was not a good time to announce a mayoral run, but the Muddites tend to do things their way. For once, it would be nice to openly visit Muddle Harbor, not to sneak in attempting to track down a murderer while trying (and failing) not to be too obvious about it.

I closed the shop and headed home, well bundled up in coat, scarf, boots, and gloves. The snow was falling heavier now, and not many people were on the streets. Traffic moved slowly down Jingle Bell Lane, windshield wipers swishing, headlights illuminating the fat flakes.

Mattie trotted contentedly at my side. Like the rest of his kind, Mattie had been bred for the snow and the cold. Winter was his happy place.

I hadn't seen Alan for days, and I missed him. I reminded myself that I could hardly complain at his lack of attention, considering I'd asked him to make more stock for my store. The holiday season might be the "holidays" in America's year-round Christmas destination, but it was not a vacation time for us.

"Right, Mattie?" I asked.

He lifted his head, eyed me, and woofed. I took that to be agreement.

The lights were on in the downstairs rooms of my house. I hadn't spoken to Mrs. D'Angelo since Wednesday. My dad had popped in yesterday to visit her, and he reported that she seemed in good spirits. Mostly back to her normal self, as she barely had time to talk to him between juggling incoming and outgoing phone calls.

The ringing of the doorbell had scarcely faded away before Mrs. D'Angelo threw open the door. She wore the pink dressing gown and fluffy pink mules I'd seen when George and I had been in the house searching for her. Her earbuds were in her ears, and her phone peeked out of the breast pocket of the gown. The sparkly pink case had not been returned to her.

"Merry! Just the person I was hoping to see. I have a report ready for you."

"A report?"

"Come in." She grabbed my arm and yanked it so hard I stumbled over the threshold. Mattie followed. I kicked snow off my boots and gave Mattie a worried look. "Is Iris still here?"

"Gone. Left this morning. Thank goodness. I won't say it wasn't good of her to come, but she can be a strain to deal with. Tea, dear? Or something stronger? It is after six."

"I won't stay, thank you. I wanted to check on how you're doing."

"Fine. Right as rain." Something twisted behind the cheerful expression, but she brushed it off. I wasn't so sure that was a good thing. She'd experienced an ordeal, one that could have ended very badly. The memory had to be constantly on her mind. But she smiled at me and said, "I won't keep you, then. Obviously, you're here for my report."

"Report?" I repeated.

"About the Torrone family. No telling, is there, how children can turn out, even in the best families. Beth and Richard, who no one ever called Rick or Rich, were always perfectly respectable people. From what everyone says, their two sons are doing fine in life. One of them is even a doctor now. Imagine that! But that Raquel." She shook her head. "Never anything but trouble."

Whenever I get my information from Mrs. D'Angelo, I have to remind myself to add a bucketload of salt. In the circles in which she moved, the more spectacular the gossip, the more it was worth. And thus the more prestige it gave the presenter of the gossip. Truth was sometimes a secondary consideration. If not tertiary.

"Beth and Richard, the parents, have arrived in town. The police are still holding their daughter's body, but that shouldn't be for much longer. So sad. They're staying at the Yuletide. You know how hard it can be to get a hotel room in Rudolph at this time of year, Merry, but they were lucky to call immediately following a cancellation. They hadn't had any contact with Raquel for several years, but she was still their daughter. So sad," she repeated.

And it was.

"In other news, they're selling the house."

"The house? What house?"

Mrs. D'Angelo pointed over my shoulder. "That house, of course. Dorothy Johannesen's house. They don't want to be bothered with a rental property anymore, never mind the tragedy they'll associate with it for the rest of their lives."

Police tape was still wrapped around the driveway, the path to the backyard, and the steps to the front door.

"When the police have finished with it, of course," Mrs. D'Angelo said. "I hope the fact that someone died there doesn't affect the selling price. Many of the old houses like that one, not to mention this one, have seen a lot of death in their time. Sure you won't have a drink, dear?"

"No, thanks. How do you know it's for sale?"

"It's not for sale yet, but it soon will be. Marlene Jones has a good chance of being chosen to be the realtor. She's done well for herself in the months since she managed to unload, I mean sell, Cole House to Vicky Casey and Chef Mark. And then double the commission when Vicky and Mark sold it so soon after moving in."

"I'm glad to see you back on your feet," I said. "If you're having any . . . difficulties dealing with what happened to you, you know you can ask for help. Professional help, I mean."

She beamed at me. "I have absolutely no idea to what you are referring, Merry. Oh, a call's coming in. I have to take this."

I gave Mattie a light tap on the head, and he followed me out the door.

Chapter Fourteen

We didn't get far.

The door to Mrs. D'Angelo's house shut behind us. Mattie and I had only gone a few steps before a car pulled up outside the house across the street.

Mattie yipped with delight, and sure enough, a moment later Detective Diane Simmonds got out. She saw us watching and lifted a hand in greeting. A man I didn't recognize emerged from the passenger side. He was tall, slightly overweight, dressed in jeans, a heavily worn coat, and much-used boots. His gray hair was cut short; his cheeks red and plump. Deep, dark circles lay under his eyes, and a network of lines radiated from the edges of his mouth. Cool gray eyes watched me, and he did not smile.

Considering Simmonds's wave to be an invitation, we crossed the street. Mattie, of course, didn't need an invitation. His eyes were bright, his ears up, his tail thumping.

"Merry. Matterhorn," Simmonds said. "Good evening." She put her hand lightly on the top of the dog's head. He just about fainted with joy.

I glanced over the roof of the car toward the unsmiling man. "Detective Frank Lopez, NYPD," Simmonds said to me. "He's following up on the Torrone murder. Detective, this is Merry Wilkinson. I told you about her involvement."

Lopez nodded at me, but he said nothing, and he did not smile.

"Pleased to meet you," I lied. I indicated the house. "Sources tell me this place is going to be put up for sale soon as the tape comes down."

"It is," Simmonds said. "We're pretty much finished here. If there are no new developments, we'll most likely take the tape down on Monday and let the owners have access. I offered to give Detective Lopez here a look before that happens. I've asked you before, but I will again. You never saw the man Mrs. D'Angelo reported as coming and going?"

"Never. All I saw were tire tracks in the snow, in and out of the garage. But that means nothing. I don't spend my days at the front window with a pair of binoculars."

She allowed a grin to touch the edges of her mouth. "Not the first time I've considered putting Mabel D'Angelo on the payroll."

"I've heard," Lopez said in the broadest of broad Bronx accents, "people who live in small towns don't always know when to mind their own business."

"I would have thought that would be of benefit to the police in situations such as this," I replied.

"Sometimes. Until they try to intervene in things that are none of their business."

"Merry has been of help to me in the past, Frank," Simmonds said quickly. "I value her input."

That came as news to me. Lopez might not have snorted. Then again, he might have kept it quiet.

"But," she continued, "the point is valid. I sense we're attracting attention simply by standing here."

I could practically feel the force of Mrs. D'Angelo's binoculars drilling into my back. I didn't think my landlady could lip-read, but nothing would have surprised me.

"We'll go around the back," Simmonds said. "Matterhorn, you may come."

Mattie leapt to his feet. If he'd been slightly more agile, he would have danced on his tiptoes before settling down to walk in a stately manner at her side, head up, back straight.

"Big dog," Lopez said. "You've got him well trained."

I decided not to mention that he didn't act like that around me.

A lock had been put on the gate to the back garden. Simmonds punched in the numbers and pushed the gate open. "Another couple of inches of snow, and we won't need the lock to keep this shut," she said.

She took a few steps into the yard and then stopped. Mattie dropped to a sit. Lopez and I also stopped. Although we didn't sit.

At first glance the back of the house appeared to be undisturbed. Snow covered the lawn and the flower beds; the deck was bare and empty. But crime scene tape was strung across the steps leading to the deck and the sliding back doors. A sheet of plywood had been hammered across the shattered glass. I thought about what I'd found in that house, and I couldn't help but shiver despite my warm coat and other winter accessories. Mrs. D'Angelo had had a lucky escape indeed.

"Anything else I can help you with, Merry?" Simmonds asked. Clearly I wasn't going to be allowed into the house for one last look.

"The man, the one who was seen coming and going. You haven't located him?"

"No. The house was rented under a false ID, but he'll be found soon enough. Plenty of fingerprints in that house, meaning a lot of work to identify them. They're still being matched and analyzed. We've been in contact with the previous tenants and taken their prints for elimination, but they had six kids and all those kids had friends constantly coming and going, and the parents entertained often. The equipment downstairs was wiped clean. Nice, careful job of it too. Of interest, not many of Raquel's prints are to be found in this house. None upstairs. A few in the kitchen, door handle of the fridge, the microwave buttons. Not much else."

"What do you make of that?"

"She hadn't spent much time in the house."

"The real Scott McNamara of NYC," Lopez said, "is an elderly gentleman who has trouble remembering what day of the week it is. The address on the ID provided when the house was rented is a retirement home in Queens. A 2015 Toyota Corolla with the license plate this so-called McNamara drove was found abandoned in a mall parking lot in Ogdensburg, New York. Owner is listed as none other than Raquel Torrone. Who, records show, bought it little over a month ago, only a couple of days before she leased the SUV found in the garage of this house."

"Mrs. D'Angelo, and others we've spoken to on this street, say the SUV was used on what was presumably moving-in day," Simmonds said. "Subsequently, the only vehicle they saw was the Toyota. Until, that is, Raquel showed up the day she died and put the SUV in the garage. No one saw both cars at the house at the same time, and half of the garage was full of empty boxes and a selection of hardware tools."

"Meaning?" I asked.

"Meaning it would appear that Raquel and this man spent little or no time in the house together. As for him, we've spoken to a few people who say they might have seen him in the grocery store or the liquor store or getting gas, but the description they provide is so vague, and so varying, as to be useless."

"What about friends and associates of Raquel herself?" I asked. "Any leads there?"

"My people are onto that," Lopez said. "Torrone's crossed our radar before. Low-level stuff mostly, but enough to keep us interested. Anyone who might have been doing business with her has gone to ground."

"You know she was running a romance scam on elderly men?" Simmonds asked me.

"Men plural? I know about George Mann's friend Bob Gravel."

"Him and a few others," Lopez said. "One man's daughter laid a complaint with the NYPD. It didn't go far. The daughter's largely estranged from her father, and the old man insists the woman he met online was nothing other than a down-on-her-luck friend in need of the occasional handout. He wouldn't press charges or cooperate with the investigating detective. But it did attract the attention of our fraud squad, and a file's open."

"Detective Lopez and his colleagues were able to have a look at Raquel's apartment when we notified them of her death and the circumstances," Simmonds said. "They found her laptop in the apartment, the one she used to run her scam. Chat groups where she found her marks and a record of plenty of FaceTime calls to men who turned out to be single and lonely. Even when the authorities contacted these men and told them she was a con artist, most of them refused to accept it. They want to know when the funeral will be held so they can pay their respects."

"Bob said he regarded any money he sent her as the price of entertainment," I said.

This time Lopez did let out an audible snort. Mattie sat between Simmonds and me, staring approvingly at the other woman. My dog never looked at me like that. I tried not to take it personally.

"Far as we can tell," Lopez said, "he didn't give her more than he could afford. Some of these guys did. Some of them have angry relatives to deal with."

"Might one of these angry relatives have taken steps to stop the scam?" I asked.

"It's possible," Lopez said. "Then again, judging by what Detective Simmonds found in this house, along with Torrone's body, she was into other activities as well."

"As for the counterfeiting operation," Simmonds said, "we've heard not a peep. Which is what I'd expect. Anyone involved should know to head for the hills and cut their losses once a murder investigation opens up."

"So you're not looking at anyone in Rudolph," I said. "That's good."

"We're looking at everyone, Merry," Simmonds said. "As a matter of interest, Raquel and her confederate were not exactly skilled counterfeiters. We found some fake money in boxes in the cellar, but not much, so I suspect he grabbed most of it when he cleaned up and ran. The sort of bills that could be handed to a bored kid working the night shift at a 7-Eleven but wouldn't pass the most causal glance of a bank clerk."

"Seems hardly worth bothering about," I said. "All that trouble, not to mention risk, to get a free Coke or packet of cigarettes."

"There are other ways of passing bad money," Lopez said. "Whether they were into that or not is still to be determined. Enough of this pleasant chitchat. If we need any more from you, Detective Simmonds knows where to find you."

"That she does," I said. "Come on, Mattie, time to go home. Mattie. Mattie!"

"Go with Merry, Matterhorn," Simmonds said.

And he did.

Chapter Fifteen

As planned, at quarter to nine Sunday morning, I pulled up to the back door of Victoria's Bake Shoppe and tooted the horn.

Vicky soon emerged, wrapping a scarf around her neck and pulling on her gloves. "Tell me again why I agreed to do this?" she grumbled as she fastened her seat belt.

"Because you're a good and loyal friend and faithful companion."

"Makes me sound like your dog."

"Not to mention you're curious about the goings-on in the Heart of Darkness, which, if my dad's plan comes to fruition, will no longer be known as such."

"Whatever."

I gave her a look. "You changed your hair color."

"Like it?"

I hesitated. Vicky kept her thick black hair cut super short. Easier to maintain that way, she always said. But, because she had to satisfy her flair for the dramatic, she kept one lock long enough to fall across her forehead and curl down her right cheek. That lock was always brightly colored. Today it was pure white. "It gives you a . . . witchy appearance. More appropriate for Halloween, maybe."

She pouted. "Tell me about it. I decided on red and green stripes to match the season. Something went wrong, and it came out looking like something Sandbanks threw up after he'd been eating grass." I attempted to brush aside that mental image.

"Aunt Marjorie told me not to try to cover it up with more color but bleach it out. So I did. Now I'm stuck with this for Christmas."

This early on a snow-covered Sunday morning, no traffic was moving on Jingle Bell Lane. We'd gotten almost a foot of snow last night, but the plows had been out, and the main streets were clear. The sun was rising in a sky of soft winter blue, and it was predicted to be a sunny day. Nothing nicer than a bright sun and blue sky shining on fields of freshly fallen snow. Trees were draped in white, and the holiday lights on the bandstand shone softly from beneath a coating of flakes.

As we headed out of Rudolph, I filled Vicky in on what Dad expected to happen this morning. "Considering it was me who started the idea of the two towns reconciling in the first place, I figured I'd like to see what goes down."

"'Me'? Meaning you and only you? Must I remind you, I've always been with you when you go to Muddle Harbor. I played my own part in promoting peace and harmony. It seems awfully early for a town council meeting. Nine o'clock on a Sunday?"

"A breakfast meeting, Dad said. Early so the hardworking Muddites can then get on with their hardworking day."

"Got it. Where's the meeting?"

"At the café, of course."

Vicky snorted. "Saints preserve us. Dare I hope they've updated the menu since our last visit?"

"They haven't updated the menu since the Eisenhower administration. And, as far as I'm concerned, that's a good thing. Nothing I love more than a gigantic, old-fashioned American diner breakfast."

Vicky shuddered. Rather than attempting to make friendly with the owner of the café—peace and harmony indeed—Vicky didn't do much other than mock the high-calorie, high-fat, high-sugar (high-taste!) meals served there.

Her disdain never prevented her from stealing a slice of my bacon, though. Sometimes two slices.

A few minutes on the road, and we were passing out of Rudolph. On our right, the waters of the lake were still open, although the shoreline was rimmed with frost. To the left, farmers' fields stretched to the horizon, dormant under their blanket of white. The ice and snow on the trees lining the road twinkled in the light of the rising sun. I'd been expecting the road between Muddle Harbor and Rudolph not to have been plowed yet, but I was pleasantly surprised. That stretch of road was so rarely traveled no one bothered to do much other than the minimum needed to maintain it.

I wondered if my dad had put in a word with the state highway people. If his and Janice's plan was successful, tourists wouldn't want to travel between the towns on a road not maintained since the horse-and-buggy era.

"Want a puppy?" Vicky said, apropos of absolutely nothing.

"What?"

"Do you want a puppy? Mattie would love a little brother or sister, don't you think?"

"Mattie would like nothing less. Why are you asking?"

"My cousin's dog is expecting. Once again, she inadvertently got loose in the company of a boy dog without suitable papers."

Vicky's cousin bred Saint Bernards, and it was from him I'd obtained Mattie. The cousin's dog was a kennel club champion, and she was expected to produce more kennel club winners. Unfortunately, said cousin tended not to keep as close an eye on his prize dog as he should when she was in the mood for canine romance.

The product of one such illicit liaison was Matterhorn and his littermates. Vicky had set about finding good homes for them all, and one of those homes had been mine.

"What type of mutt did she hook up with this time?" I asked.

"A standard poodle."

"The mind boggles."

"The poodle does have suitable papers. Just not suitable for mating with a Westminster-winning Saint Bernard."

"The mind continues to boggle. Why don't you take one of the puppies? Sandbanks needs company in his old age."

"He does not. His old heart couldn't take the excitement."

Come to think of it, when homes were being sought for Mattie and his siblings several years ago, Vicky said she couldn't take one because Sandbanks was too old to have a puppy around.

I was prevented from inquiring further as the speed limit changed as we reached Muddle Harbor, and I slowed to drive into town.

Main Street was as cheerful as ever. Meaning not. A few scraggly green-and-red Christmas lights graced shop fronts, and tattered wreathes with faded ribbons hung on doors, but many of those stores were boarded up, the signs over the doors or in the windows dirty and fading. The streets were empty and unplowed, forcing me to take care as I concentrated on driving in the ruts made by previously passing vehicles.

"Has anyone ever suggested using Muddle Harbor as a movie set?" Vicky said. "Perfect for a postapocalyptic tale of the supernatural."

"They might have," I said, "but the actors would refuse to stay here."

The only signs of life on the street were in front of the Muddle Harbor Café, the town's hot spot and center of all activity. Cars and trucks were parked outside. That stretch of the sidewalk had been cleared of snow, the windows were trimmed with twinkling lights, a big wreath made from fresh greenery and adorned with a bright-red bow hung on the door, and lights from inside shone through clear windows.

I recognized my dad's car and parked next to it. "Now, remember. We're here to make friends. To support Janice, without appearing to be taking sides in whatever goes down. We're not here to talk."

"I like to talk."

"Yes, Vicky, I know."

"Okay. Whatever you say. I take it that this time we're not here to accuse anyone of murder. That'll be a change."

"I can see no connection between Muddle Harbor and Raquel's death or Mrs. D'Angelo's kidnapping. Raquel's great-aunt's brother lived in Muddle Harbor, but if you go back far enough, most people have relatives on either side of the divide. Sort of like Germany when it was separated by the Berlin Wall."

I opened my door and was about to step out when I saw someone I hadn't expected to see here. Kyle Lambert, hurrying down the sidewalk toward the café. His big black Nikon camera hung around his neck.

He passed in front of my car, and I jumped out and said, "Kyle. Hi. What brings you here?"

"Oh, Merry. Hi, Vicky." He grinned and touched the camera. "I'm with the *Muddle Harbor Chronicle* now. Staff photographer."

"Muddle Harbor has a newspaper?" Vicky said. "Does that mean they have news? Other than the obituary pages, that is."

"Important meeting today in the café," Kyle said. "I'm taking photos for the paper. As outsiders, you two might not be allowed in."

"We're with the band," Vicky said.

"Huh?"

"Have you quit the *Rudolph Gazette*?" I asked. His camera looked familiar. It also looked like a very expensive one.

"In these days of increasing online content, declining revenue for local newspapers, and the general decimation of the profession of journalism," Kyle recited, the lines obviously memorized, "a good photojournalist is required to seek jobs where he can find them."

"Does Russ know you're using the *Gazette*'s camera to do work for the *Chronicle*?"

Kyle's eyes widened. He put his hands over the camera and glanced around, as though fearing Russ Durham was watching from behind a lamppost. "Uh . . . uh . . . No. Not this one. It looks the same. But it's not." He ran into the Muddle Harbor Café, and Vicky and I followed.

The place was the same as every time we'd been here, except for the number of people. The big round table that normally occupied the center of the room had been pulled to the front and extra chairs placed around it. Every one of those chairs was taken. A handful of townspeople occupied the booths lining the walls, lingering over their Sunday breakfast and coffee, but most people seemed to be here for the meeting. Chairs had been pulled away from the tables and arranged in two lines facing the counter. Groups of people stood around, clutching coffee cups, waiting for the festivities to begin. The waitstaff were busy clearing the tables of those who'd come for breakfast before staying for the meeting.

My dad sat alone at a booth, a cup of coffee in front of him. I couldn't help but notice a few suspicious glances being thrown his way. I also couldn't help but notice more suspicious glances being thrown at Vicky and me.

The café didn't just resemble an old-fashioned diner; it *was* an old-fashioned diner. Black-and-white-checked floor, stools covered in red plastic pulled up to the chrome-trimmed Formica counter. Serving hatch cut in the back wall to the kitchen, pies and cakes under glass domes, advertising

posters of men on horseback smoking cigarettes on the walls.
The scent of coffee and grease. Even the apron-clad, sensible-
shoe-wearing waitress who called everyone *hon*.

"Thanks for coming, hon." Janice Benedict greeted us
from behind the counter. "Grab a stool. Can I get you your
usual?"

"Thanks," I said. "Okay if we sit with my dad?"

"Sure. One order of poached eggs, soft, bacon, and sau-
sages. Rye toast. Potatoes done to the point of very crispy,"
Janice called through the serving hatch. My order placed,
she turned to Vicky. "What can we get you, hon? Water
and a handful of oats?"

Vicky cleared her throat. "As I've been up for hours and
I had breakfast at work, I'll have . . . a slice of that carrot
cake, please. And . . . a cup of . . . coffee."

Janice grinned.

"Nice of you to make the effort to be polite," I said to
Vicky as we crossed the floor to Dad's booth. "Not that
having carrot cake counts as an effort in anyone else's
books."

"It's past nine," a man yelled. "Let's get this show on the
road. I've places to be and got things to do."

"Must we?" another man said. "My wife expects us to
go to her mother's for lunch, and I told her I might be
delayed."

"You wish, Fred," a woman called.

Kyle walked around the room, ostentatiously displaying
his camera, tilting his head, holding his hands up as though
composing a picture frame. A few people straightened their
shoulders, stretched their necks, and preened, but he moved
on, leaving them disappointed.

"What do you expect to happen?" I whispered to my dad as Vicky and I slid into the booth.

"This is the monthly meeting of the town council," Dad said. "Randy assumes it will progress as usual, meaning everyone will argue about everything, nothing will be decided, Janice will serve pie, and then they'll adjourn until next month to do it all again."

"Why do they have council meetings in a restaurant?" Vicky asked. "Why not town hall?"

"The town hall burned down. This is temporary until they can rebuild."

"Gosh, I didn't hear about that," I said. "When did it happen?"

"Nineteen eighty-four. That they're still gathering here might have something to do with the aforementioned post-meeting serving of pie."

The man seated next to Randy Baumgartner, resplendent in the chain of office worn over his denim shirt, stood up. He was a hefty guy in his late thirties, at that stage of a man's life when muscle competes with fat to see which will dominate as he moves into middle age. His goatee was neatly trimmed and his brown hair combed. He gave me a quick glance, a slight smile. I smiled back, just being polite. Then he turned his attention to the matter at hand and pounded the table with a gavel. "Shut up, everyone. As I believe Ralph so astutely said, let's get this show on the road." Another quick glance at me. "For those who don't know me—"

"Everyone knows you, Graham. Get on with it," a woman called.

He cleared his throat. "Just going through the formalities, Edith. I am Graham Johannesen, here to conduct this meeting and take the minutes. This is the monthly meeting of the Muddle Harbor town council. Anyone who's not here for that is welcome to leave." This time he pointedly looked at my father.

"Carry on," Dad said. "You all know me, Noel Wilkinson of Rudolph. I'm here today as an observer, as I have a keen interest in local politics."

"Yeah, okay. Whatever. I call the meeting to order." More pounding of the gavel.

Kyle stood in front of Graham. The town clerk straightened, lifted his chin as well as his gavel. He attempted to look stern and serious as his photograph was taken for the official record.

"Johannesen," I whispered. "That's the name of Raquel Torrone's mother's family. I'd heard Dorothy's brother lived in Muddle Harbor. Heck of a coincidence."

"Not really a coincidence, honeybunch," Dad said. "You heard the name recently, and thus you noted it next time you heard it. Happens all the time."

"If our honored guests would keep their chatter to themselves, we can get on with it," Graham said. "Thank you for your consideration. First on the agenda is to approve the minutes of the November meeting. Any comments? Any objections?"

No one commented or objected. Someone approved the minutes, and someone else seconded. Graham jotted their names down on the laptop open in front of him. Then he said, "First item of business—"

"I'll have another coffee," Randy shouted. "Janice, coffee!"

Janice stepped forward. She was not carrying her ever-present coffeepot. "The order of business has changed." She shifted her feet and wiped her hands on her apron. My dad sat straighter.

"You can't do that," Graham said. "We have to follow the agenda. As you can see, the first point to be discussed is the issue of that big-box store chain wanting to open a location in our town."

"Which," Janice said, "brings me directly to my point, thus keeping to the agenda as outlined in crayon on a bar napkin last night." She cleared her throat and shifted again. A few people exchanged questioning looks. Randy peered into his cup, disappointed coffee hadn't magically appeared.

"Those people have no intention of opening a store in Muddle Harbor," Janice said. "Not the way things are now. That meeting was eight months ago, and you haven't heard a word since."

"They're playing it cool. A negotiating ploy," Randy said. "Common tactic in business at our level. Get back to your kitchen, Janice. I see the Rudolph folk haven't got their food yet."

A collective gasp went up from the women in the room.

"Not a politically astute comment," Vicky mumbled gleefully.

If Randy's intention had been to force Janice to retreat, he only managed, as could have been expected, to put the fight into her. She lifted her chin, turned away from him, and addressed the room. "No one is investing in Muddle

Harbor. This town is dying, and our useless mayor hasn't a single idea about how to save it. I do."

"Order, order." Graham pounded the table with his gavel. "We'll put your concerns under new business, Janice."

"I want to hear what she has to say now," a woman yelled. Ohers murmured their agreement. Randy opened his mouth. He closed it again. Graham looked unsure and lowered the gavel.

Janice didn't wait for permission to continue. "We live next to one of the fastest-growing, most prosperous towns in this area. Are we taking advantage of that? No, we are not. We've let old resentments and old thinking by old men—and that means you, Randy Baumgartner—let every opportunity we've had to seek new opportunities pass us by. Noel Wilkinson!"

Dad stood up, obviously prepared for this. "Yes?"

"What's the current vacancy rate of hotels and B and Bs in Rudolph?"

"Zero," Dad said. "In fairness, I will point out that it is the holiday season. At other times of the year, the vacancy rate varies between five to fifteen percent."

"Rhonda, what's the current vacancy rate at the motel?"

A wild-haired woman stood up. "I don't know about the arithmetic of it, but maybe we're quarter full for the next two weeks. Almost every one of those folks said they couldn't get a room in Rudoph so they booked with me."

"Noel, what would you say is the current number of vacant stores on your main street?"

"One," Dad said. "Due to unexpected circumstances, the specialty olive oil and balsamic vinegar shop had to suddenly close before Thanksgiving."

"How many olive oil and balsamic vinegar stores do we currently have in Muddle Harbor?" Janice asked, somewhat redundantly.

"There are stores selling nothing but oil and vinegar?" someone asked.

"A tourist favorite," Dad said. "They make attractive gifts for people who enjoy cooking."

"Graham," Janice demanded, "as the town clerk, part-time, unpaid or otherwise, can you tell us what percentage of the stores on Main Street are currently vacant?"

"I don't have that information at my fingertips. I'll have to check."

"Anyone want to venture a guess?"

"A lot?" a man said.

"Yes, a lot. I don't need to guess, nor do I need to check. Half. And you wonder why you haven't heard from the big-box store people in eight months?"

"She's got a point," Rhonda said. "The only reason I can keep my business going is my parents bought the land the motel stands on back in the sixties."

"We have no need of any help from Rudolph." Randy's face was turning a decided red, and a vein pulsed in his forehead. I checked my phone was at hand in case of the need to call 911.

"We do, and you're too darn proud to admit it," Janice said. "But someone has to. I hereby announce my candidacy for mayor of Muddle Harbor."

"You . . . can't," Randy gasped.

"Of course I can. My hat is in the ring. I will be raising funds for my campaign and asking for volunteers. In the meantime, I am open to bringing anyone onto my team who has intelligent, modern solutions to our problems. And that includes working with the good citizens of Rudolph, always ensuring the interests of Muddle Harbor come first and foremost. Now, who wants pie?"

The room burst into an uproar, everyone talking at once. People leapt to their feet and slapped Janice on the back or shook her hand. The woman looked slightly stunned, and I hoped she wasn't going to come to regret taking on the task. I heard plenty of comments along the lines of "about time."

The waitress began bringing out plates, napkins, and forks and arranging them on the counter. Next came an assortment of pies.

"Likely the first time in the history of Muddle Harbor," Vicky said, "no one's rushing to be front of the line for pie. As I still don't have my carrot cake, I might check them out. Research purposes only, of course. In case I do a second book." She stood up and made her way through the excited crowd.

"A picture for the *Chronicle*," Kyle yelled. "You, Casey, get out of the way; I want a photo of the mayor-to-be."

"Been thinking about doing some shopping in Rudolph." An elderly woman stopped at our booth and spoke to my dad. "My husband always says Rudolph's no place for a decent woman, but I figure why not see for myself."

"Why not indeed," I said. "You must drop in at Mrs. Claus's Treasures and then have lunch at Victoria's Bake Shoppe."

Graham Johannesen abandoned his gavel and joined the crowd around Janice. Randy Baumgartner stayed where he was, sunken into his seat. Not a single person approached him offering their support.

143

"Good job, Noel." Vicky returned with a slice of blue-berry pie and another of pecan. "I would have brought a piece for you, but I didn't know what you wanted and several varieties are on offer."

"Hard work's still to come," Dad said. "People get excited at new possibilities easily enough, but soon interest begins to fade and it all seems like too much bother."

"Poached eggs, soft, bacon, sausage," a young waitress said. "Potatoes browned."

I lifted my hand, and she put the laden plate in front of me. "Carrot cake?"

"That would be me," Vicky said. The cake was arranged next to her two slices of pie. It was triple layered, bursting with shredded carrot and nuts, lavishly filled and decorated with thick coatings of cream cheese icing. I refrained from making a comment as we both picked up our forks.

The breakfast was as delicious as ever, and I finished it. I'd regret having it all later, but right now, my tummy was content. Vicky managed to eat all her carrot cake, including scraping up the last of the icing, and she'd enjoyed half of each diner-size slab of pie. Dad helped her finish off the pie. Vicky, I knew, would not regret eating so much. Life, as I often reflected, was not fair. Vicky made her living baking, and thus tasting, wonderful things, yet she remained model slim. Whereas I tried, and usually failed, to watch everything I put in my mouth, which quickly made its way to my hips.

The meeting was breaking up now. People yelled their encouragement to Janice as they left or assured her they'd be in touch about working on her campaign. Janice had taken a seat at a booth with three middle-aged women.

Pens and pads of paper and phones were brought out and heads bent as they made their plans.

I hadn't seen Randy Baumgartner slink away, but he was nowhere to be seen. "Do you think Randy will give in gracefully?" I asked Dad.

"Hard to tell. He should have known Janice was interested in his job; she's been asking questions about the running of town council and what's involved in doing the mayor's job. That he was so obviously completely blindsided is, once again, an illustration that he truly doesn't know, or care, what goes on in his town. He likes the limelight. Being the big fish in an excessively small pond."

"Seems to me as though all the enthusiasm is on Janice's side," Vicky said.

"For now," Dad said. "We will see."

Vicky chuckled. "He didn't do anything to keep the women on his side, not with that crack about Janice getting back to her kitchen."

Dad slapped his hands together. "My work here is done. Time to be heading home. I offered to put in a shift on the sleigh today. Sit up front with the driver and wave to passersby." On weekends in December, the Yuletide Inn provides a horse-drawn sleigh to ferry guests between the hotel and town and up and down Jingle Bell Lane.

"I got some great shots." Kyle stood by our booth. "Sorry about not including you, Vicky and Merry, but . . . uh . . ."

"We're not news in Muddle Harbor," I said.

"Right." He had a firm grip on Graham Johannesen's right arm and pulled the man forward. "Here's someone who'd like to meet you. Graham, these are the ladies I told you about."

Graham smiled at me for a beat longer than polite before turning to Dad and Vicky. "Nice to meet you." He and Dad shook hands.

"Vicky and Merry were the ones who found Raquel," Kyle said.

"Oh," I said quickly, "I'm sorry. Were you and she close?"

Graham looked down. "I won't say close, not really. I hadn't seen her in a few years. She was my cousin. Sort of a cousin. My granddad and her great-aunt, Dorothy, were brother and sister, so we had the same great-grandparents. Is that second cousins?"

Before anyone could try to work out the family tree, Kyle sucked in a sob. "I still can't accept it." His eyes unexpectedly filled with tears. "I hadn't seen her for a long time either, but I always hoped she'd come back to Rudolph someday. That we'd . . ." He started to cry. He grabbed my arm. His eyes were wide and wet, his focus intense. "You saw her, Merry. After . . . after . . . How did she look? Even in death, was she as beautiful as ever? She was the most beautiful girl I'd ever . . ."

My dad got to his feet. He took Kyle's hand off my arm, not unkindly. "Why don't you have my seat. We're leaving now. Take a couple of minutes to yourself."

Kyle sat, and his head dropped to the tabletop. He wrapped his arms around his head, and he began to weep. Great racking sobs. Dad, Vicky, and I looked at each other. Graham backed slowly away. "Okay, then. Sorry buddy. Uh . . . see you around. I get to Rudolph now and again. I'll look you guys up next time I'm there."

Kyle lifted his head. His face was streaked with tears, his eyes and nose red. He sniffled heartily. "Wait! Graham! You're her cousin, right? That means you're family. I went to the hospital after . . . after it happened. I asked to see her, but they wouldn't let me. I'm not a relative, they said."

"I don't know if distant relatives can get into the morgue," Dad said. "The police will be releasing the body soon, and her parents will be in touch with those who want to pay their respects."

"But I wasn't just anyone to her," Kyle insisted. "We were . . . we had something really special. Truly deep. Soulmates. Sure, she went away for a while, but I always knew she'd remember what we meant to each other and come back someday."

Embarrassed by the sudden display of emotion, Graham continued to back away.

"Why don't you and Vicky be off home, honeybunch?" Dad said. "I'm in no hurry, so I'll stay with Kyle for a while."

Vicky and I grabbed our bags and slipped away.

"Who is that guy?" Graham said as we passed him. "Do you know him? I thought he was part of Janice's press team, and then, out of the blue, he started blathering on about Raquel."

"I don't know that Janice has a press team," I said. "When did you last see Raquel?"

"It's been years. I didn't even know she was back in Rudolph. I haven't had any news of her since Aunt Dorothy died."

"Since Dorothy died? That was a few years after Raquel left town. Did she keep in touch with Dorothy?"

"A bit, yeah. I knew Raquel sometimes skirted the law. Nothing serious, though. Aunt Dorothy thought it was a great lark, and she loved to tell me all about it."

"She did?"

"I used to go round to the house to do errands for her. Cut the lawn, that sort of thing. No one else would do it. Aunt Dorothy never got on with the rest of Raquel's family. Only Raquel herself, so they kept in touch even after Raquel left town."

This came as news to me, although I had to admit there was no reason for me to be aware of what Raquel, a person I hadn't seen or heard of since high school, was up to. Still, everyone said no one had heard from her since she left Rudolph. Such would appear not to be the case. "Did she ever say anything to her aunt about counterfeiting?" I asked.

"Counterfeiting?" His eyes widened. "You mean printing money? Was she?"

"It would appear that might have been going on in the house where she died, yes."

He chuckled. "Can't say that comes as a total surprise to me, but Aunt Dorothy never mentioned anything like that. It was mostly about how easy it was for Raquel to get money out of lonely old men. Aunt Dorothy liked to hear stories like that. Aunt Dorothy didn't like men much. She didn't like many people, come to think of it. Other than Raquel, and maybe me. She told me many times to keep a firm hand on my wallet and not let some cheap floozy know how much I had."

"Can't say I've heard the word *floozy* for quite some time," Vicky said. "If ever."

I, however, had. It was the exact word Bob had used when trying to convince his late wife to change her hairstyle. Clearly, a generational thing.

Graham grimaced. "I won't deny I was disappointed when Aunt Dorothy died and she left her house to Beth Torrone, who never had the time of day for her. Not to Raquel or even to me. All those times I cut her lawn or shoveled snow because she didn't want to pay for some neighborhood kid to do it. Not that I minded, of course," he added quickly. "Always happy to help out. Raquel would phone her from wherever she was living and tell Aunt Dorothy about what sort of scams she was up to. That amused the old lady no end. And then Dorothy cut her out of the will in favor of people who didn't want anything to do with her. Dorothy wasn't the easiest person to get on with, but you have to make the effort, right?" He gave me a crooked smile. He wasn't bad looking, but I didn't care for something about that smile. I doubted he helped out his elderly aunt from the sheer goodness of his heart. He was clearly hoping to be mentioned in the will and angry when that failed to happen.

Not the first person to be disappointed when the will was read, and unlikely to be the last.

Which made me wonder if Raquel had also been disappointed and angry not to inherit at least part of the estate from her great-aunt. Yes, she might have gotten some of it, eventually, when her parents passed on, but her parents were not elderly, and she had two older brothers. It would be a long time before even a portion of the value of the house came to her. I couldn't see how that might relate to her murder, but I put the idea in the back of my mind to ponder later.

"Will you look at the time," Vicky said. "I have a business to get back to, Merry. And the store will be opening soon."

"You work in a store?" Graham asked me.

"I own Mrs. Claus's Treasures on Jingle Bell Lane. Pop in one day, next time you're in Rudolph. To shop, I mean," I added quickly.

"I haven't been to Rudolph since my aunt Dorothy died and strangers moved into her house before she was barely cold in her grave."

"Nice way of putting it," Vicky said in a low voice.

He paid her no attention and smiled at me. "But, now that our towns will be working together, I might do that."

We were almost the only people left in the café. Kyle had stopped crying, but he remained sitting in the booth, staring at nothing, while my dad hovered uncertainly over him. Janice's newfound supporters had left. A few customers wandered in in search of Sunday breakfast, and Janice called to them to take a seat anywhere they liked.

Nothing remained of the pies, and the waitress whisked away the empty dishes and used cutlery.

"Gotta go," I said. "Nice meeting you, Graham."

"Kyle told me you're tight with the police," he said.

"He did? I wouldn't exactly put it that way."

"I said I hadn't been to Rudolph for a long time, but that's not strictly true. I went yesterday, drove past the house, just wanting to have a look. For old times' sake, like. It's wrapped in police tape. What do you suppose is going to happen to it now? Are Beth and Richard going to keep renting it out? I'm thinking they won't want to live there. Not after what happened to Raquel in that house."

"Last I heard, the police plan to take the tape down tomorrow and let the Torrones in. I heard they're planning to sell it."

Something lit up behind his shrouded eyes. "Is that so?"

"You interested?" Vicky asked.

"In buying it? No, not me. Big place like that in Rudolph is way out of my budget, even if I wanted it. I have to admit my business has been struggling lately, and I've been thinking of cutting my losses. Selling up and moving away. Finding greener pastures. I own a farm supplies store, inherited it from my dad. But big changes are coming to Muddle Harbor. I might stick around and see what happens."

"Are you going to work on Randy Baumgartner's campaign?" Vicky asked.

He winked at her. "Me? Oh, no. I'm Team Janice all the way."

Chapter Sixteen

"Did you find Kyle's reaction to be slightly over-the-top?" I asked Vicky once we were back on the road to Rudolph.

"I find Kyle Lambert over-the-top at the best of times," she said.

"Specifically in regards to Raquel."

She snorted. "Kyle's a jerk and an idiot, and he's also an attention hound, Merry. He took a few pictures of boring people looking boring, and then he got bored and wanted to liven up the festivities."

"I'm not so sure," I said. "Men rarely turn on the waterworks as a way of attracting attention. His emotions seemed genuine to me."

Vicky laughed. "Yeah. Right. All that about soulmates and her eventually seeing the light, returning to her hometown to fall into his manly arms. The man watches too much TV."

I wasn't convinced. Was Kyle that upset about Raquel's death? Had he genuinely carried a torch for her all these years? Was he now forced to confront the end of his dreams?

Or was Kyle Lambert going through the throes of delayed shock because he himself had killed her? Had Kyle seen Raquel driving into town? Had he followed her to the house on Broad Street? Did he ask her why she hadn't told him she was back, or did he assume they'd simply pick up where they left off? When she rejected him, probably even laughed at him, did he . . . ?

You never knew what a spurned man was capable of.

I debated taking my thoughts to the police. Obviously, I had no proof at all, nothing but my observations and speculation. That wasn't enough to lay charges, never mind get a conviction, but it might get the investigative ball rolling in a new direction. It took a cold-blooded person to lie believably to the police when being questioned about a murder. Not only cold-blooded but a sharp thinker, someone able to skillfully dodge tricky questions and come up with believable explanations on the fly. Kyle Lambert had never been what I'd call quick on his feet.

"You expecting a busy day?" Vicky asked me.

"Hope so. Jackie and Melissa are both scheduled to be in all day."

"I wonder what Jackie'll have to say if she hears about Kyle's little meltdown back there. Nothing good, I suspect. Doesn't matter. She won't hear it from me, and despite Janice and your dad's attempt at municipal rapprochement, it'll be a long time before Rudolphites and Muddites exchange casual gossip. Smart move on Janice's part to casually point out that although she's willing to take advice from your dad, she'll keep the interests of Muddle Harbor first and foremost."

I scarcely heard what Vicky was saying.

I wouldn't go to the police with my suspicions about Kyle. Not yet. If Kyle could be accused of killing Raquel because she rebuffed his romantic intentions, it could be argued Jackie also had a reason to have done the deed.

Jealousy.

You never knew what a spurned woman was capable of either.

Chapter Seventeen

The forces of law and order came into Mrs. Claus's Treasures that afternoon, and Detective Simmonds asked Jackie if I was free.

I was in one of the alcoves, helping a customer choose a gift for her new daughter-in-law's first Christmas with them. It didn't take long for the customer to tell me she didn't much like her daughter-in-law, disapproved of the woman's profession (financial adviser, and not very good at it), thought she was a bad influence on her son, and she spent far too much of their (i.e., his, as she was so bad at her job) money on frivolous things. "She's trying to talk him into a Caribbean vacation after Christmas. Those places are far too expensive in January and February. Wait until you can take advantage of off-season rates, I told her. But does she listen to me? Never. You'd think my son would have more sense, but he's besotted with her."

"This serving platter looks most attractive at the center of a properly set holiday table," I said. So far, I'd shown her jewelry, linens, crystal glassware, a couple of vases, candlesticks, winter hats, leather gloves, and even holiday decorations.

It isn't normally a good thing when the police walk into a shop. But this time, I was almost grateful for the interruption. "Excuse me," I said. "Something seems to require my attention."

She sighed. "I don't see anything suitable here. I'll try some of the other stores. I would like to find the perfect gift for her. A way of showing her I truly do want us to get on. Particularly if, as I suspect, they have big news to give us."

She left. I peeked around the corner of the alcove. Simmonds was with Detective Lopez from New York City. I briefly wondered if, in speculating as to whether Kyle or Jackie had killed Raquel, I'd inadvertently telepathically summoned the detectives to my place of business. When Jackie arrived to start work, I must have been looking at her strangely, because she'd said, "Everything okay there, Merry?"

"Perfectly fine. Yes. Just wondering . . . wondering . . . where I put the train sets Alan dropped off yesterday."

"You put them beside the children's table," Jackie said. "Right over there. Next to the nicely arranged display of trains."

"Right. So I did. Carry on."

She'd given me another curious look before going into the back to put her bag away.

I took a breath and walked out of the alcove. The shop was busy. I glanced out of the window to see the sleigh pass by—the high-stepping horses with red and green satin ribbons braided through their manes; the wooden sleigh with hay bales for seats, now full of children and their families; my dad, in full Santa gear, sitting next to the driver, dressed in a heavy black cape and long woolen scarf of the sort that might have been worn by Bob Cratchit.

I turned my attention to the detectives. "Good afternoon . . . uh . . . Ms. Simmonds. And Mr. Lopez. How can I be of service?"

"I see you're busy, Merry," Simmonds said, "but we're hoping you can spare a minute."

"As long as it's not much longer than a minute. Come this way." I led us through the curtain into the back.

Simmonds eyed the office door, from which emerged no sounds of overly excited dog. "Matterhorn not here today?"

"I had an errand to run this morning before opening, so I didn't bring him." I'd come to the shop directly after dropping Vicky off at the bakery following our trip to Muddle Harbor.

"An errand in Muddle Harbor."

"How'd you know that?"

"I'm the police, Merry. I know everything."

She was here to arrest Jackie! Or at least accuse her.

Simmonds grinned. "On the other hand, maybe I only know because the chief of the Muddle Harbor PD attended this morning's meeting and she called to tell me about it. She's pleased at the possibility of a change in the town's leadership."

"She didn't say anything at the meeting. Not in her official capacity."

"She likes to keep a low profile. Not that she'd say anything about her political bosses, not publicly anyway. Privately, she's had plenty to say about Mayor Baumgartner over the years. But that's not why we're here." She nodded to Detective Lopez.

"We've just spoken to Mrs. D'Angelo," he said. "We asked her if she remembered anything more about the man she saw coming and going at the house across the street from hers in the days preceding the attack on her, or about anything else she overheard in that house while she was confined. She had nothing new to tell us."

"The experience had to have been highly traumatic," I said. "I'm not surprised she can't remember many details."

"That's normal enough," Simmonds said.

"I'm leaving after this," Lopez said. "Back to the city. Before I go, I want to ask you the same."

"I didn't see anyone going into or leaving the house in all the time they were—supposedly—there. It's a busy time of year, and this shop takes up all of my time. Once I was inside the house itself, in search of Mrs. D'Angelo, I didn't see anyone, except for Mrs. D'Angelo in the pantry and . . . Raquel in the cellar."

"You still maintain you didn't, at any time, go into the cellar?"

"No. I mean, yes. I maintain that. I would have gone down to check on Raquel once I saw her lying there, but Vicky was calling for me to help Mrs. D'Angelo and Raquel was not moving."

He studied my face, as though willing me to suddenly remember something important. If he'd asked me if I had any suspicions, I might have blurted out what I'd been thinking earlier. But he didn't. And so I didn't.

"You will contact Detective Simmonds if anything comes to you," he said.

"I will. You're going back to New York City. May I ask if that means you believe the investigation needs to focus elsewhere? Not on Rudolph?"

"We do," Simmonds said. "Raquel Torrone was involved in a lot of things she shouldn't have been. People make enemies that way. They also make rivals, who can be as dangerous as outright enemies."

"We've been attempting to locate the man she was most recently known to be in a relationship with," Lopez said. "He doesn't seem to want to be found. Mabel D'Angelo mentioned overhearing reference to someone named Lou. That mean anything to you?"

"No. Does it to you?"

"Raquel's most current boyfriend, that we know of, was a man named Jean-Claude Lefevre. Recognize the name?"

I shook my head.

Simmonds took out her phone and showed me a mug shot. A man in his late thirties, short hair, strong jaw, thick neck. He might have been good looking if not for the suppressed rage in his narrow eyes. In the photo he was not smiling. "You said you didn't see anyone at the house, but might you have noticed this man around town at any time?"

"No," I said. "I'm positive I've never seen him."

She put the phone away. "We showed this picture to Mrs. D'Angelo. She said it might have been him who'd been carrying furniture and boxes into the house. But it might not have been. It was a cold day, and he wore a hat and scarf."

"Irrelevant," Lopez said, "as Lefevre's prints were found on pieces of furniture in the house and some pizza boxes in the trash. He, if it was him, took pains to wipe his prints off the counterfeiting equipment and the money, but he didn't worry about the rest of the house."

"Likely the whole house was too much to worry about, if he was intent on getting out of there in a hurry," Simmonds said. "He only wiped down evidence of criminal activity."

"Lefevre happens to be married," Lopez said. "His wife's name is Louisa."

"Could that be the Lou Mrs. D'Angelo heard being referred to?" I asked.

"Louisa Lefevre is usually called Lou, yes. She says she hasn't heard from him in a couple of weeks. Which, according to her, is a regular occurrence. They have a fight, he leaves, he comes back, they have another fight, he leaves again. We've spoken to the neighbors, and they confirm Jean-Claude is often away, sometimes for weeks or more at a time. For what it's worth, the couple have two young kids. Louisa herself hasn't been in trouble, that we know of, for a couple of years, but she has a record of minor theft and embezzlement."

"Curiouser and curiouser," I said.

"It is."

"Did she know about her husband and Raquel?"

"She claims not. I don't know if I believe that. Regardless, the focus of the investigation is now on Lefevre and his known associates in New York City. We're keeping an eye on Louisa in case he comes home and she neglects to tell us about it."

"Good luck," I said.

"You've got a nice little town here," he said. "I might come back next year, bring my family for a holiday. Love the whole Christmas Town thing." He broke into a huge smile. "Imagine, I saw Santa Claus earlier, riding in a sleigh. Diane tells me you have an in with the Jolly Old Elf."

"The in-est of ins," I said.

"This town is not what I was expecting. Acquaintances of Raquel Torrone told our officers she did nothing but disparage Rudolph. 'Run-down backwater,' she called it. 'Occupied by nothing but a bunch of hillbillies trapped in time.'"

I wished the detective good luck with his investigation, and the police left. Before going back out front, I allowed myself a sigh of relief. Raquel had gotten herself involved with a married man, and they'd embarked on an illegal operation together. Was it possible he'd come to the house to discover, to his considerable shock, Raquel had a neighbor tied up in the pantry? What did he do then? I thought back to the conversation Mrs. D'Angelo overheard. The man wanted to get rid of the "temporary inconvenience." If Mrs. D'Angelo was correct in assuming the "temporary inconvenience" meant her, he wanted to kill her. Raquel, to her credit, refused. And so he must have killed Raquel and fled the scene.

He couldn't stay hidden for long, and the police would soon have him.

Nothing to do with Jackie or Kyle or anyone else I knew.

* * *

The next visitors to Mrs. Claus's were my own parents. No one who didn't know them would ever suspect they were together. My parents are total opposites in almost every way, not the least in how they dress. Following his shift on the sleigh, Dad changed out of his full Santa regalia into one of his beloved ugly Christmas sweaters, this one showing a tree fully adorned with bouncing balls of wool and flashing lights. He still had on the red trousers and high black boots. His curly gray hair was tossed by the wind, his blue eyes sparked with the cold, his cheeks were rosy, and his beard was trimmed with bits of ice.

Mom, in contrast, wore a calf-length, midnight-blue velvet cape lined with white silk. Her blue leather gloves matched the color of the cape. Her fake-fur hat was pure white, with a thick band of dark blue. Her black leather high-heeled boots reached the hem of the cape.

"That man looks like Santa Claus," a wide-eyed child said.

His mother giggled. Dad gave the boy a big smile. "Have you been good, young man?"

The boy nodded frantically, and his mother said, "Most of the time, Santa."

"Glad to hear it," Dad said. "Ho ho ho."

My mother refrained from rolling her eyes. She loved her adopted town of Rudolph, and she enjoyed the Christmas spirit, but she had occasionally been heard to complain it could go a mite toward excess at times.

Jackie gave Dad a broad wink as she rang up the boy's mother's purchases.

"Are you really Santa Claus?" he asked Dad.

"What do you think?" Dad asked.

"I'm not sure. Some of the kids at school say Santa isn't real."

"I'm real," Dad said. "You can decide for yourself if Santa is real."

The boy's forehead wrinkled, and his little nose crinkled in thought. Then he nodded seriously. "Yup, he is."

His mother took his hand and said, "Merry Christmas, Santa," as they left the shop.

"Another true believer," Jackie said. "Like me. I know Santa is real. I can't wait to see what Santa gives Kyle to give to me this year. I'm thinking it's about time for a lovely little—but not too little—diamond."

I coughed.

"Are you all right, dear?" Mom asked.

"Fine. Something stuck in my throat. Not to be too rude about it, but we're busy here. Is there anything you need?"

"Alan's taken over on the sleigh," Dad said. "He left his phone in the truck, so he asked me to pop in and ask how you're set for the six-inch nutcracker soldiers. He has some ready for painting, and he can do that tonight if you need them."

"I do," I said. "Only one set left."

Mom wandered over to the jewelry display, and Dad cast a critical eye around the shop. "Once again, you've let the book rack get pushed out of the line of sight as people come in the door."

"I need the space," I said. "This is a decor and gift shop, remember. As I've told you before"—many times before—"I have a few holiday-themed books for one-stop shopping, but I'm not competing with the bookstore. I'm looking forward to having a big splashy display of Vicky's cookbook next year, though."

Mom selected a pair of handmade silver earrings and a matching bracelet. "These will go nicely with this cape, don't you think, dear?"

"Absolutely perfect." I went behind the counter to complete the sale.

"Any updates on the murder of the woman who kidnapped poor Mabel?" Mom asked in a low voice.

"The police are pretty sure she was killed by her partner in crime and sometime boyfriend. He's from New York City, so the NYPD are taking on the focus of the investigation."

She laughed. "Donalda will be disappointed to hear it. She was rather enjoying all the attention that strange business was sending her way."

"Donalda? You know someone named Donalda?"

"Yes, I do. She has two children in my classes."

"She has little children? Are we talking about the same Donalda? A friend of Mrs. D'Angelo?"

"I believe so. Donalda Reynolds. They live not far from you. Dreadful gossip, she is. Some of the parents wait in the outer room while their children are having lessons, and sometimes they go for coffee together. They've learned not to say anything around Donalda they don't want the entire town to know. With much embellishment."

"Jackie," I called, "will you mind the till for a few minutes?"

She looked up from arranging linens. "Sure."

Dad was examining the bookshelf. He moved the table containing flower vases and candlesticks over a few inches and called, "Melissa, can you give me a hand here?"

I ran around the counter and pulled my mom into a corner. "Donalda took a casserole to the house where everything happened. No one answered the door, so she left it on the step and went home. Mrs. D'Angelo told me that. Was Donalda involved in other ways?"

"Not that I know of. Simply standing on the front steps to deliver her casserole means, according to her, she barely escaped with her life." Mom gave me a wicked grin. "She has a very delicate constitution, don't you know?" The grin died. "I shouldn't mock. I do find her tiring at times, but she's a deeply unhappy woman."

"In what way?"

Mom glanced across the busy shop floor to where my father was admiring his handiwork. Melissa had helped him reposition the bookshelf. I didn't want it there, but I'd wait until he left before moving everything back to where I did want it. My mother smiled. "What is most likely to make a woman unhappy? A bad marriage."

"Do you know this for sure, about Donalda?"

"As any teacher will tell you, dear, young children don't keep secrets. Nor do some of their mothers. Mr. Reynolds, it seems, has a reputation for not strictly sticking to his marriage vows."

"Huh?"

"He's a philanderer, Merry. Some of my mothers say he's flirted with them to the point at which they became uncomfortable." She grinned again. "At least they say they became uncomfortable. They are not going to tell me if they accepted his advances, now, are they? He brought the children to their class at my house once. When supposedly Donalda was ill. Slimy fellow, I thought. All false charm and sly insinuations. You learn to recognize men like that fast enough in the world of show business. You do if you want to survive. And I did. I remember a famous tenor, from Russia as I recall, he had a terrible reputation backstage. On one occasion—"

"Never mind the tenor. Does Donalda know this about him? Her husband, not the Russian tenor."

"We're not friends, Merry. She doesn't confide in me. But I consider it highly unlikely she would not know. Everyone else does."

"I don't. Didn't. I guess I do now."

"You don't move in the right circles, dear. As I said, I sense Donalda is deeply unhappy, despite the cheerful chattering front she presents. She has that aura about her. I suspect that's why she's so keen on gossip. She wants to believe everyone else is as unhappy as she is."

"Does Mrs. D'Angelo know?"

"I'd be shocked if she doesn't. For all her own love of gossip, Mabel does have her standards. She doesn't repeat anything told to her in confidence, and she never betrays a friend. Now, let me collect your father, and we'll be off."

Books arranged to his satisfaction, Dad was advising a man on choosing a gift.

"I don't suppose you know if Mr. Reynolds has been seen recently?" I asked my mother.

"Seen? What does that mean? I told you he doesn't usually bring the children to their classes."

I began to contemplate all that information, but then I mentally gave my head a good shake. No point in letting my imagination run away with me. I had absolutely no reason to think that Donalda, who I wouldn't recognize if I saw her walking down the street, had knifed her husband's potential lover and calmly gone back to her casseroles and children's music lessons. Or that Mr. Reynolds, who supposedly had an eye for an attractive woman, had for some reason killed Raquel and fled.

The customer Dad had been talking to put a Christmas-themed teapot on the serving counter. Dad joined my mother and me, and he gave me a broad wink with a jerk of the head toward the customer. "Ready to go?" he said to my mom. "Don't forget we have dinner with Sue-Anne and Jim tonight."

"How could I possibly forget," Mom said with a deep sigh.

The shop door flew open, and the woman I'd been helping earlier, the one with the disliked daughter-in-law, ran in. "Nothing!" she said to me. "I can find absolutely nothing in this town to get her for Christmas. I was hoping to find something truly special, something that says we might be able to start over again on a fresh new footing. But I can't think of a thing. I'll have to get that vase after all." She turned to point at it and let out a gasp. "I . . . I . . . That's it! Perfect. I can't believe I didn't see it the first time I was in." She ran to the bookshelf and snatched up a large hardcover. She held it out in front of her, stared at it, and then clutched it to her chest. A child's illustrated edition of *A Christmas Carol* by Charles Dickens.

She brought the book to the counter, eyes brimming with tears. "My son told me *A Christmas Carol* is his wife's absolute favorite movie. She loves the one with the Muppets the most, but she'll watch any version, or all of them, over the holidays. This book will be the perfect gift."

I stared at my father. He stroked his beard, took my mother's arm, gave me a wink. And they left.

I know my dad isn't Santa Claus. But sometimes I wonder.

Chapter Eighteen

My sister phoned me as I was preparing for Sunday closing.

"Got any plans for tonight?"

"Early to bed, early to rise. Another working day tomorrow."

"Feel like a girls' night in?"

"Not particularly."

"What time do you expect to get home?"

"The store closes at six, but I—"

"Come on, Merry. You need it. All you do this time of year is work. I'll be at your place at six thirty. I'll bring the wine. Why don't I call Vicky and invite her to join us? I bet she's alone tonight too. Bye!"

I stared at the phone in my hand. *What just happened there?* Alan was spending his evening finishing off nutcracker soldiers, and I was looking forward to a quiet night in with microwaved pizza, a boring movie, and a snoozing dog.

"Must be nice to have a sister," Jackie said.

"Sometimes it is. Sometimes it's not," I said. "I have two."

"And you have a brother. I liked getting to know Chris better when he was here the last time." All of a sudden she looked uncharacteristically sad. "Must be so exciting, what he does. Building sets on Broadway. Eve, being in movies. Isn't your other sister a singer?"

"Carole. Yes, she followed our mother's footsteps into opera. She's in England right now, performing in some avant-garde thing my mother isn't entirely sure of."

"They all have such exciting careers." Jackie let out a deep sigh; her eyes focused on something far away. "You did too, didn't you? But you gave that up to come back to boring old Rudolph."

"Boring old Rudolph is where I want to be, Jackie. Chris is doing okay, and he loves what he does. But Carole and Eve? Not the life for me. Always competing for roles, always being passed over for the big parts, grabbing for the crumbs, trying to be grateful for getting those crumbs."

"But Eve was in a Cate Blanchett movie!"

"She had a walk-on part; she never even met the stars." Jackie's mouth twisted. Her eyes teared up.

"Are you okay, Jackie?" I asked.

She let out a deep, shuddering sigh. "No. Not okay. I'm worried about Kyle. About me and Kyle, I mean. I've never lived outside of Rudolph. I've never been further away than family holidays to Cape Cod. I've always been okay with that, but . . . not if Kyle's not with me."

"Why don't you come to my place tonight? Girls' night in, right?" I made the offer without thinking it over, but as soon as I said it, I realized it was the right thing to do. Jackie rarely let anything intrude on her bubbly, cheerful view of the world. Shortly after Mom and Dad left, she'd taken her break. When she came back, I could immediately tell something was wrong. She didn't say anything, but her smile was forced, and for the rest of the afternoon she engaged in the barest minimum of acceptable chatter with our customers. I suspected she'd had a phone conversation with Kyle and he said something that made her realize an engagement ring might not be forthcoming this Christmas.

"If you don't have anything on, I mean," I added.

"That would be nice, Merry. I don't have any plans. I did, but . . . things changed." She dipped her head and went into the back for her bag.

I didn't have to tell Jackie where I lived. On one memorable occasion, she'd hidden in my garden shed for several days while the police—and I—were hunting for her.

I locked up the store, and we headed out. The snow had stopped some time ago, leaving everything white and pristine. "People are saying this season's going to be one of the best in Rudolph for a long time," Jackie said. "All this snow helps get people in the mood."

Two couples passed us. Laden with shopping bags, wrapped up warmly, laughing. It was after dark, but lights in the town park lit up the tiny toboggan hill and the skating rink, both fully occupied. The lake, rimmed with ice, stretched to the horizon like black velvet.

"There truly is," I said, "no place like Rudolph in the wintertime."

"I would miss it," Jackie said. "If I went away."

I turned my head and looked at her. "Are you thinking of doing that? Moving away?"

"Nah. Not really. Rudolph's home, right? Although . . ." Her voice trailed off.

We reached my house and turned into the driveway. Mrs. D'Angelo was on her front porch, wiping a dusting of snow off the railing with a handheld broom. The bandages had been removed from her wrists, and all that remained to mark her ordeal was slight bruising. She called out to me and waved, and I had another sudden impulse. "I'm having some impromptu guests around for drinks," I called. "Would you like to join us?"

The surprise and joy on her face was something to behold. "Oh my goodness. What fun. I'll change my shoes and be right with you."

She disappeared into her house and was back before I'd taken more than another couple of steps. She waved a bottle at me. "I've had this in the back of the fridge for simply ages, waiting for a chance to use it."

I thought that was incredibly sad. Mrs. D'Angelo had her network and she had her contacts, but she didn't seem to have many real friends. I'd never before considered that tuning in to the town gossip the way she did might be her way of having a social life.

"George brought it," she said, shattering my image of a sad, lonely woman. "He only drinks beer, and this was such an expensive bottle I didn't want to drink it by myself. I will confess, but only to you, Merry, I hid it when Iris was visiting. No need to cast pearls before swine. Not that my sister is swine, that's not what I'm saying, but you get my meaning."

I unlocked the door at the bottom of the steps, and we went in. Mattie caught our scent and yipped in greeting.

Once we were inside my apartment, I accepted the offering from Mrs. D'Angelo. I texted Eve: *Bring more wine.*

Mattie loves nothing more than having company, and he allowed Jackie to scratch vigorously behind his ears while I rummaged in the fridge and cupboards to lay out what I had in the way of snacks. I found a couple of types of cheese and crackers and nuts and put them on plates. I then got down the wineglasses. Before pouring, I checked the label on Mrs. D'Angelo's offering. A middle-of-the-road California chardonnay.

Eve and Vicky soon arrived. My sister carried a tote bag that clinked when she walked. She held it up proudly. "Dad won't be happy next time he checks his wine cellar."

"Your parents have a wine cellar?" Jackie said as I handed her a glass. "That's cool."

"Not a wine cellar, but he likes to pretend he's a connoisseur of fine wines," Eve said with a laugh. "Not a problem. I'll replace these tomorrow."

Eve knew Jackie from the store, but I introduced her to Mrs. D'Angelo. Vicky came into the kitchen with me to get more glasses. "I picked up Eve, so I'll just have a sparkling water, please." She lowered her voice. "What's with the additions to the guest list?"

"Jackie's depressed, and Mrs. D. is feeling lonely," I whispered back. "I thought they both could use some cheering up."

While Vicky poured drinks, I put the plates of snacks and some cocktail napkins on the coffee table, and we all took seats in the living room. Mattie settled on the rug at my feet.

Mrs. D'Angelo politely asked Eve what she did, and Eve said, "I'm an actor. Movies, TV. I live in LA now."

"That's exciting. Have you been in anything I've seen?"

"As I don't know what you've seen," my sister said a touch sharply, "I can't say, can I?"

Mrs. D'Angelo thought this over.

"It must be so exciting," Jackie said. "Being in the movies. I considered acting at one point. I was in a couple of plays at school, and the teacher said I was a true original."

"Oh yes," Eve said. "I remember. That performance in *The Sound of Music* was definitely memorable."

Jackie smiled and said, "Thank you." Eve was not being polite, but I didn't bother to point that out to Jackie. My sister was uncharacteristically brittle, and I took a guess as to what the reason might be. And as to why she suddenly decided she needed company—and wine—tonight.

"You were better off staying here," she said to Jackie. "Acting's not for everyone. The business is heartless; the competition can be brutal, and you only have friends as long as you're not auditioning for the same role."

She twisted her wineglass in her long fingers and stared into the depths.

"Did you hear about the part?" I asked, fearing the answer.

"Yeah. I didn't get it. Not that there's anything to get. Not anymore. They canceled the second round of auditions. They've eliminated the female-cousin-visiting-from-the-countryside role altogether."

"I'm sorry," I said.

Vicky and I exchanged glances.

Eve's eyes filled with tears. "At least it wasn't because they didn't like me, right? So, that's good. Never mind. There'll be other parts." She tried to be brave, but her heart wasn't in it. My sister was over thirty. Before much longer it would be too late for her big break.

"Didn't Raquel Torrone act in some of the plays at school?" Jackie helped herself to a handful of nuts, oblivious to the sudden tension swirling around the room.

"Yeah, she did. Not a scrap of talent." Eve sniffed. "She would have been perfect for Hollywood, though. Talent is hardly a job requirement."

"If I haven't seen you in anything," Mrs. D'Angelo said in an attempt to make amends for her earlier slip, "that doesn't mean much. I rarely go to the movies these days, and I prefer watching the nice English mystery shows on TV. But I'm sure your parents are very proud of you."

"Yeah. They are. That'll look good on my tombstone." Eve took a long drink. "Your friendly local detective brought a guy from New York around to talk to me about Raquel. I don't know why they're wasting their time with me. I had absolutely nothing to tell them, and I told her that the first time she asked. I haven't seen or heard of Raquel since we left school. I hadn't so much as given her another thought in all these years."

"Seems strange they'd talk to you twice," Vicky said.

"Digging up old dirt. Isn't that what the cops do? Just like Raquel to pop back into town and now everyone's in an uproar."

"She is dead," I said.

Eve turned to me. "Dead and still causing trouble. Someone, I don't know who, told them about Raquel and me having a big fight. As if I'd wait thirteen years and then swoop down and exact my revenge."

174

"Revenge? For what? What happened thirteen years ago?" I asked.

"That blasted drama club. We were both after the role of Maria in *West Side Story*. Raquel's singing made an out-of-tune violin sound good, but she was a contender because she was *sooo* pretty and *sooo* charming. Charming. More like manipulating."

"Which of you got the part?" Mrs. D'Angelo asked.

"Neither of us. They chose Samantha Schwartz. Who had a minimal amount of singing talent and no acting chops at all. But she wasn't being backbitten all day long, with everyone in school taking sides, so the teacher thought she was a safer bet. The play was a mess. Total flop. I, like the professional I am, accepted a smaller role and kept my head high. Raquel quit school in a huff."

"Is that the reason she left before graduating?" Vicky asked.

"Probably not the only one, but she was likely only staying in school for the play, and when she wasn't going to be the star, she left."

I vaguely remembered tears and tantrums. Doors slamming; Eve screaming into the phone with her friends, weeping on Dad's shoulder. But I was an older sister. Whatever trauma my younger sibling might have been going through meant nothing to me. By then I was in college, home for the holidays and far too worldly to be concerned about any small-town high school drama club.

Eve reached for the wine bottle. "All water under the bridge now. At least I have an acting career, no matter how much of a failure it might be. And Raquel was reduced to trying to fleece old men out of a couple of hundred bucks here and there."

"Where did you hear about that?" I asked.

"Everyone's talking about it, Merry," Mrs. D'Angelo said. "George's friend, Bob Gravel, reported it to the police, at George's insistence, and George hasn't been shy about warning other unmarried men of his acquaintance to be alert for scams."

"Bob lives in New York City, right? Is there any indication someone in Rudolph might have been one of Raquel's intended victims?" I asked. "Is it possible she came here to get closer to him? Maybe she finally met someone with the money to support her in the style to which she wanted to become accustomed, and naive enough to fall for it?"

"Not that I've heard; then again, he—provided there is a person—might be keeping it under wraps, particularly in light of what happened to Raquel. As for her, folks can put two and two together. I feel sorry for Raquel's parents. In their time of grief, they have gossip about their girl to hear."

"As for whoever killed her," Eve said, "there are a lot of better suspects than me. I told the cops that."

"I'm glad I didn't know her," Jackie said. "Sounds like she was a nasty piece of work. Only goes to show what fools men can be."

"Some of them," Mrs. D'Angelo said. "Mr. D'Angelo had an eye for a pretty girl, and he never let anything like common sense interfere with that."

"You were married?" Vicky asked.

"Of course I was, dear. But not for long, let me assure you. I saw the writing on the wall soon enough and showed him the door." She grinned. "I got the house out of it, didn't I?"

Jackie burst into tears.

"Goodness," Mrs. D'Angelo said. "What did I say?"

"Kyle," Jackie gasped. "It's all Raquel this and Raquel that. This afternoon, I called him to suggest we go to a movie tonight, and he said he doesn't think it would be appropriate to see me for a while, as he's in deep mourning. The light of his life has been extinguished."

Vicky glanced at me and raised her eyebrows. I suppressed a shudder. That had been a mighty thoughtless thing to say, even for the witless Kyle. I'd never liked Kyle, but surely even he couldn't be that oblivious to the effect those words would have on Jackie's feelings.

Yeah, he could.

"'I thought I was the light of your life,' I said." Tears flowed down Jackie's cheeks, and she didn't wipe them away. "'You'll do,' he said, 'but . . . but . . . you're not Raquel.'" Deep sobs.

Mrs. D'Angelo snorted. "My point exactly. You're better off without him."

"I don't want to be without him. I love him. He's the light of *my* life."

Okay, so my plan to cheer Jackie up wasn't working. Still, better her getting it out here with us than home alone. I headed for the kitchen to get her a glass of water.

When I returned, Vicky had left her chair and was crouched on the floor in front of Jackie. She held the other woman's hands in hers. "I doubt he meant it. It's the shock, right? Raquel dying reminded him of what thinks he lost when she went away. He'll get over it soon enough."

Jackie lifted her head. She sniffled. "You think so?"

"For sure," Vicky said.

I kept my opinion to myself. Once again, I had to wonder if Kyle's over-the-top reaction to the death of someone he hadn't seen in a decade was more one of guilt than grief.

I handed Vicky the glass, and she gave it to Jackie. Jackie accepted it and took a long, deep drink. She settled back in her chair. "Sorry. I don't know what came over me. Too much wine, maybe."

"That's all right, dear," Mrs. D'Angelo said. "Sometimes we all need a good cry in the company of sympathetic friends."

"Soon as I saw her," Jackie said, "driving into town, as bold as brass, I knew she was here to make trouble."

I dropped into my chair in something approaching shock. Was Jackie saying she'd seen, and recognized, Raquel?

"When was this?" I asked.

"Not long after the parade," Jackie said. "I don't remember exactly what day. I was coming to work and waiting to cross at the light near the library when Raquel, of all people, drove by, in a big fancy SUV."

"Are you sure it was her?" I asked. "If she was in a car?"

Jackie's face crunched up in thought. "I thought so at the time. Maybe not. It might have been someone else. She was wearing a hat and a scarf."

"Was she alone, this woman? Anyone else in the car?"

"Not that I noticed, but I can't be sure. It happened so fast, and whoosh . . . she was gone."

"Jackie," I said. "Did you tell the police this?"

"Tell them what?"

"That you saw Raquel in town."

Jackie blinked. "Why would I do that? They never spoke to me about her or what happened. No reason they would. I mean, it's not as if they were trying to find her. They knew she was in Rudolph. She died here, right?"

No one said anything for a while. Jackie wiped her eyes and sipped her water. Mattie resumed his place on the rug and settled down. Mrs. D'Angelo scooped up a handful of nuts. Eve went into the kitchen for another bottle. Vicky stifled a yawn.

I decided to process what Jackie'd said later and decide if it mattered. Jackie was right that no one had any doubt Raquel had come to Rudolph. If someone had been in the car with her, that might be highly significant, but Jackie hadn't seen anyone.

"Turns out my mom knows your friend Donalda," I said to Mrs. D'Angelo. "Her children take vocal classes from her."

"Yes, I knew that. Donalda is very proud of those children. She never passes up an opportunity to brag about how well they're doing in school or how talented they are."

"Did the police speak to her? About the goings-on at that house, I mean?"

"I believe they did. Donalda was delighted at the chance to be of help. Unfortunately, she had no more to tell them than anyone else. She saw a car coming and going, garage doors closing and opening, shapes moving behind the curtains, but nothing more. No one even bothered to drop by to thank her for her casserole, as would have been the least you'd expect from new neighbors."

"I've heard Donalda's husband has a reputation."

Mrs. D'Angelo's lips tightened. "Is that so?"

"What sort of a reputation?" Vicky asked.

"Fooling around. Having affairs. That sort of thing."

"Oh, yeah," Jackie said. "He fancies himself quite the ladies' man. Too bad for him none of the ladies agree."

"As I believe I said earlier," my landlady said, "men aren't worth the trouble."

I thought of my parents' marriage, but I didn't bother to argue the point. I thought of Alan, who made me happy. I glanced at Vicky. Newly married and blissfully content. Sometimes, men were worth the bother.

Mrs. D'Angelo, who lived for gossip, changed the subject. "Eve, you must have met many famous people. Can you tell me about them?"

"I have, yeah. Some of them can be really stuck-up, but some are very nice. Always thoughtful and kind. I was on set one day with—"

I changed the subject back. "Did Donalda mention if her husband tried to meet the new neighbors?"

Mrs. D'Angelo looked at me, her eyes wary. "Why are you asking me this, Merry?"

"I'm wondering if it's possible he went over to introduce himself to Raquel and . . . whoever was with her . . . and Donalda didn't like that."

"Donalda is a perfectly respectable woman." Mrs. D'Angelo's tone turned as cold as the night air outside my windows. "She keeps a lovely home, has a good job and well-brought-up children. It is not her fault her husband is a scallywag and a layabout."

"Scallywag?" Eve said.

"I prefer not to talk about my friends," Mrs. D'Angelo said. "And I don't care for what you're implying."

Vicky caught my eye and wiggled her eyebrows at me.

"I'm not implying anything, I'm just asking. We're all wondering what happened over there." I waved my index finger in the general direction of the Johannesen house.

"You told us the police believe Raquel's boyfriend did it," Jackie said. "She'd obviously forgotten all about Kyle, the fool. She didn't make any attempt to get in touch with him over all those years, did she? He wouldn't have liked that one bit. He—" She slammed her mouth shut, and her eyes widened as she realized what she'd been about to say. That Kyle might have reacted badly if he came to understand Raquel hadn't come back for him.

Which, of course, raised the question as to why Raquel returned to Rudolph in the first place. And not only to Rudolph but to a house her parents owned, without bothering to let them know she was here. Had she chosen her hometown for a particular reason? Surely one could set up an illicit counterfeiting operation in any house, just about anywhere. Did Raquel specifically come to Rudolph for a man? A man the illusive Jean-Claude didn't know about?"

"What are you thinking, Merry?" Vicky asked. "You've come over all serious like."

"Serious? I suppose I am. We've started talking about a serious subject, right? The police are focusing their attentions on Raquel and her counterpoint's criminal activities in general, beyond Rudolph. Which is good, for us, right? But—"

"But you, being you, won't let it go until you know for sure what happened."

"We may never know," Eve said.

"Mrs. D'Angelo," I said. "Can I get you another glass of wine?"

She lifted her glass. "That would be very nice, dear. Isn't this pleasant. It's been a long time since I've sat around and chatted with a group of young women."

"On to other topics," Eve said, "I have to confess, I'm not looking forward to Mom finding out I didn't get the part. She'll launch into another one of her stories about someone she knew who persevered after many disappointments and eventually had a marvelous career."

"She means well," I said from the kitchen. "You know that."

"I do. I also know because her career path was pretty much straight up the ladder at a rapid pace to the very top, she thinks anyone should be able to do the same with enough strength of will."

"Your mom knows luck plays an important part in anyone's career," Vicky said.

"I don't know if she does know that," Eve said.

I handed her a refilled glass and touched her shoulder lightly in sympathy.

Vicky struggled to think of something neutral to talk about. "Did you know Raquel's aunt well, Mrs. D'Angelo? When she lived across the street from you?"

"Dorothy Johannesen. I can't say I knew her well, but we had a casual acquaintance. She wasn't one for making friends or for getting involved in the community. More the opposite. She kept herself to herself. I heard she was independently wealthy; she had a substantial trust fund from an inheritance, folks said."

"Was that true?" Vicky asked.

"I can't say for sure, but I never really believed it."

"I remember that," Eve said. "When Raquel and I were hanging out together, she told me her aunt was a millionaire. I didn't pay much attention, but Raquel constantly prattled on about how her aunt Dorothy was going to set her up in an apartment in Manhattan and pay for her to go to drama school." She laughed. "We all know how well that turned out."

"If Dorothy did have money," Mrs. D'Angelo said, "goodness knows what she did with it. She never traveled. Didn't have a car. Didn't put more money into that house than was needed to do the most basic of maintenance. For example, she could have hired a landscaping firm to cut the grass and trim the bushes, but she relied on the unpaid labor of a distant nephew. She didn't get on with her closest relative, Raquel's mother. Although, in the end, she left Beth the house. Dorothy's supposed riches were nothing but a small-town rumor, one that grew in the telling."

"Might have had a grain of truth," Vicky said. "Once upon a time. A million dollars sure isn't what it was forty or more years ago. My grandfather is always exclaiming at what price houses around here are going for these days. It's sort of his hobby now."

"I don't believe any additional money went with the inheritance," Mrs. D'Angelo said. "Just the house itself. The Torrone family had moved away by then, but only as far as Rochester. They didn't act as though they'd come into a windfall. Andrea—you know Andrea O'Callaghan, of course, Merry—and Beth were good friends, and Andrea visited them several times after they moved. She said they lived in a nice but modest home in a nice but modest area."

"Maybe Dorothy left her money to Raquel," Jackie said.

"Unlikely," Vicky pointed out, "if Raquel was reduced to cranking out twenty-dollar bills in a Rudolph cellar and fleecing lonely old men."

"My dad said Dorothy was considered a pest at town hall," I said.

Mrs. D'Angelo laughed and sipped her wine, relaxing once again now she was back in comfortable territory: gossiping about people she didn't consider personal friends. "Goodness yes. She wasn't at all popular on the street. She complained that the neighbor to her right cut the hedge between their properties back too much."

I drew up a mental image of the streetscape. "There's no hedge there. Just a tall wooden fence."

"Indeed there is. Tired of her complaints, he cut the entire hedge down. Which was within his rights, as it was planted on his side of the property line. She was furious. She then attempted to get revenge by complaining to the town if their trash bins were left out too long after collection or if they were put out too early."

"Sounds like the neighbor from hell," Vicky said with a laugh.

"She could be, if she took against you. She never caused me any real problems. Like I said, she kept to herself. She could even be kind on occasion. When I broke my foot, she brought over an endless stream of casseroles, some of which were quite good, and she took a list of things I needed from the supermarket for her nephew to get when he next did her shopping.

"The neighbors, however, eventually moved, tired of the endless complaints. As for Dorothy herself, she was one of those people who suspect everyone is out to get them. She didn't trust banks. She paid cash to any contractors she might hire, and even went to town hall twice a year with an envelope containing a wad of bills to pay her taxes. Not that she wanted to pay her taxes. She didn't trust any level of government either. She believed the town had installed listening devices in the lampposts so they could listen in on her conversations." Mrs. D'Angelo shook her head. "Although what, being a suspicious lady living on her own, she had to talk about that would be of interest to the town council, or anyone else in authority, she couldn't say. Now, enough of that. Vicky, what's happening with your book? I simply cannot wait to get my copy."

* * *

I thought about what Vicky had said as Mattie and I took our nightly excursion through the dark, quiet streets of our neighborhood. The police had determined that Raquel's death didn't have anything to do with anyone in Rudolph. That should be sufficient to allow me to forget about the entire situation. But . . . pesky little niggling thoughts continued to run around the back of my mind. Was it as cut-and-dried as it seemed to appear? Perhaps not. Why had Raquel come back to Rudolph? And did the fact that she died in Rudolph have anything to do with her *being* in Rudolph?

What did I know about her relationship with Rudolphites? Just about nothing.

Jackie had known Raquel was in Rudolph. Had she taken steps to ensure Kyle didn't go running back into the welcoming arms of his high school crush?

No. I dismissed that. Jackie was many things, but she was not devious and she was no actor. If she had killed Raquel, or anyone else, she'd confess to it.

As for Kyle, was it possible his high school crush wasn't at all welcoming and he acted out of anger and disappointment?

As Mattie and I approached our house, I was thinking that although I might *want* to do something about investigating Raquel's murder, December in Rudolph didn't give me a heck of a lot of spare time to do so. Thinking about it was likely all I'd be able to do. A figure stepped out of the shadows of the blue spruce in front of the Johannesen house and walked rapidly in the opposite direction, head down, shoulders hunched.

Mattie paid him no mind, so I didn't either, and we crossed the street toward the forest of holiday lights. I'd enjoyed myself tonight. Nothing like simply sitting back and relaxing with friends, but I feared I'd come to regret having that last glass of wine.

Chapter Nineteen

The following day the town of Rudolph hosted an unusual group of visitors. People from Muddle Harbor came to take a tour of Jingle Bell Lane. My dad invited them to breakfast at Victoria's Bake Shoppe, and following that he planned to show them the highlights of Rudolph's business district.

"Strictly an unofficial visit, honeybunch," he said to me over the phone as I was having a quick breakfast of coffee and muesli while regretting some of the choices I'd made last night. "Janice called me late yesterday afternoon to propose the idea. I told Sue-Anne about it last night. Sue-Anne is unsure as to how much we should encourage growth in a neighboring town. I reminded her that growth is good for everyone, but I fear an excess of imagination has never been one of Sue-Anne's strong points. On the other hand, to be fair, she doesn't want to be seen to be playing favorites in the Muddle Harbor mayoral race, so she told me to handle the visit as I think best."

Which Dad would have done with or without the mayor's permission.

"Are you playing favorites?" I asked. "Surely Randy and his team would be entitled to the same courtesies. If they ever bothered to be interested."

He chuckled. "Which is the entire point. Randy, and what he has of a team, has never asked and has rebuffed any gesture I've made at friendship. I'm meeting Janice and her group at nine thirty at Vicky's place. You're welcome to join us."

"I just might do that. Thanks, Dad."

At 9:25, I left Melissa to open the shop and headed to the bakery. Monday morning was normally a quiet day in Rudolph, but with little over a week to go until the big day, people were up early, and the bakery was busy with people enjoying coffee and muffins before embarking on an intense day of shopping.

Dad had pushed two tables together and was arranging chairs for his guests when I came in. He gave me a big grin when he spotted me. He was happy a few cautious steps were being taken between the two towns. It might come to nothing—Janice might not win the mayoral race, and Muddle Harbor would retreat back into their shell of resentment—but Dad was nothing if not optimistic and willing to give everything a try.

"Mom coming?" I asked.

"I believe her words at the invitation were along the lines of 'Over my dead body.'"

"I can believe that." Even during the many years my dad had been mayor of Rudolph, the role of politician's spouse was not my mother's thing.

The chimes above the door tinkled, and the Muddle Harbor delegation entered precisely on time. Along with Janice Benedict, her brother, John, a real estate agent, had come, as well as the town clerk, Graham Johannesen, and the two women I'd seen huddling with Janice after the breakfast meeting yesterday.

Janice had moved quickly, and I thought that was a good sign. She wasn't fooling around in establishing her candidacy in the mayor's race.

Everyone shook hands and found seats. A smiling young waitress took drink orders, and Marjorie brought platters heaped with tempting breakfast pastries. Vicky came out of the back, rubbing her hands through her short hair. "Welcome to my place," she said to Janice with more than a touch of pride in her voice.

"Looks nice," Janice said. "I suggested we come here on a Monday morning, thinking it would be quiet, a good time to talk. But—" She indicated the occupied tables, the line up at the service counter, the hissing and gurgling espresso machine, the waitress collecting used dishes, a kitchen helper bringing out a tray of breakfast sandwiches to be arranged behind the glass display case. "Are you this busy all the time?"

Vicky took a seat and glanced at Dad. He gave her a slight nod. "To be honest, no, we're not. Not on Monday mornings most of the year. But it's almost Christmas, the town's full, people are eager to get a start on their day, and so yes, this is pretty normal. And"—she cleared her throat— "if I may say, very few of these people are regulars. The regulars, the people who work in town, at the banks, town hall, the stores, have already been in for their coffee. The stores open at nine thirty, so these people are shoppers. Many of them are tourist shoppers."

One of the women activated her phone and started jotting down notes.

"I get it," Janice said. "I do a good breakfast business with people going to work or farmers in for their shopping, what little shopping they do in town, but the café's pretty much dead the rest of the day."

I studied the offerings of breakfast pastries and selected an almond croissant, plump and glistening.

"Don't compare apples and oranges." John Benedict pointed his coffee cup at the handwritten menu on the blackboard behind the counter. "The two places are totally different. I don't see any bacon and eggs and hash browns on the menu here. These here muffins are well and good"—he'd selected a blueberry one for himself—"but not what a working man needs to get a start on his day."

"Marjorie," Vicky called, "can you bring one of the all-in breakfast sandwiches over, please." She turned to John. "All the fat and calories a man, or a woman, would want in a convenient handheld packet."

"They're very different businesses, yes," Dad said. "But the point is still valid that Vicky's place is busy and yours . . . is not."

"Point taken," Janice said. "Which is why we're here."

"Are you going to be helping Janice on her campaign?" Dad asked John.

"Yeah, I am. Randy and I have been friends for a lotta years, but something has to change in Muddle Harbor. I haven't had a solid offer for a commercial property in months. He's going to regard that as a betrayal, but business is business, right?"

Marjorie placed the requested item in front of John. Sausage patty, several slices of bacon, fried egg, slab of melted cheese, all spilling over the edges of the toasted store-made bun.

"Point definitely taken," John said as he tucked his napkin into his shirt front. The look on his face reminded me of Mattie when dinner was about to be served.

I'm not particularly interested in small-town politics, despite my father's lifelong involvement, so I found my attention wandering as they talked. Janice asked Vicky questions about the local restaurant scene; John and Dad talked hotels and B and Bs. One of the women, whose name I never did get, asked about what state grants might be available for new businesses while the other typed away on her phone, taking notes.

I sat next to Graham Johannesen, who hadn't had much to say. I was about to make my excuses and head back to the store when he said, "I heard you live across the street from what had been my aunt Dorothy's place."

"What the neighbors still call the Johannesen house. Yes, I do. I didn't know your aunt, though. I only moved there a couple of years ago, some time after she died."

"I was fond of the old bat. And I mean that in a good way. She could be difficult. Extremely difficult. Maybe I liked that contrarian feistiness about her. You always knew where you stood with Aunt Dorothy."

"My landlady, Mabel D'Angelo, was telling me the same the other day. She and your aunt got on fine, she said, but not everyone on the street did."

He grinned. "Sounds like Aunt Dorothy." The grin faded, and he asked, "Have the police said anything more about Raquel? About what happened, I mean?"

"Last I heard, they're looking for a sometimes boyfriend and known criminal acquaintance of hers. He seems to have disappeared, which they consider highly suspicious."

"Poor Raquel. She never wanted to do anything the hard way. Always on the lookout for the main chance. I've seen how that turns out." He nodded toward the end of the table where Janice and my dad had their heads close, talking quietly. "Which is why I'm on Janice's team in this. As town clerk, even part-time, I'm supposed to be neutral. But, as a businessman, I can't stay neutral much longer. Not while our town dies around us. About this boyfriend, is he from this area?"

"No. New York City. The NYPD has taken over the lead on the investigation. Have the police spoken to you?"

He shook his head. "No reason they should. I haven't seen Raquel in years. Haven't even heard anything about her since Aunt Dorothy died."

"My cookbook's been accepted by a major publisher, and it comes out next fall," Vicky said to one of the Muddle Harbor women. "It's called *Holiday Favorites From America's Christmas Town*, and we're hoping it will bring even more business to the bakery. If anyone buys it, that is."

"They will," I said. "Guaranteed."

"I'll buy it," the woman said. "Janice, have you considered writing a cookbook?"

Janice turned her attention from Dad and laughed. "No one needs a recipe for bacon and fried eggs. I have no intention of turning the Muddle Harbor Café into anything other than what it is. A solid, good old-fashioned American diner. I'd like more business, that's all. What happens here in January and February, Noel? The number of visitors must drop right off."

Around us, people began gathering up their bags and paying the bill. The line up at the counter was down to two people. I checked my phone. Twenty after ten. Shoppers were heading out, and that meant it was time to get back to work. I downed the last of my coffee, hesitated over taking another croissant (the platter had been topped up), gave in to temptation, grabbed one, wrapped it in a paper napkin, and pushed my chair back. "Sorry, all, but I have to run. Please drop in to Mrs. Claus's Treasures later, and I'll give you the grand tour."

Graham leapt to his feet. "Why don't I walk with you? I'd like to have a stroll down your main street. Check things out on my own. Catch you back in MH, Janice."

We said our goodbyes and left the bakery together. A soft snow was falling. As we stood on the steps, pulling on gloves and wrapping scarves, the sleigh passed, horses stepping high, bells jingling, ribbons threaded through manes blowing in the light wind. Across the street, the windows of Candy Cane Sweets glowed with red and white lights shaped into candy canes. Party gowns sparkled in the window of Jayne's Ladies Wear. Next to the clothing store, Kyle Lambert was setting up the butcher's hot dog cart.

"Christmas Town indeed," Graham said. "I don't see a lot of promise here for growing my own business, being a farm supplies store, but I hope Muddle Harbor can learn something."

He fell into step beside me as we walked down the street. "I heard Aunt Dorothy's house is going to be put on the market soon. I'd love to buy it, but I fear it's going to be way out of my price range, and Beth Torrone isn't likely to drop the price to help out a distant relative she doesn't even remember."

I thought of Vicky and Mark buying the grand old house on the huge, treed property close to the lake they thought was the house of their dreams. They could only afford it because it was practically falling down. The dream hadn't lasted once reality hit, and they were now happy in their small, modern bungalow. "Not so much grass to cut," as Mark put it.

"It can be tough for a young person starting out," I said. "Finding the right house at the right price."

"I might have liked to rent it," he said. "But I never even heard it was available until the opportunity was gone."

I glanced over at him. The tone in his voice had turned bitter. He must have realized how he sounded, as he gave me a bashful grin. "Silly sentiment, I suppose. Probably just as well. The drive between Rudolph and Muddle Harbor isn't long, but it could be a tough commute on bad winter days."

We arrived at Mrs. Claus's Treasures. The windows were cheerful with their display of a holiday picnic basket being enjoyed by a stuffed Santa and Mrs. Claus, nutcracker soldiers, elf dolls, and a collection of reindeer ornaments. Inside, Jackie was helping a customer at the till while Melissa hung a newly arrived collection of jewelry on the stands.

"This is your place," Graham said. "Nice."

"I owe, I owe," I sang, "so it's off to work I go. I hope you enjoy the rest of Rudolph."

"Thanks, uh, before you go . . . Would you like to have dinner with me tonight?" He spoke quickly, the words tumbling all over themselves. "Strictly in the interest of improving the relationship between our two towns. Hands across the municipal border and all that?" He gave me a charming, shy, crooked grin.

I didn't hesitate with my reply. "Thank you for the invitation, Graham, but I'm going to decline. I'm in a relationship."

His face fell. "Oh, I'm sorry to hear that. Dare I hope it's not a serious relationship?"

"We're not engaged or anything, but it's serious enough. For now."

"If things change, let me know," he said.

"I will. But they won't." The chimes over the door tinkled as I went into my shop.

Chapter Twenty

My day only got more interesting from there. And not in a good way.

Not long after I left the bakery, I spotted Dad and the crowd of Muddites strolling past. Dad was talking and gesturing, the woman with the phone taking notes while trying to watch her footing at the same time. Not many people paid them any attention, but I noticed the jaws of a few Rudolphites hit the snow-cleared sidewalks. Dad and his group did not come into Mrs. Claus's Treasures and about ten minutes later they passed by again, going in the opposite direction. Graham Johannesen was not with them either time.

Shortly before three a highly distressed Mrs. D'Angelo burst through the doors. "Merry! The most ridiculous, unbelievable thing has happened. I can scarcely credit it!" Her hair was wild; her coat hung askew, as she'd matched the wrong buttons with the right buttonholes. A well-worn black boot was on her left foot, a new brown one on the right. She sucked in great gasping breaths, as though she'd run all the way from the house.

I abandoned the customer I was helping and hurried toward my landlady. "What on earth? Are you all right? Should I call an ambulance? Jackie, call 911."

"No. No. Nothing like that," Mrs. D'Angelo cried as her legs gave out beneath her. I grabbed her arm before she crashed into a display of glass tree ornaments.

"I'm a doctor, can I help?" my customer asked.

The store was full. Everyone abandoned their browsing to stare.

"Betrayed! I've been betrayed!" Mrs. D'Angelo wailed.

I looked her over quickly. No blood, no broken bones, no bruises.

"Why don't we find a seat in my office?" I said as Melissa took her other arm.

"I'm . . . I'll . . . be all right. It's the shock, just the shock. Such a shock."

"Are you sure, madam?" the doctor asked. "You don't look well."

Mrs. D'Angelo took a deep breath. She gave her head a good shake and almost visibly began to recover. She patted the approximate vicinity of her heart. "The shock. The shock. I'll be all right in a moment."

"Jackie, get her a glass of water," I ordered, and my assistant ran for the back. Mattie woofed.

I guided Mrs. D'Angelo to the stool behind the counter while Melissa hovered nervously nearby.

"If you're sure," the doctor said.

"We're okay here," I said. "Thank you."

Jackie was soon back with the water and handed it over. Mrs. D'Angelo took the glass in shaking hands and drank deeply.

"Melissa," I said, "can you see if any of these nice people need help?"

No one moved.

"Melissa?" I repeated.

"What? Oh, right. Help. Uh, does anyone need any help here?"

"You too, Jackie. Back to work. We're fine now."

Jackie gave Mrs. D'Angelo a last questioning look before she turned and gave the circle of onlookers a broad smile. Everyone immediately turned away, back to chatting among themselves or admiring the goods. The doctor hesitated and then joined them, still keeping a cautious eye on us.

"Can you tell me what happened?" I said to Mrs. D'Angelo when we were alone. "Were you in some sort of an accident?"

Mrs. D'Angelo shook her head. "No. Nothing like that. The . . . the"—her voice broke—"police. Came to my house. They . . . she . . . accused me of killing that poor young woman."

I didn't know what I was expecting, but it certainly wasn't that.

"Okay. Let's grab a coffee or something, and you can tell me about it."

"That would be nice. Yes, thank you." Mrs. D'Angelo climbed off the stool, but her breathing and her legs weren't quite back to normal. She must have run all the way here. Mrs. D'Angelo was not a woman who spent a great deal of time in the gym.

"Jackie, Melissa," I called. "I'm taking a break. Call me if you need anything."

Once again everyone in the shop, including my two employees, stopped what they were doing to watch us.

I led the way out of the store and immediately began to turn right, to Cranberry Coffee Bar next door, but Mrs. D'Angelo gasped. "No. Not there. It's not safe. I don't trust that Mary-Ellen who works there."

I knew Mary-Ellen. A pleasant middle-aged woman with two kids in primary school, a member of the local amateur dramatic society. Her husband coached kids' soccer in the summer, hockey in the winter. I could think of no reason she was not trustworthy. Trustworthy, or not, about what? Had the police truly accused Mrs. D'Angelo of murder? Or had she suddenly come down with a serious case of out-of-control conspiracy theories?

"Okay," I said. "Is the bakery . . . uh . . . safe?"

"Yes. It should be. If we get a quiet table."

I kept a solid grip on her arm as we walked down the street. Gradually, I could feel her strength coming back, and I released her when we reached Victoria's Bake Shoppe.

The lunch rush was over, with no line at the counter. A handful of tables were taken by people chatting over the last of their tea and cakes, shopping bags piled around their feet. More than a few of those bags were from Mrs. Claus's Treasures.

I spotted a table at the back, tucked next to the doors leading to the restrooms, and pointed it out to Mrs. D'Angelo. "You take a seat, and I'll fetch the drinks. What would you like?"

"A latte, I think, dear. One of those ones with the chocolate syrup and whipped cream and chocolate sprinkles on the top."

"Everything okay?" Marjorie asked me as I approached the counter.

"I don't know. Can you tell Vicky I'm here? I'll have a low-fat latte and one large mocha. Heavy on the whipped cream and chocolate sprinkles. On the mocha, not the latte."

"Take a seat, and I'll bring it to you. Vicky! Merry's here."

My friend's hairnet-covered head popped out of the kitchen. "What's up?"

"I honestly don't know," I said. "If you have a minute, come and join us."

The head retreated, and a moment later all of Vicky came out. She'd pulled off the hairnet and was drying her hands on the front of her apron. "Bring me a cappuccino, please, Aunt Marjorie."

"Coming up," Marjorie said.

We took seats at the table. I studied Mrs. D'Angelo's face. Some of the color was returning, her breathing almost back to normal. She gave me a weak smile. "I might have overreacted a fraction there. Sorry, dear."

"Overreacted about what?" Vicky said.

"Here you go." Marjorie placed three mugs on the table. "Can I get you something to eat, Mabel? We have a couple of mince tarts left, and you know how unusual that is at this time of day."

"A tart would be nice, thank you."

Marjorie bustled off. Vicky gave me a curious look. I shrugged in response.

Mrs. D'Angelo took the first, long welcome sip of her drink. "How's your cookbook coming along, dear?"

"My book? To be honest, Mrs. D, it's mostly out of my control now, and I don't handle that too well. My editor wants some changes I don't want to make."

"What sort of changes?" I asked.

"She phoned me this morning, not long after you and that weird lot from Muddle Harbor were here. She doesn't want three recipes for Christmas cake. She says no one eats fruitcake these days. I said they do at my place. She said the readers won't be at my place, will they, but baking for their families. And their families don't want fruitcake. One fruitcake recipe is enough, although she'll accept two at a pinch. She wants another cookie recipe to replace the third cake. I told her I've given the book the best cookie recipes I have and I have no time to develop any more. I fear we left things at an impasse." Her face crinkled up in thought. "Do you suppose they'll dump me and the book if they think I'm being difficult?"

"They're not going to dump you, Vicky. Not only do you have the advance in your dough-covered little hands, but they're invested in the book. They understand; you all have the same goal here. To produce the best book possible. Some back-and-forth is not only acceptable but desirable."

"Donalda told the police I was the mastermind behind the counterfeiting ring!" A line of whipped cream covered Mrs. D'Angelo's top lip.

Vicky's mouth snapped shut. I stared at Mrs. D'Angelo open-mouthed.

"What?" we said simultaneously, once we'd recovered our wits.

"They came to my house. Detective Simmonds and little Candy Campbell." I doubted Officer Campbell would be all that pleased at being called *little Candy*, but I supposed she was used to it, trying to be a police officer in a town where people remembered seeing her pee her pants onstage in the first-grade Christmas play.

Heck, even I remember that. I'd been standing next to her.

"Without naming names, Detective Simmonds said I'd been seen in the vicinity of that house in the days before Raquel's death. *Sneaking* was the word their source used. As if!"

"What did you say?"

"I denied it, of course. Quite firmly. I might have been attempting to pay a neighborly call, as one does in this town, but I was most definitely not *sneaking*."

"Here you go. A nice mince tart. I took the liberty of getting one for you too, Merry. And Vicky." Marjorie put a plate on the table between us.

"Thanks," Vicky said.

"We'll be closing in a few minutes," Marjorie said.

"We're fine here," Vicky said. Marjorie slipped away after giving Mrs. D'Angelo a questioning look.

"First things first," I said. "We know you weren't running a counterfeiting ring out of a house on Broad Street. Or anyplace else."

"Don't jump to conclusions," Vicky mumbled around the rim of her mug. I ignored her.

Mrs. D'Angelo took a bite of her tart. "Yummy."

"You said Donalda told them so, but you also said the police didn't name their source."

"Who else but Donalda? Always watching, always gossiping."

Vicky gave me a wink. I ignored her once again. Yes, the description could easily apply to Mrs. D'Angelo herself.

"In major cases such as this one, the police ask everyone who might know something to let them know about anything they observe, no matter how inconsequential it might appear to be. Anyone of the people on the street could have seen you . . . uh . . . paying attention to the goings-on. Delivery people, the letter carrier maybe."

"No. It was Donalda. I'm sure of it. What you suspected, Merry, about her husband is absolutely true. But you don't know the half of it. He travels extensively for work, and we all know what that leads to."

"We do?" Vicky said. Vicky, I realized, was not taking this seriously. But it was serious. Serious for poor Mrs. D'Angelo.

"Donalda pretends not to know what he gets up to, but I've seen the tears in her eyes when she watches him drive away and heard the shake in her voice when she tells me on the phone he's been delayed getting home. He didn't even make it in time last August for her birthday party. So there! Some feeble excuse about plane cancellations and delays. As if that ever happens in August."

"It does. But that has nothing at all to do with why she'd tell the police you're a counterfeiter," Vicky pointed out. She studied her mince tart, out of which she'd taken one small bite. "Not half bad, if I do say so myself."

"Have you included a mince tart recipe in your cookbook?" Mrs. D'Angelo asked.

"Yup. It's going to be the cover photo."

I took a bite myself, and I was not disappointed. Vicky's mince tarts are the best I've ever had. Flaky pastry, rich spicy filling packed full of fruits and the essence of rum and brandy, a light dusting of sugar sprinkled on the top crust before baking to give it a bit of crunch.

I forced my attention away from the delights happening in my mouth and back to the matter at hand. "What exactly did Detective Simmonds say about this accusation?"

"She started by wanting to know if I'd been in that house at any time prior to being knocked over the head and stuffed into the pantry. I told her I visited Dorothy on occasion before she passed away—"

"Glad you didn't visit her after she passed away," Vicky said.

I threw Vicky a warning glare. She grinned in return.

"But not since," Mrs. D'Angelo continued. "Not even once. The first bunch of renters were that stuck-up lawyer and his brittle, skinny wife. The next lot, who stayed longer, had a large family, always rushing about with hockey equipment or baseball bats and soccer balls. No time for stopping for a chat to get to know their neighbors. Those without children, at any rate." She sniffed in disapproval. "Although they could be polite enough if we met on the sidewalk or in town. I told Detective Simmonds that. She apologized for taking my time and left."

"So they didn't actually accuse you of being a member of the gang?" I licked pastry crumbs off my fingers.

"Well, no. But why else would she have asked that question?"

Why indeed.

"The police have to follow up on any tip they get," I said. "It would be negligent of them not to. You know that. From what you say, Detective Simmonds told you about this tip, she asked if it was true, and then she left."

"You think I overreacted?"

I chose my words carefully. "I think you've been through a highly traumatic experience and you're still struggling to come to terms with it. As would anyone in that situation. Seeing the police on your doorstep"—even in the form of "little Candy"—"brought it all back."

Her eyes filled with tears. "Thank you, Merry."

"As for Donalda and her husband. What's his name again?" Vicky asked.

"William."

"William Reynolds. Has he been seen since the curious incident of the cellar in the nighttime?"

"The what?"

"Has Mr. Reynolds been seen since you were kidnapped and Raquel murdered?"

Mrs. D'Angelo thought. Her mocha and tart were finished. Around us, Vicky's staff were going about the business of closing up at the end of the day. The display cases were almost empty, and on the blackboard behind the counter, chalked lines had been drawn through the soup of the day—sausage and sweet potato—and the day's lunch special—sliced roast turkey and cranberries on a baguette.

"I haven't seen him," she said at last.

I exchanged a look with Vicky. Earlier, I'd wondered if it was possible Raquel had come to Rudolph for a man, either a genuine relationship or one of her marks. Could it be? Was that man the illusive William Reynolds?

"That might be an avenue to pursue," Vicky said. "Did Donalda accuse you to cover up her own guilt? Or his?"

My landlady's eyes brightened. "I'll get onto that straightaway. I'll make some calls. Not to Donalda, of course. She will rue the day she set the police on me, let me tell you."

"If it was her," I said. "You don't know for sure. Don't ruin your friendship without proof."

Marjorie began collecting the used mugs and plates. "I couldn't help but overhear. You need to talk to someone, Mabel D'Angelo, and I know just the person. My cousin Rose, who would be Vicky's mother's cousin also, is a trained and registered therapist. I'll make an appointment today for you to see her."

"I don't need—"

"Yes, you do," the three of us said at once.

"Come along, Mabel," Marjorie said. "Merry will take care of your bill."

"I will? I mean, okay, I will."

"We'll call Rose this very minute and get you in as soon as possible. Everything you tell her will be under the strictest of confidence, so no need to worry about it getting around."

"Hey!" Vicky said. "Before you go, I've had the best idea ever. Molasses spice cookies!"

"What about them?" Marjorie asked. "Are you thinking of putting those on the rotation?"

"I need a new cookie recipe for the book if I'm going to drop one of the fruitcakes. Mrs. D, your spice cookies are fabulous. Would you share the recipe with me? I'll mention your name in the notes in the book. Something about how neighbors in Rudolph help each other out, usually over coffee and cookies."

Mrs. D'Angelo's eyes lit up. "Oh my goodness. Why, yes. That would be marvelous. Imagine, my mother's recipe in a New York–published cookbook."

Marjorie took Mrs. D'Angelo by the arm and helped (forced?) her to stand. "My phone's in the back. Come along now."

"If you're okay," I called after them, "I need to get back to the store."

Behind Mrs. D'Angelo's back, Marjorie lifted her right thumb.

When they'd gone, Vicky let out a bark of laughter. "Mrs. D'Angelo, criminal mastermind. It doesn't bear thinking about. Let me think about it again." She laughed again.

"I don't know why you find it so amusing. She's obviously highly disturbed about her ordeal, anyone would be, and anyone would know she would be. Mean trick sending the cops after her."

"Live by the gossip, die by the gossip, Merry. I agree it wasn't very nice, but I don't have all that much sympathy for her. She's quick enough to dish the dirt about everyone else."

"That's sort of my point, Vicky. She doesn't so much dish the dirt as spread the news. In the old days, Mrs. D'Angelo would have been the town crier. Walking up and down Main Street in a tricorn hat and brass buttons, ringing a bell and shouting, 'Hear ye, hear ye.' I'll admit sometimes the news gets exaggerated a bit, but she's never genuinely nasty. Far as I know, anyway."

"Okay. I'll buy that."

"You're not as unsympathetic as you pretend. When was the last time you had one of her cookies?"

"Let me think." She put her chin in her hands and twisted her face in what she thought was a thoughtful expression. "Never." The thoughtfulness disappeared, the hands dropped, and she laughed. "She brought some out when we had iced tea with her the other day, but I wasn't hungry. You say they're good, and that's enough for me, so I thought the offer would cheer her up, and I do need a new recipe, at least according to my editor. A win-win. Back to the subject at hand. What do you think Donalda, if it was Donalda, was playing at? I'd say deflecting blame."

"Blame from who?"

"From whom. Her. Her husband, who's gone missing all of a sudden."

Vicky was thinking along the same lines as I was.

"He travels a lot," I said. "Or so we've been told."

"Suspicious, I say. Let's suppose he ran into Raquel in town. Suppose she suggested they get to know each other better, and by the way, could he lend her a couple of thousand bucks. Suppose Donalda got wind of this and decided to put a stop to it. Suppose he realized his new friend intended to cheat him and he decided to put a stop to it. A permanent stop."

"It's possible, if she got wind Raquel and William were up to something." Like Mrs. D'Angelo, Donalda had been keeping an eye on the house on Broad Street. She'd have been eager to have the honor of making "first contact" with the new people on the street. To be the first to find out what was going on to make them so elusive.

Raquel was a young, attractive woman. Had Mr. Reynolds decided to do the neighborly thing himself and make her acquaintance? Had Raquel invited him in even though he, presumably, came without an offering of a casserole or homemade cookies? I remembered the couple of times I'd seen a lone man outside the house. Could that have been the wayward Mr. Reynolds, watching for Raquel to return? Had Donalda seen him entering the house? Had he perhaps stayed longer than it took to say *Welcome to the neighborhood*? Had she followed him, intending to put an end to his straying once and for all? One way or another?

It made sense, in a strange sort of way, but it was mighty extreme. "Isn't it more likely that of the two of them, William's the killer? I've been wondering why Raquel not only came to Rudolph but to her parents' own house. Maybe the house itself wasn't the attraction, but its proximity to William Reynolds. If she was scamming him, it must have been going on for a while. It takes time to set up that sort of confidence trick, and Raquel and her friend were only in that house a short time."

The more I thought about it, the more I liked the idea. A married man like William would have far more to lose than someone like Bob Gravel, who'd seen straight through Raquel and regarded his involvement with her as a form of entertainment, costing him nothing more than he could comfortably afford. But what if William had been spending money on Raquel? Money that should go to support his family, money that belonged to both him and his wife? Not a laughing matter. Did Raquel start demanding more? Did she want payment for out-and-out blackmail? Did she move into a house in his own neighborhood as a way of making sure he realized she was serious and would expose him if he didn't pay up? What would William have done to put a stop to that?

"Maybe he was having a legitimate affair with her," Vicky said. "Not that any affair is legit, but you know what

I mean. She wanted to break it off. Maybe she threatened to tell his wife."

"That might be possible, if they knew each other before the move. The time frame's way too short for them to have started an affair after her arrival in town. As far as we know, she didn't spend much time, if any, in the house and the guy who did spend time there was apparently her boyfriend. If, and of course it's still a mighty big if, William Reynolds is our guy, I'm thinking she came to town after him." I explained my reasoning to her. How William would have far more to lose than a man like Bob Gravel.

Vicky ran her index finger across her plate and scooped up the last of the pastry crumbs. I sipped my latte. We thought.

"Let's slow down here," I said at last. "We're getting way ahead of ourselves. We've never even met this William Reynolds, and now we find ourselves at the point of accusing him of murder. We're making a lot of assumptions here. Beginning with the fact that we don't even know if it was Donalda who talked to the police about Mrs. D'Angelo. Could have been anyone. Attempting to deflect blame or for any number of reasons."

"True."

"Do you know what Occam's Razor is?"

"No."

"It means the simplest solution to any problem is more often than not the correct one. It means don't make things more complicated than they have to be. We know Raquel was into illegal stuff. I've heard criminals don't aways operate on the up-and-up and they sometimes fall out. Raquel had a boyfriend, right? One who was also her accomplice. He's in an off-again, on-again marriage, with kids, and he's known to the cops as a small-time crook. He's disappeared. The New York police are looking for him."

"Yes, but—" Vicky said.

"No buts. It's Christmas week in Rudolph, and we both have more than enough on our plates."

"True enough," Vicky said.

I changed the subject. "You'll never guess what happened this morning."

"What happened this morning?"

"You remember Graham Johannesen from Muddle Harbor? The young guy. Young compared to the rest of them, anyway. He was with the group this morning."

"Yeah, I do. Reasonably okay-looking guy. I didn't know they had such a thing in Muddle Harbor. What about him?"

I leaned back in my chair with a grin. "He asked me out. Like on a date."

"Ooh. Do tell."

"Nothing more to tell. I told him I was in a relationship, which I am, and he accepted that graciously."

"Never hurts to be asked, does it?"

"Nope."

"Speaking of being asked, did you know your mom invited me for Christmas Eve?"

"I didn't know, but I'm not surprised. Is Mark coming?"

"No. He's working that night, but he's taking all of Christmas Day off. Which means we'll wake up in our own house and run into the living room together to see what

Santa put under the tree. We'll spend all morning opening presents with coffee and mimosas and a big, cooked breakfast. Then we'll go to my parents' for a light lunch and more presents, maybe a walk in the snow-covered woods, a good restaurant for dinner, followed by postprandial liquors." She glowed with the joy of anticipation.

And that, dear reader, is the spirit of Christmas in Rudolph.

Chapter
Twenty-One

I'd been longer than I intended at the bakery, and it was after four when I got back to Mrs. Claus's Treasures. Jackie gave me a disapproving frown when I came in. I held up the bakery bag I'd brought, and the frown disappeared. "Sorry to be away so long. Anyone for leftovers?"

Jackie took the bag. She opened it and peered in. "A cupcake and a fruit tart. No mince tarts left?"

"You know how it is in mid-December," I said cheerily. "They're so popular they run out early."

"The cupcake will do. Mabel okay?"

"She'll be fine. The police had some follow-up questions about the goings-on in the house across the street, and she overreacted."

Melissa took the bag from Jackie and peered in. "No gingerbread? That's my favorite."

"It's everyone's favorite, which is why none was left."

"That cupcake looks good."

"No way," Jackie said. "I have first dibs. You get the raspberry tart."

"Don't like raspberries."

"Tough."

"Gee," I said, "I'm sorry I bothered." I left them to fight it out and glanced around the store. Customers browsed happily. I couldn't help but notice how many items were missing from the book display.

"Did we have a run on the books?"

"We did." Jackie triumphantly lifted the coconut cupcake out of the bakery bag. "That woman who bought *A Christmas Carol* yesterday came back with a man who's probably her husband, and they got a whole bunch of the other titles."

"Nice."

A woman put an armful of Christmas tree ornaments onto the counter, and I said to my employees, "Why don't you take a break and enjoy your snack. I'll handle this."

"I suppose I can pick the berries off," Melissa said.

* * *

Not long after, Alan texted me to say he was pulling into the alley behind the store, and I ran out to meet him. I helped him unload boxes of stock and carry them into the storage room to be unpacked and put on display after closing.

"I was at the bakery earlier," I said. "If I'd known you were coming, I would have brought you some leftovers."

He gathered me into his arms and said, "Always love leftovers." He kissed the top of my head. "Can you take a few minutes for a walk?"

"No, but I will anyway. Mattie could use a stretch."

Mattie's always delighted to see Alan, and after effusive greetings (more on Alan's part than Mattie's), we went back to the alley. We didn't stay long, just long enough to enjoy some brief moments in each other's company and let the dog sniff trash cans to his heart's content.

"I gotta go," Alan said at last. "I have a delivery for the toy store. I had stuff to drop off in Rochester earlier, and that chewed up a good part of my day. I'm seriously thinking I should have hired a driver for the season." He let out a puff of air. "But it's hard to find someone looking for part-time work at this time of year. Other than a high schooler who might not even have a driver's license."

"If my dad's rapprochement with Muddle Harbor comes to fruition, maybe some Muddites will be willing to work around here."

"There's always Kyle."

"Who will always be wanting work," I said with a laugh.

He didn't laugh in return.

"Are you serious?"

"Nothing I can do about it this year. If business is as good next year as this, I'll have to do something, Merry. I can't keep burning the candle at all ends from August to December." He turned to me, his eyes dark and thoughtful. "Not if I want to spend serious time with you."

Mattie abandoned whatever he found so fascinating at the back door of Cranberry Coffee Bar and barked at Alan.

Alan's eyes widened as he looked at the dog. "Do you suppose he's telling me to back off?"

"I do not," I said.

"Glad to hear it. Gotta run. We still on for Christmas Eve at your parents'?"

"Command performance. Try getting out of it."

He kissed me lightly, and then he climbed into his truck. He gave me a wave before backing out of the alley.

Serious time. What did that even mean?

I decided to think about that later, and I went back to work.

* * *

The number of shoppers dropped off toward the end of the day, as it usually does, so I left Melissa in charge of the shop with instructions to text me if she got too busy, and Jackie and I unpacked the delivery boxes. As well as the nutcracker solders, Alan had brought angels, train sets, and components of his highly individual, much-sought-after Santa's village.

The soldiers were painted in the traditional design with red jackets, blue trousers, black boots, and tall red-and-gold hats. Bushy eyebrows, big mustaches, wide blue or dark-brown eyes. They came in all skin tones and all sizes, from about six inches to five feet tall. The latter were designed to stand on either side of an entranceway or next to a towering tree.

My phone buzzed, and I checked it. Melissa, asking for backup.

I pushed myself to my feet. "Can you stay for a few minutes after closing, Jackie? Help me put these out."

"Sure." She pouted, and it was not an attractive look. "Not as if I have anything better to do tonight, is it?"

"Are you and Kyle still on a break?"

"You could put it like that." She went out front without another word, and I followed.

As though summoned by our words, who should appear no more than two minutes later but Kyle Lambert himself.

"Hey, Jack," he said. "What's up?"

"Nothing in particular," Jackie said with a sniff. "Not that it's any of your business."

A large group of last-minute shoppers had come in and spread throughout the store, chattering to each other and exclaiming over everything. Melissa stood behind the till, ringing up purchases, while another customer hovered, clearly wanting to ask a question.

"Hi," I said, "welcome. May I help you?"

"We're going to a Christmas Eve dinner party at the home of people I don't know very well. I want to bring a nice hostess gift, but I truly have no idea what they would like. Do you have any suggestions?"

"Something practical yet seasonal is always nice on Christmas Eve. Let me show you some of our table settings." I led the way to the display of linens and dishware.

"I want to take something to Raquel's mom," Kyle said to Jackie. "My mom said flowers would be best, but that's not very original."

"It's not at all original," Jackie replied in an icy tone. "Which is why you take flowers to a mourner. It's not a present, for heaven's sake, you idiot. Get her flowers."

Not the way I normally wanted to hear my staff speak to our customers, but I let it go and smiled at my own customer. "These napkins make a nice addition to the holiday table." Bright-red linen, with a stylized design in white thread showing flying reindeer pulling a sleigh.

"I like them. They're cute, but I don't know what color their dining room is. I've never been in the house."

"How about cocktail napkins, then? Paper ones don't have to match the decor."

Her face twisted. "That seems cheap."

"Aren't you supposed to be the expert in buying gifts?" Kyle said in a voice that could be heard by everyone in the store. "That's what you're always going on about."

"Why are you taking something to Raquel's mother anyway?" Jackie snapped back. "Not like you've been in touch with them over the years."

"It's the decent thing to do, Jackie. You know what that means, don't you?"

"Decency. You're talking to me about decency? When all you can do is blather on about how beautiful and how wonderful she was and—"

"She was beautiful. She was wonderful. She was—"

"Yeah, yeah, I get it. The light of your life. Never mind that she walked out on you ten years ago and never so much as sent you a text again."

Customers were abandoning their shopping and turning to see what the commotion was. The louder Jackie spoke, the louder Kyle spoke back. Melissa stared at them. Her customer turned around, hand frozen in the act of handing over her credit card.

Kyle lowered his voice. "True love stands the test of time." Not low enough we didn't all hear it.

"True love! Is that what you call it! You don't know what true love is. I thought I was the one you love." Yup, we all heard that.

Kyle blinked. He glanced around at the shop full of women, everyone staring at him. He might have finally come to realize that Jackie had a point. And the audience was not on his side. "I do," he said. "I . . . love you too, Jackie."

"You love me too! Me too!" Jackie's rage was terrible to behold. Her face had turned a bright red, her eyes wild. She threw up her hands and took a step toward Kyle. Spittle flew out of her mouth. "Your precious Raquel was a two-bit hooker!" Jackie bellowed. "She got nothing more than she deserved. Murdered either by one of her marks or her criminal boyfriend."

"Maybe the cocktail napkins will do after all," my customer said. "And a couple of wineglasses to go with them." She edged toward the display of paper products, which just happened to be closer to the combatants.

I crossed the room. "Why don't you two continue this discussion outside?"

No one paid the slightest bit of attention to me.

"The police say she was killed by her boyfriend," Jackie said. "Are they right about that, Kyle? But are they concentrating on the wrong guy?"

"Huh?" he said. "What does that mean?"

"Did you kill her, Kyle, because she laughed at you? As I should have done years ago."

"That's enough," I said. "Please, you two, take it outside."

"Don't know why you think you're so special," Kyle said. "You're lucky I've bothered with you."

Jackie let out a roar and reached for the closest thing at hand: a wide-mouthed crystal vase piled high with brightly colored glass ornaments. Before I could move, she grabbed the top ball and threw it. Kyle ducked, and the ornament hit the door behind him. Glass tinkled cheerfully as the ball shattered into a hundred pieces and shards fell to the floor.

One at a time, Jackie grabbed balls and threw them. Kyle dodged and dipped and tried to cover his head and face with his hands. Glass shattered. Some customers screamed. Some laughed. One called, "You go, girl."

I grabbed Jackie's arm as she pulled back to make another throw. "Enough! Enough! Kyle, get the heck out of here."

He spread his fingers and peered through them at me. Fortunately, he didn't appear to have been hit. "Yeah. Okay." He threw the door open and stumbled out. "Uh . . . call me sometime, Jackie. When you've cooled down."

She roared and jerked forward as though to follow him, but I had a good grip on her arm. "Leave it!"

The fight went out of her. Jackie looked around. At fragments of colorful glass sprinkled across the floor. The staring women. Wide-eyed Melissa behind the counter.

At me. Steam must have been coming out of my ears. "Go home, Jackie." I released her arm.

"Uh . . . Sorry about that, Merry. I'll clean it up."

"No. I'll clean up. I'll also finish unpacking today's delivery. Go home, and be glad no one got hurt. I will be charging you for the damage."

She stepped toward the door. I grabbed her arm again and pulled. "Your coat and bag are in the back. Take the door to the alley."

"Okay. Sorry. See you tomorrow." She slunk away.

"Goodness," one of the customers said, "that was exciting."

"Did he honestly tell her he loved another woman and expect her to be okay with that?" someone asked her friend.

The woman with the credit card turned back to Melissa and said, "Here you go, dear. Get that sort of thing often in this town, do you?"

"Not quite the true spirit of the holidays, I'd say," my own customer said as she turned to the display of paper napkins and made a selection.

"In my family it's exactly the holiday spirit," another woman said. "Although we usually get to the bottom of the dinner wine bottles before all the grievances start coming out. How fondly I remember the time Granddad hit his brother over the head with a beer bottle. Needed ten stitches, Uncle Ned did. My mother never did get the blood out of the tablecloth. A nice Christmassy red it was." She put a stuffed reindeer doll on the counter. "Which is why I never buy breakable holiday ornaments."

I went into the back for the broom.

Chapter
Twenty-Two

Melissa apologized profusely for not being able to stay after work to help me unpack and arrange Alan's delivery. Her mom was minding the kids today, and she had plans for as soon as Melissa got home.

I told her that was okay. Not to worry. I bid her a good night.

When I was alone in the shop, I looked around for something to kick. As this was a gift and decor shop, not a sporting goods store, nothing came immediately to hand. Or rather to foot. Instead I went to the office and got Mattie for a brief break in the alley.

My phone lit up with incoming texts.

Vicky: *OMG. Marjorie told me major blow-up at MCT.*
Mom: *WHAT HAS BEEN GOING ON? And they say opera singers are divas!*
Dad: *All okay, honeybunch?*
Sue-Anne Morrow, mayor of Rudolph: *Once again, a disturbance at Mrs. Claus. Really Merry, this is a respectable town.*

I replied to each in turn.

To Vicky: *I'm going to fire that Jackie!* 😫
To Mom: *Non issue.* ☺
To Dad: *All Okay. Crisis passed. No one injured.* 👍
To Sue-Anne (reluctantly): *No harm done. Excess of Christmas spirt.* ☺ 🎅

The phone rang. Mrs. D'Angelo. I considered not answering. Then I decided she might once again be in some sort of crisis, so I said, "Hello?"

"Good heavens, Merry. Are you all right? Is it true? Kyle Lambert killed Raquel?"

"Where did you hear that?"

"Mary-Ellen from Cranberries was walking past your store and heard Jackie accusing Kyle and Kyle admitting it."

"He didn't admit anything. Jackie was angry and making no sense. Besides, I thought you didn't trust Mary-Ellen."

"I don't trust her to keep what she hears spoken in confidence over coffee and sandwiches to herself. She didn't hear it at Cranberries, and it was hardly in confidence. I've had more than one report. I told Mary-Ellen Kyle is an unlikely candidate for murder. He might be sneaky and lazy and not at all clever and the despair of his poor mother's life, but he's no killer. Besides, if he had killed Raquel, he wouldn't be able to stop justifying himself to anyone and everyone."

Which, I had to admit, was pretty much the conclusion I'd come to. Kyle might not be too bright, but he wasn't devious.

Then again, what did I know? He and I weren't what anyone would call close.

"Gotta run." I hung up without waiting for her to say goodbye or to ask for more salacious details.

I called Mattie to come away from a patch of weeds on the far side of the alley, and we went back inside.

I tried to enjoy unwrapping Alan's pieces, the wood so pure, the paint so fresh, each item crafted with such care, but I couldn't stop thinking about the incident. I was undecided about what to do about Jackie.

That earlier display was a firing offense if ever there was such a thing. My shop was full of breakable objects. Never mind the stock—if broken glass or china had started flying and customers had been struck, Mrs. Claus's Treasures (meaning me) could have been in a lot of trouble.

On the other hand, it was a week before Christmas. If I fired Jackie, I wouldn't be able to find anyone to replace her.

It was her first offense. Jackie could be difficult, and she could be opinionated, and she didn't take instruction well. But she'd never before endangered my customers.

As I was putting out the last of the big nutcracker soldiers, my phone rang. Jackie. Once again, I considered not answering it, but I gave in. I kept my voice as cool as possible. "Hello."

"Merry. It's Jackie here."

"I know."

"I'm really sorry."

"You should be. Jackie, someone could have been hurt. And I don't mean you or Kyle. Never mind subjecting my customers to that display of personal . . . whatever."

"Some of them seemed to enjoy it."

"Jackie! That's hardly the point."

"Sorry. Sorry. I know. I'll pay for the broken balls. I can come back now and clean up, like."

"I've taken care of that."

"Oh. Okay. Uh, see you tomorrow?"

I sighed. "Yes, Jackie. You're scheduled to start at noon. Be here."

"Merry?"

"What is it now?"

"Do you think I should call Kyle and check if he's okay? He was really mad when he left."

"No!" I hung up.

* * *

My mood hadn't improved by the time we headed home. Usually, I like being my own boss. Running my own business. Being responsible for myself.

Sometimes I wonder why I left a good job at a magazine in Manhattan.

Today was one of those days.

I tried to cheer myself up by thinking of Alan's soldiers, toys, and angels. They were lovely. Handcrafted with care and genuine love and attention, and that showed.

Like the man himself.

The morning's snow had stopped some time ago, but the thick cloud cover hadn't moved on. The streetlights and holiday decorations did their best to lighten the dark of the night.

My house came in sight, and Mattie picked up his pace. Dinner, he knew, was waiting.

As soon as the police took down their tape at the house across the street from mine, a FOR SALE sign had been erected on the lawn. A lamp shone above the front door, but otherwise all was dark. Mattie's attention was caught as something moved under the blue spruce; his head swiveled and he let out a warning bark.

A man stepped out of the shadows. He was dressed in a long black coat, black scarf, black gloves and boots. I sucked in a breath and put my hand on the phone in my pocket.

"Hey, Merry," he said, and I relaxed. Mattie edged forward to sniff at his boots.

"What are you doing here?" I asked Graham Johannesen.

He bent over and gave Mattie a pat on the top of his head. The pat was awkward and rough, and Mattie stepped out of the way. I wondered if Graham was avoiding my eyes.

Then he lifted his head and smiled at me. "Just checking out the old place. Memories. You know how it is." He indicated the sign. "I see Beth and Richard wasted no time in putting it up for sale."

"No reason for them to delay, not if they don't intend to live there."

"I guess."

"Did you have further business to do in Rudolph today?"

"No. Why?"

"No reason. Just wondering why you came back."

His grin widened, but it didn't reach his eyes. "Like I said, memories. I was fond of Aunt Dorothy. I told you that."

"You did. Good night."

226

He pointed to the big Victorian on the other side of the street. "Is that where you live?"

"Yes, it is. I have an apartment there. My neighbors and my landlady are almost always home." Lights shone from Wendy and Steve's half of the upper floor and from Mrs. D'Angelo's living room. Wendy's car was in the driveway, next to mine.

I didn't know why I added that detail, but something about the way Graham was watching me made me uncomfortable. For some reason, I didn't believe he didn't know where I lived. Next to me, Mattie let out a low whine.

Graham looked down. "Big dog."

"Yes."

"How about inviting me in? I bet you had a long, tough day. Isn't that what everyone says, the holiday season in Rudolph is nothing but hard work? A beer'd be nice. Coffee if you don't have beer."

"Sorry, but my boyfriend's coming for dinner. He'll be here soon."

"Another time, maybe."

"Sure. Another time."

He gave Mattie a tap on the nose and walked away, heading toward the lights of town.

Noticeably, Graham had not parked his car on our street.

Chapter
Twenty-Three

"Tell me if you think I'm being paranoid," I said to Vicky.

"Just because you're paranoid doesn't mean they're not out to get you. Although I don't think anyone's out to get you. What happened? Did Jackie and Kyle return to finish their spat?"

I leaned back against the cushions and cradled my wine glass. The phone sat on my lap, on speaker. Mattie was in the kitchen gobbling up his dinner. "No, this has nothing to do with them. Remember I told you Graham Johannesen asked me out earlier today?"

"Yeah. And you turned him down. Did something more happen?"

"Like I said, maybe I'm paranoid. But I think he might be stalking me."

"What!" Even over the phone I could hear her feet hit the ground.

"He was at the house across the street when I got home, standing there in the dark. I think he might have been watching for me. And I suspect it was not the first time."

"Meaning?"

"With all the comings and goings after the death of Raquel and what happened to Mrs. D'Angelo, I didn't pay a lot of attention. I mean, plenty of the neighbors have been watching the police activity, and people drove or walked by to have a look. Some of them lingered, like it was a TV show or something, even when the police packed up and there was nothing more to see. That's normal, right?"

"Normal enough. Look at all the activity on Lakeshore Drive when that person died at our house around Easter. We could have sold tickets. Should have sold tickets; it would help to pay the mortgage on the new place. Never mind that now. Go on."

"I'm only saying I might have seen him there before, but I can't be positive. I might be wrong."

"You're not wrong. Not if you get a bad feeling from him. Do you?"

"I didn't at first. When he asked me out, I was sort of flattered. But tonight, I wasn't comfortable. He wanted to come up to my apartment, for a beer he said. I told him I was expecting Alan any minute."

"Good move. What did he say to that?"

"'Another time, maybe.'"

"And?"

"And nothing. He left."

"Okay. Sounds innocent enough, but sometimes these things are innocent until they're not. Are you going to tell Alan?"

"I don't think so. Alan's not the sort to overreact to anything, but I don't want to start something if something isn't there to be started."

"Have a word with Diane Simmonds."

"You mean lay a charge? I don't know if I can do that. The guy was standing under a tree on a city street at six in the evening."

"Nothing official. Just mention it. You and her get on okay. You might almost be friends."

"I wouldn't say that."

"I would. If she knows anything about this guy, she can give you a heads-up. If not, no harm done."

* * *

I didn't call the detective that night. If I was reading something into nothing, I wouldn't want to get an innocent man into any sort of trouble.

Then again, I reminded myself, isn't that what women always say in this sort of situation? *I didn't want to cause trouble.* And then trouble arrives, and they're the ones at the end of it.

I decided to wait until morning and see how I felt then. Before going to bed, I ran downstairs and checked that the lock on the door at the bottom of the steps was secure. Sometimes, if Wendy's tussling with Tina when they come in or Steve is laden with groceries, they forget to come back down and lock up.

Satisfied all was secure, I went upstairs and double-checked the door to my own apartment. Mattie was snoozing in front of the TV, his breathing deep and content, his legs twitching as he dreamt he was chasing squirrels across the lawn. He was no guard dog, but his sheer size should frighten away any intruder.

Unless that intruder has met him and knows what a softy he is.

I pulled back the curtains and peeked outside. It was early enough that traffic still moved down the street, people heading home from working late or enjoying a night out. A few pedestrians strolled by. An elderly couple, still holding hands after all these years. A woman being dragged along by a still-to-be-trained puppy. Two teenage girls, skates tossed over their shoulders, running and laughing.

Apart from the light over the door, the house across the street was wrapped in darkness. Nothing moved beneath the trees.

I let the curtain drop into place.

Rudolph, New York, the week before Christmas, and all was right with the world.

*   *   *

My dreams had nothing to do with intruders or stalkers, counterfeiters or murderers, or even gossipers. Instead, I cowered on the shop floor as colored glass flew all around me and customers ran screaming into the glass-coated streets while shards of clear glass fell from the skies and Alan's nutcracker solders laughed in glee and hurled tree decorations from their wooden hands.

I woke to a bright winter sun streaming in my windows and a big slobbery dog staring into my eyes.

"Ready for another fun-filled day?" I asked Mattie.

He licked my face, and I threw off the covers.

First things first. I poured myself a mug of coffee from the maker I'd set before going to bed, pulled a coat over my pajamas and slipped my feet into rubber boots, went downstairs, and let Mattie into the enclosed backyard.

I leaned against the doorframe, sipped my coffee, and watched him investigate if any intruders had broken onto our property last night. I couldn't help but notice his attention was attracted to the base of the trees and not the path from the driveway or the ground around the door.

I considered that to be a good thing. Squirrels on the property, not men.

Back upstairs, I fixed myself a bowl of yogurt, granola, and berries and poured another cup of coffee. I checked the online news but could find nothing fresh about the progress of the investigation into the murder of Raquel Torrone.

The weather report predicted light snow, barely-below-freezing temperatures, and sunny skies until Christmas Eve. Always a good thing in Rudolph.

Breakfast finished, second cup of coffee going cold, I prepared for a day at work. I debated with myself how to handle yesterday's incident with Jackie. Should I ignore it, pretend nothing had happened? Should I reprimand her severely?

I decided on the former course of action. She'd had the grace to call me to apologize, so I'd accept that and consider the matter closed.

At the bottom of the driveway, as we were about to turn left toward Jingle Bell Lane and the shop, a car I recognized drove slowly past, heading in the other direction.

Detective Diane Simmonds saw us and lifted her hand in acknowledgment.

At first I thought she was here to have another look at the Johannsen house, but she kept going. I decided I could be late to open the store this morning, and I turned to the right instead, calling to Mattie to pick up the pace.

He must have caught a whiff of the detective's scent as she drove by, and he almost galloped off in pursuit. And believe me, Mattie never gallops.

I was well aware the police have more than one case to deal with at a time, and the Torrone murder had been handed over to the NYPD, but I couldn't help but wonder if Simmonds's call on Mrs. D'Angelo yesterday was more significant than the older woman had told me.

Ours is a traffic-calmed neighborhood, so Simmonds didn't drive much faster than Mattie and I hurried. After about two blocks, I realized this was a waste of time, and I was going to call the chase to a halt when her turn indicator came on and the car slid against the curb.

She was getting out of the car when Mattie and I ran up. Both of us out of breath.

"Training for a marathon?" the detective asked me.

"Do they have those for dogs?"

She didn't answer. She looked at Mattie, his tongue lolling, ears up, eyes bright with adoration. "Sit, Matterhorn."

He instantly dropped to a sit.

"As I just happened to see you passing," I said, "I wanted to ask you a question."

"Go ahead."

"Mrs. D'Angelo came into my shop yesterday. She was highly upset. She said you accused her of killing Raquel because she, Mrs. D'Angelo, was the mastermind of the counterfeiting operation."

The edges of Simmonds's mouth curled up. "A slight exaggeration. I did not accuse her of anything. I asked a few general questions. I didn't even think to ask how she managed to kill Raquel after Raquel left her tied up in the pantry."

"A minor detail. If she was a criminal mastermind."

"I'm sorry if Mrs. D'Angelo was upset by my questions. But she has to realize that if I get a tip, I'm required to follow it up."

"Who gave you this tip?"

Her eyes flicked to the house we were standing in front of and then almost immediately focused once again on me. "I'm not going to tell you that, Merry. Even before I spoke to her, I decided the tip had no merit. But considering how closely involved Mrs. D'Angelo was in the events of that case, I wanted to ask her about it in person rather than phoning or sending a uniform around with routine questions."

Many of the old houses at this end of the street had either been torn down, to be replaced by modern ones, or updated extensively. This house was a large bungalow, of the sort they call midcentury modern. Long and low, with a gently pitched roof, centrally placed chimney, attached garage. The front door, garage door, and window frames were painted a bright, cheerful orange. The large lot was full of burlap-covered bushes and ancient trees, bare winter branches making a sculptural display.

A figure moved behind the front windows.

"Now," Simmonds said, "if you'll excuse me."

"This is the Reynolds house, isn't it?" I took a guess by the way her eyes moved when we talked about the call accusing Mrs. D'Angelo. Simmonds wouldn't reveal the name of the person who called her with the so-called-tip, but Mrs. D'Angelo was pretty sure she knew, and she told me. She'd likely told half the town.

I wondered if that would elevate Donalda's status among the local gossips or cause her to be blackballed.

"This is the residence of William and Donalda Reynolds, yes. Hardly a secret. You are obviously wondering why I'm calling on them. Information has come forward that needs to be followed up on. The matter of who exactly killed Raquel Torrone has been handed to the NYPD, but as the crime happened here, in my town, I have plenty of local details to pursue. In any high-profile case, we get a lot of tips. Many of them are made by well-meaning citizens misinterpreting events; some by people who simply get a chuckle out of muddying the waters. And, occasionally, someone who is hoping to, at the least, play a prank on a friend or enemy by sending us on a wild-goose chase."

"Yet you yourself are here. You didn't phone or send an underling."

"Maybe because I had some free time this morning, and I'm the curious sort. Now, I assume it's time you were heading to work. Matterhorn, you may go."

He jumped to his feet.

Simmonds pointed down the street. He woofed slightly, might even have given her a knowing nod, and started off.

I gripped the leash tightly. "Wait just a minute. Mattie, hold up."

He stopped and looked over his shoulder, clearly conflicted.

Simmonds lifted her right hand, palm up. "What is it now, Merry?"

The front door of the house in question opened. A man came out. I'd seen him around town before but didn't know his name. The very definition of an ectomorph, he was kinda hard to miss. Excessively tall at about six foot seven, barely more than a hundred and twenty pounds, all arms and legs, knees and elbows. Big ears, long thin nose, enormous Adam's apple.

"That's William Reynolds?" I said.

"It is. You sound surprised."

"Maybe I am. I'm going to go out on a limb and guess someone told you he was seen at Raquel's house. Entering or leaving. Talking to her on the front step, maybe. I don't know about other times, but that man is definitely not any of the people I saw in the vicinity of the house before the incident." I felt compelled to add, "I mean, I didn't see him there. For what that's worth."

"Hard to prove a negative, Merry. You yourself have said you didn't pay a lot of attention to activity on the street, it being such a busy time at work."

"True," I said.

"Detective!" William called. "I don't have all day here."

"Be right there, sir," Simmonds replied. "If there's nothing else, Merry?"

"People say, or so I've heard, that Mr. Reynolds travels a lot for business. The town gossips also say he's known to be a womanizer—is that still a word?—and a philanderer. That bit of gossip was related to me by none other than my own mother. Who is not normally part of the town network."

Simmonds looked at me. She said nothing, but she didn't dismiss me either.

"You know, from Bob Gravel and probably others, Raquel was not above online scamming of men out of money."

"Your point is?"

"Until this week, I didn't know William Reynolds from any of the other men who live with their wives and families on this street. But his name has come up." More in conjunction with his wife and her relationship with Mrs. D'Angelo, but I skipped over that and raced to complete my thoughts before she got bored. "Bob Gravel brushed off the incident as a piece of harmless entertainment. That is, he says he brushed it off, but did he really? Maybe he exacted his revenge. Have you considered that?"

"Such has been considered, yes. Mr. Gravel has been spoken to, and his alibi is good. Other likely contacts of Raquel Torrone are being investigated and spoken to."

"Glad to hear it," I said. "Consider the implications if she'd gone after a married man. A man with a family to support. A man with far more to lose if word gets out or Raquel ups her demands."

"Where is this going, Merry?"

"The NYPD are satisfied Raquel's death is related to her criminal associates and activities, but I consider it highly significant that she rented a house on this very street. And not just any house, but one owned by her parents? Out of all the houses for rent in New York State, why come here?"

Simmonds's expression indicated she wasn't discarding my idea outright. "That is a point, Merry. And a good one. It might be that she missed the old neighborhood. That she wanted a walk down memory lane. Bear in mind, she didn't have time to reconnect with her parents or her old school friends. Perhaps she intended to. You've given me something to think about."

"Glad to be of help," I said. "Have a nice day. Merry Christmas, if I don't see you before then."

"Same to you. Matterhorn, you take care of Merry."

He barked.

Chapter
Twenty-Four

Over the next few days, I had little time to worry about Raquel Torrone and what happened to her. Christmas was fast approaching, and everyone was desperate to get their hands on that perfect gift.

From her post in her front window, my landlady reported that the realtor and her photographer had been to the house across the street, but so far, they'd had no showings. According to Mrs. D'Angelo, Beth and Richard Torrone were asking far too much for the house, but I considered it more a case that no one was looking to buy in the middle of December.

Diane Simmonds called to tell me Raquel's body would be released to her family on December 23. She also told me Raquel's parents would be taking her to Rochester, where they now lived, and the funeral would be strictly limited to immediate family only.

"I feel sorry for them," she said to me over the phone. "Stuff's coming out about Raquel they shouldn't have to know."

"What sort of stuff? More than what we've already learned?"

239

"She had a few convictions for shoplifting; she'd been present at parties where items were found to have disappeared once the party was over. Of the later cases, nothing could ever be proven. Most of her indiscretions related to online fraud. Word went out in New York that the police are looking for known associates of hers, and they've been getting calls. Late middle-aged or elderly men, mostly widowers, who were friends with her online and gave her money. The police have spoken to them, but they don't have evidence of any of them following her to Rudolph, never mind killing her. Generally, the men she fleeced were sorry to hear about her death. In more than a few cases, they've offered to pay for the funeral expenses."

"What's that saying? There's a sucker born every minute."

"Something like that. A lot of sad, lonely people in the world, and a lot of schemers ready to take advantage. I feel sorry for the rest of the Torrone family. They seem like genuinely nice people. As for your point about her fleecing a man who might have a lot to lose—nothing we've found points to that."

"William Reynolds is in the clear?"

"I'm not talking about anything specific, Merry. Don't jump to conclusions."

"Any more news of the counterfeiting gang?"

"Some," she said. "Although by *gang*, we're thinking it's likely only Raquel and Jean-Claude Lefevre, involved in a small-potatoes operation. He drove across the border near Montreal, on a Canadian passport, the day after Mrs. D'Angelo was kidnapped. Obviously, at that time we weren't looking for him, so he wasn't stopped. There's no indication he later crossed back into the US, but he can't be found by the Canadian authorities. Not yet, at any rate."

I thanked her for the update.

* * *

"Kyle," Jackie said to me with some degree of relish, "has his nose seriously out of joint. Raquel's parents went home to Rochester, and Kyle paid a call on them there. Her mother accepted the flowers he brought her on the front stoop, but she didn't even let him into the house. She told him the funeral would be private, and she shut the door in his face." Jackie chuckled. It was almost opening time on the day before Christmas Eve, and we were expecting a busy day.

"Understandable," I said. "I feel awfully sorry for them. Raquel's parents. Raquel had a reputation, and it wasn't a good one. They don't need the curious or the gloating coming to their daughter's funeral." Or a bunch of lonely old men who only wanted to have a friend.

Eve had called the family to express her condolences. They thanked her for her thoughts and hung up without mentioning funeral arrangements. "For the better, I guess," Eve said to me. "If I went to the funeral, I wouldn't know what to say. Raquel had a lot of promise when we were young and carefree. What a total waste of all that."

"Mrs. Torrone didn't even remember Kyle from back in school," Jackie continued. "Raquel never brought him around to her house to meet the parents." Another chuckle.

"What are you planning to do about him?" Melissa asked. "Are you going to take him back?"

Jackie lifted her head high and pronounced, "I am undecided."

I wondered if she was genuinely undecided or if she intended to drag the reconciliation out as long as she could. To make Kyle grovel. Groveling could be expensive. I hoped his job at the hot dog cart in front of the butcher was paying enough.

With a jolt I realized I had a reason (another reason) to wonder if Kyle had killed Raquel. Had Kyle found out what Raquel and Jean-Claude Lefevre were up to? Did he want in on their scheme? Kyle wasn't terribly bright, and he was always in need of money. The concept of printing his own cash would appeal to a guy like him. Had Kyle seen Raquel in town and approached her, not in an attempt to win her back to his affections but as a business deal? Did things get out of hand? Did she laugh at him? Tell him to get lost?

And then . . .

I had to admit I was reaching with that line of thought. The counterfeiting equipment was kept in the basement. Unlikely Raquel would have casually invited Kyle down to have a look. Not if she didn't intend to let him in on the operation. I supposed she could have mentioned it in a strange sort of bragging way, but it was a big step from that to murder. Raquel was likely not all that smart either, but she would have had a substantial amount of street smarts. She would have known better than to let Kyle get so emotional about being left out of her criminal operation.

Then again, what do I know about what people are capable of believing or knowing?

If Kyle didn't kill Raquel but he'd been at her house, had someone else overreacted?

"Why are you looking at me like that?" Jackie asked.

I blinked. "I'm not looking at you like anything."

"Sure you are. You have that suspicious questioning look on your face."

"Yup," Melissa said. "You do."

"I do not."

"It's her detective face," Jackie said. "She comes over all serious when she's sorting through a case."

"Does she do that often?" Melissa asked.

"Pretty often, yeah. You wouldn't believe the number of times she's run out the door in pursuit of a clue, leaving me in charge. That's why I got promoted to assistant manager with a commensurate increase in salary. Take my advice, Mel; if she tries it on you when I'm not here, hold out for a promotion. You can be chief assistant to the assistant manager."

"You two do know I'm standing right here," I said. "Like two feet away, and I can hear every word."

"No secrets between us, are there, Merry?" Jackie gave me a grin and a wink.

I laughed. No, Jackie, of all people, had not killed Raquel Torrone in a jealous rage. I wasn't dismissing the act as impossible, but Jackie was no actress. She wore her emotions on her sleeve for all to see. I could see not a trace of guile on her small-town pretty face.

"It's almost nine thirty," I said. "No time to stand around gossiping. Plaster those smiles on, throw open the doors, and let's do this!"

"She likes giving that sort of inspirational talk," Jackie said to Melissa.

"Be right back." I slipped into my office and made a quick phone call.

"Merry!" Mrs. D'Angelo said. "Are you calling on a matter of some urgency or importance? I'm on the line to

Eileen. You know Eileen, of course, lives not far from your parents."

Never heard of her. "Not critically important, but I have a quick question. Do you know Kyle Lambert?"

"I know him, but not well. Can't say I'm surprised at the way he turned out. I mean, look at that father of his. Never did have a lick of sense. Why, I remember the time—"

"A story for another day. Have you ever seen Kyle on our street? Recently, I mean."

"Oh yes. Several times."

My heart leapt. Was I onto something?

"I couldn't believe it when I heard Russ Durham hired Kyle Lambert as the paper's photographer. Still, I suppose the silly boy comes cheap and the paper is desperate. I was in the hospital in the critically important days after the discovery of poor Raquel, but the police tape was up at the house for some time, and Kyle was likely hoping something dramatic would happen for him to photograph."

"Not then. I meant before . . . what happened happened."

"Oh. No. Not that I recall."

"When you were in the pantry, you heard Raquel arguing with a man. Is it possible that man was . . . a voice you recognized?"

I wasn't trying to lead the witness, as they say in the legal dramas, but Mrs. D'Angelo was no fool. "You mean Kyle Lambert?" She laughed. "Heavens no. Kyle's voice is high-pitched. Squeaky almost. That man had a deep voice. In other circumstances I might have found it quite attractive. Mr. D'Angelo had a deep, rolling voice. Charmed the socks right off me, I can tell you. He had a faint accent—the man in the kitchen I mean, not Mr. D'Angelo; French Canadian would be my guess."

"Did you tell the police that? About the accent?"

"Of course I did. But, as I said, the accent was not strong, and accents can be faked, can't they? Why are you asking this? Surely you don't think Kyle, of all people, had anything to do with it?"

"Just a thought. Gotta run. Bye." I hung up. It was a long shot, and I was, truth be told, happy to strike Kyle from my virtual suspect list. I'd never liked Kyle, but that didn't mean I wanted him to be arrested for murder.

* * *

The week had been a good one saleswise, and at closing time on Christmas Eve Eve, I was feeling very pleased. Along with the many other items Mrs. Claus's stocked, Alan's toys and wooden statues had done extremely well. I was looking forward to telling him tomorrow night when he picked me up to go to dinner at my parents'. Alan lived simply and happily in his century-old stone farmhouse deep in the woods. He was a hard person to get gifts for, so I'd bought a certificate for dinner at the Yuletide Inn. Not entirely an unselfish gift, as I hoped he'd take me with him. Once the holiday rush and the post-holiday sales period died down, it would be nice to have a long, lovely, leisurely night out, just the two of us.

I was looking forward to that when Graham Johannesen came in. Melissa had left for the day, and Jackie was standing at the window, watching the parade of last minute shoppers hurrying past. "Hi." Graham looked around with approval.

"I'm glad I caught you before you closed for the day. Nice place." He didn't have a Quebecois accent, but as Mrs. D'Angelo had noted, accents could be faked. Plus, at the time the unknown man and Raquel were arguing, Mrs. D'Angelo wasn't in much of a condition to be thinking coherently. Graham's voice, I thought, wasn't particularly deep, and it wasn't rolling. Did that mean anything? What did deep and rolling mean anyway?

"How can we help you?" I asked.

Jackie turned from the window to check out the new customer. Her eyes lit up with interest.

"I'm looking for something for my mom," Graham said. "A present, I mean."

"Happy to help," I said. "Do you have any idea of what she'd like? Jewelry, table linens, dishware, wine or cocktail glasses, maybe? Not everything we stock has a Christmas theme."

"Jewelry might be nice. Care to show me what you have?"

I led him to the display. He eyed everything but didn't seem particularly interested. That's not uncommon, I've found, in a young man trying to get his mother a present. They're simply out of their depth.

"That necklace?" He pointed to one of the pieces made by a former store employee, Crystal Wong, intricate twisting strands of silver.

I lifted the necklace off the display and held it up. "A good choice. Made by a local woman. So local she worked in this very shop when she was in school."

"Great, I'll take it." He reached out and took the necklace out of my hand. He looked directly into my eyes, and his fingers brushed against mine. The touch lingered slightly longer than necessary, and then he smiled and pulled away.

I felt Jackie's eyes on me as I scurried behind the sales counter. I rang up the sale, found a small box for the item, folded it in tissue paper, and popped it into a paper bag with the Mrs. Claus's name stamped on it.

Graham watched me. Instead of handing him the bag, I put it on the counter between us. "Merry Christmas," I said.

"Same to you. I'm going to my parents' tomorrow night for dinner. We always exchange our gifts on Christmas Eve. What time do you finish here tomorrow?"

"Officially we close at three when the staff leave, but I . . . I mean my . . . my father and I hang around until four for last-minute shoppers." Dad had no intention of coming in to help me close, but the moment the words were out of my mouth, I realized that if I was worried Graham had an unwelcome interest in me, I'd better not mention I'd be here alone.

"And then?"

"Same as you. My *boyfriend*"—emphasis on the word— "and I are going to my parents' house."

"Merry's parents always make a big deal out of Christmas Eve," Jackie said. "I've always wondered how Noel fits it in, what with delivering presents to little children all over the world and then having to settle the reindeer in the barn for the night. But that's all part of the Christmas magic."

"What's she talking about?" Graham asked me.

"Just a normal Christmas Eve for me," I said. "Early dinner, presents, sing a few carols."

"I'm sure you'll be busy over the next few days, but how about I give you a call next week? Maybe we can have dinner sometime. Or just a coffee, if you'd prefer."

"Busy. Yes, busy. It never ends. The minute Christmas is over, the sales begin." I smiled.

"It's a date, then. I don't have your number, but never mind. I know where you live." He picked up his bag and left the shop.

My smile crumbled faster than the stiffness in my shoulders.

"Oh my gosh," Jackie cried the moment the door shut behind him. "It's so hot in here I'm surprised you didn't burst into flames." She waved her hand in front of her face. "The heat. The heat."

"I have no idea what you're going on about." I had to admit, I was feeling rather warm. Okay, hot.

"He was so into you, Merry. I hate to imagine what would have happened if I wasn't here. Okay, I love to imagine it. Are you going to go out with him? I notice you didn't say no, and I can guarantee he noticed too."

"Time to lock up. Tomorrow's going to be busy. And no, I am not going to go out with him. I'm in a relationship, Jackie."

"Yeah, I know, but it never hurts to keep them on edge, does it? Alan's getting too comfortable, if you know what I mean. You can't let him start taking you for granted. A casual mention of having coffee with a new guy in town should straighten him up quick enough."

"I have no intention of trying to make Alan jealous. And that's not a new guy in town. He's from Muddle Harbor."

"Muddle Harbor." The gleam disappeared from Jackie's eyes. "Oh dear. Really?"

"Really. I met him when my dad dragged me along to a meeting about the mayoral election in that town."

"That must have been deadly boring."

"It was. He's a cousin of Raquel Torrone."

"Is that so? No surprise, I guess. Everyone in these parts is related somehow to everyone else. See you tomorrow, Merry."

"Bright and early," I said.

Chapter Twenty-Five

On Christmas Eve, Jackie and Melissa left work at three, pulling gloves on hands and wrapping scarves around necks, calling "Merry Christmas" over their shoulders. I stayed for another hour in case of last-minute shoppers. We always had last-minute shoppers, those who suddenly realized they'd forgotten to buy a gift for wives or mothers. Always middle-aged or older men. They ran into the shop moments before I finally locked up, eyes full of panic, credit cards extended.

Easy pickings. I could sell them the store fittings if I was so inclined. Instead I did a nice trade in jewelry and table linens.

Finally, a few minutes after four, I flipped the sign to CLOSED and locked the door. Up and down Jingle Bell Lane, other shop owners were doing the same, while in the windows of the restaurants, staff were laying tables and serving early arrivals. Only four o'clock, but the long winter night was setting in. A light snow was falling and people hurried past, laden with brightly wrapped packages or shopping bags bulging with things still to be wrapped.

I glanced around the quiet, empty store. The decorations on the tree sparkled, the colored lights gleamed. The rows of stuffed reindeer and elves, the porcelain Santas and Mrs. Clauses, the carved and painted nutcracker soldiers and angels watched me. I wondered if they were waiting for me to leave before leaping down from the shelves and getting the party started.

It was a pleasant thought. And that gave me an idea for next year's parade float. My version of Fezziwig's Christmas Eve staff party.

I switched out the main lights, leaving on the ones in the front window and those decorating the tree. Then I went into the back and got Mattie and we headed home. Alan was due to pick me up at five to go to my parents' house. As we walked, I found my thoughts wandering. For no reason I was aware of, they settled on Graham Johannesen. He'd made me uncomfortable yesterday, and I didn't like that in my own store. I didn't like that anyplace. But I had to admit, he hadn't done anything other than indicate a mild, polite interest in possibly spending some time with me.

So, I asked myself, why did that make me uncomfortable? Our house came into view, as did the Johannesen house across the street. The light over the front door was on, as well as one in the living room and another on the second floor. The driveway and path had not been shoveled, leaving several inches of fresh, undisturbed snow. The FOR SALE sign on the lawn swayed in the light wind.

At our house, as could be expected, the pavement was clear and deicer had been liberally scattered. To my surprise, lights were on in the living room and the kitchen. Mrs. D'Angelo was notoriously parsimonious. When she left a room, she turned off the light. When she left the house, she made sure everything was off.

I hesitated at the top of the driveway. She was supposed to have gone to spend Christmas with her sister. I didn't have a lot of time to get ready, and I feared if I knocked on the door to check on her and she answered, I'd find myself dragged into an extended, one-way conversation.

My conscience told me not to be so selfish. She might be sick or in need of help.

"Quick detour, Mattie," I said as I made up my mind. We climbed the front steps. Rather than anyone needing help, the door flew open before I'd lifted my hand to ring the bell.

"Merry! How nice of you to call. Merry Christmas." Mrs. D'Angelo was dressed for an evening at home in jeans and a badly pilled brown sweater with yellow stripes. She looked down. "And a very merry Christmas to you too, Mattie."

He woofed.

"I thought you were going to your sister's tonight. Is everything okay?"

"Oh yes. How kind of you to check. I'm going tomorrow instead. A close friend of Iris was in a car accident earlier today. She's not harmed but badly shook up, as you can imagine, so Iris offered to spend the night at the friend's house so she wouldn't be alone."

I almost wished her a good evening and turned away, but instead I said, "Now you're alone on Christmas Eve. Would you like to come to my parents' for dinner? You know you'd be welcome."

"Thank you, dear, but I'm fine. I'll enjoy my Christmas tomorrow, and I want to get on the road first thing."

"Are you driving?"

"I've rented a car for the journey. I parked it at the Smiths' house to leave room in the driveway for you and Steve and Wendy to get in and out as you need."

"That was thoughtful of you. Merry Christmas, then," I said.

"Same to you, and please give your parents my best wishes."

* * *

I showered, applied makeup, and dressed in record time. That done, I gathered up my gifts and put them into a tote bag to take with me. Mattie would not be going to the party, but he and Ranger would enjoy a special Christmas treat at breakfast tomorrow. I fed Mattie and waited for Alan to arrive. He'd drop off Ranger and then drive us to my parents' house for the festivities.

It was unlike Alan to be late, and I was looking out the front window for signs of his truck approaching when he phoned. "Sorry, Merry, but I don't think I'm going to make it tonight."

"What's happened? Are you okay?"

"I'm fine. Well, sort of fine. Ranger is not. He's been sprayed by a skunk."

"What!"

"Yup. Full on, right in the face. As for me, I went outside to see what he was barking at, and I caught some of the, shall we say, fallout."

It was awful, but I couldn't help but laugh. "When did this happen?" The sounds of doggy moaning and groaning came down the phone line.

"Like two minutes ago. I let him out for a romp before we left, and . . . boom."

"I didn't know skunks were active in the winter."

"They don't hibernate, but they usually stay pretty close to their dens. Something must have brought this one out and he encountered Ranger. I should be able to clean myself up and be nice and fresh tomorrow morning, but Ranger will likely be confined to home for a few days. Sorry, but I don't think your parents would appreciate having me in their house tonight."

I was disappointed, but it was only one night, and no matter how stinky Alan might be, we could still spend Christmas Day together as planned. "How about I come around to your place tomorrow morning? I have all the brunch things I bought; easy enough to throw them in the car."

"That'd be nice. You don't want Ranger in your apartment."

"I wonder what Mattie will think of it."

"Nothing good, Merry, nothing good. Can you drive yourself tonight?"

"I think I'll walk. It's a nice night, and that way I can enjoy a couple of glasses of wine. Mom's sure to have bought some champagne to toast the season."

After exchanging seasonal greetings, words of affection, and a few skunk jokes with Alan, I hung up.

"No company for you tonight," I said to Mattie as I pulled on my coat and boots. "I won't be too late. If you hear Santa coming down the chimney, don't do anything to scare him away."

The walk, I decided, would do me good. It was a nice night. Cold and crisp with a sky full of stars.

Poor Alan would not be enjoying it.

I ran lightly down the stairs, swinging my tote bag. I'd bought a bottle of top-shelf whiskey for Dad, leather gloves for Mom, hand-painted silk scarves for Vicky and Eve, and a few small tokens for whoever had been invited to join us tonight and might have bought something for me.

I walked down the driveway. One car drove slowly past, but otherwise no one was in sight. The front door opened before I reached the sidewalk, and Mrs. D'Angelo's head popped out.

"Merry!" she called in some combination of a whisper and a shout. Thinking she'd changed her mind about coming with me, I started toward her before I realized she still wore the same clothes as earlier. Christmas Eve at my parents' house is a formal affair. Formal as far as Rudolph goes, at any rate. Mom would be in an evening gown and diamonds, Dad in a tux with a bow tie featuring a Christmas image of some sort. (The tie changed every year.) Not all the guests would be quite so done up, but everyone would wear their festive best. I was in the dress I'd last worn to Vicky's wedding. Vicky told me she was going to wear her wedding party dress—the cute little pink tulle thing she'd worn for dinner and dancing after the church ceremony.

Mrs. D'Angelo beckoned frantically to me as her eyes darted around, searching for I didn't know what.

"Is something the matter?"

"Come inside, quickly."

I moved, quickly, and she shut the door behind me. "Someone's in the Johannesen house."

"Why?"

"I don't know why. And that is the point, Merry. It can't be a prospective buyer. Even Marlene wouldn't work this late on Christmas Eve, and besides, her car isn't parked out front."

"I mean, why do you think someone's in the house?"

"I saw a light."

I peeled back the thin curtain next to the door and peered out. I saw no more lights on than I'd noticed earlier. "Maybe the lamps are on a timer."

"This light was not very bright, and it was moving."

"Moving? Like a flashlight?"

She nodded.

I looked again. I could see nothing. A car came slowly down the street, heading into town. Its headlights washed across the sign on the lawn of the house across the street and the unshoveled driveway and continued on their way.

I sucked in a breath. A single line of footsteps marched up the driveway and turned onto the small path leading to the rear of the house. They did not come back.

"You might be right," I said. "Those footprints in the snow were not there earlier. I'm positive."

"Should we call the police?"

I hesitated. It might be anyone. A kid taking a shortcut. A prospective buyer who wanted to check out the neighborhood and property before contacting the realtor. Beth or Richard Torrone checking on their own property, although it was unlikely they'd come on foot.

The light Mrs. D'Angelo thought she saw might have been a reflection from the flashlight of a dog walker or a neighbor hurrying to a party.

"Why don't I have a quick look around first?" I said. "You stay here, and if I'm not back in ten minutes, call the police. If you hear me screaming before that, call the police."

Mrs. D'Angelo reached for her coat. "You are not too stupid to live, Merry Wilkinson. Isn't that what they say about young women in the movies who go into haunted houses alone?"

"That house isn't haunted."

"It might be now. And not by a ghost. I'm coming with you."

"Then we'd both be too stupid to live. Okay. I'm going to send Vicky a text and tell her if I don't send another text in twenty minutes to call the cops."

I pulled out my phone, typed the message, and sent it as we slipped out of the house.

The street was empty of traffic, and we crossed quickly. The town sidewalk had been plowed earlier, and the snow that had fallen since was crisscrossed with footprints and paw prints. One set of prints—human, not animal—stepped off the sidewalk, and I studied them. They were about average size for a man, big for a woman, but not impossibly big. Thick treads in a zigzag pattern with solid heels, indicating winter boots.

"Maybe the killer came back to get the counterfeiting equipment," Mrs. D'Angelo whispered. "It must be worth a lot."

"The police would have taken it away. It isn't something to be left lying around for the new buyers to use if they so choose."

"Or they're after something they hid, maybe."

And then I knew. Memories tumbled all over themselves in my mind. Events fell into order.

I'd first seen Graham Johannesen on our street *before* I met him at the Muddle Harbor Café. He hadn't been watching my house because he was so enamored of my feminine charms. He hadn't been watching my house at all. He'd been watching what had been his aunt Dorothy's house, and meeting me later was a convenient pretext in case he was asked what he was doing here. He told me he'd been close to his aunt and was visiting the house to capture his memories. I might have bought that excuse once, but it had been a long time ago he'd cut the lawn and done odd chores for Dorothy Johannesen.

Town rumor said Dorothy had had a substantial income, but she didn't appear to spend it on anything. That she didn't often leave the house and never traveled far from Rudolph. That she spent little more than the minimum required to maintain her house and property. That she didn't trust banks and paid her property taxes in cash.

What, then, I asked myself now, did she do with that substantial income?

Hide it?

Graham had expected to inherit the house on his aunt's death. Instead, it had gone to Beth Torrone, Dorothy's niece. Beth was, in the order of things, a closer relative to Dorothy than Graham. I remembered the trace of bitterness in his voice when he said Beth Torrone never had the time of day for her aunt Dorothy. Yet she, Beth, Raquel's mother, inherited the property rather than Graham, who'd faithfully cut the lawn and helped with chores. Had he done the work in expectation of inheriting? Possibly. But, in the end, he hadn't inherited, and more than ten years had passed since Dorothy died and the ownership of the house passed to Beth Torrone. Beth and her family never lived there; instead, they rented it out, and it was now for sale to anyone with the funds to buy it. It was a big house, with a substantial lot, in a good neighborhood in a prosperous town. Was it more than Graham Johannesen could afford? Again, possibly, as he was still in his thirties, trying to make a go of a small business in Muddle Harbor.

If Graham had been in and out of the house over the years, likely doing minor jobs such as hanging pictures or changing lightbulbs, did he know what Dorothy Johannesen was doing with all the money she wasn't putting in the bank? Again, possibly.

My phone buzzed with an incoming text.

Vicky: *What on earth does that mean!*
Me: *Graham Johannesen killed Raquel.*
Vicky: *So?*

I suddenly realized that while I'd been remembering, putting it all together, and texting Vicky, Mrs. D'Angelo had gone ahead without me.

Head down, watching where she was placing her feet, she was following the path of the footsteps in the snow.

I shoved my phone into my coat pocket and ran after her. I reached her as she opened the gate to the backyard. "I've decided we need to call the police after all."

"Just a quick little peek first." She went through the gate and tiptoed around the house. What could I do but follow?

The single line of footsteps went directly to the back deck and climbed the stairs. The glass in the sliding doors leading to the kitchen had been replaced since I'd broken it, but whoever had done that might as well not have bothered. Tonight broken glass was sprinkled across the clean snow, glittering like diamonds tossed onto white silk sheets. More glass sparkled on the kitchen floor. The footprints we were following went into the house, and the sliding door had been closed after them.

The blinds were pulled down, but the edge of one was caught on a fragment of broken glass, leaving a large gap in the window coverings. From deeper inside the house, a dim light flickered. We heard a muffled crash, as though wood was being torn up or a sledgehammer applied to the drywall.

"What's happening?" Mrs. D'Angelo whispered to me.

"He's tearing the house apart. Looking for Dorothy Johannesen's hidden cash."

"That makes a strange sort of sense. Everyone said she was well off, but she never spent a cent she didn't have to. I agree, we've seen enough. Let's go." Mrs. D'Angelo turned and half ran across the deck. I snapped a quick picture of the broken panes of glass, but before I could turn and also flee, the hammering stopped, replaced by a cry of triumph.

At that moment, I heard a loud noise from behind me and a startled shout. I whirled around to see that Mrs. D'Angelo had slipped on the snow-covered top step and tumbled the rest of the way to the ground. She lay on her stomach, arms and legs flailing, moaning loudly.

"Are you okay?" I ran across the deck, taking care to watch my own footing on the steps. I was still carrying my bag of gifts, and I dropped it, ready to help her get up.

"I . . . I think so. Nothing seems to be broken. Let me catch my breath." She rolled over. She blinked up at me, and I was relieved that she didn't appear to be in any pain and her limbs were all at the correct angle. I bent over her and was holding out my hand, ready to help her up, when she caught her breath and braced herself. Her eyes widened in fear as she saw something behind me, but before I could react, I felt a strong hand grab the collar of my coat and I was jerked backward.

"What do you think you're doing?" a man yelled as he shook my coat.

"Let go of her," Mrs. D'Angelo shouted.

"You keep quiet, you nosy old woman. And don't move."

I struggled to turn around. "Graham, let's talk this out."

"Talk. I have nothing to talk to you about." He released me, but before I could run, he grabbed my right arm and pulled me around to face him. I stared into his face. His eyes gleamed with rage and perhaps a touch of madness. Spittle flew from his mouth. A layer of dust was sprinkled across his cheeks and in his hair; wood chips were trapped in his goatee.

He lifted his left hand and showed me what was gripped in his fist. A hammer. A big, heavy one. "You, into the house, or the old lady gets it."

"What are you going to do, Graham?" I struggled to keep my voice calm and level, my expression neutral. "You can't kill us both. I called the police. I told them someone was in the house."

"No, you didn't. If you had, you would have waited for them before being stupid enough to poke around where you don't belong. Get up," he ordered Mrs. D'Angelo.

Keeping her eyes fixed on him, she slowly and painfully rolled onto her stomach, pushed herself to her knees, and then stood. "You're a nasty man."

"You don't know the half of it."

"I suspect we do," I said. "You killed Raquel, didn't you? Why? To get her out of the way, at a guess, so you can have access to the house alone?"

"Keep guessing." He let go of me and gave me a shove toward the deck. I stumbled forward but managed to remain on my feet. He grabbed Mrs. D'Angelo's arm and held up the hammer. "If I killed Raquel, I have no reason not to kill you two, do I?"

"No reason, except you can claim you killed her in a rage during an argument. But the two of us? No way anyone would buy that."

"I'll kill you if I have to, Merry, but I don't need to. I've found what I'm after, and all I need now is time to grab it and get away."

I climbed the steps. Mrs. D'Angelo followed while Graham walked behind her, ready to bring the hammer down on her shoulder. Or even her head.

The sliding door stood open, and I stepped into the kitchen. The air was thick with dust.

"You spent a few days in there, I hear." Graham spoke to Mrs. D'Angelo and nodded toward the pantry.

The last bit of color in her face drained away. "I . . . I can't . . ."

"Good place to hide someone. Raquel was clever like that. Clever like a fox. Too clever, in the end."

I didn't know whether or not to believe Graham when he said he wouldn't kill us. He likely didn't know himself.

The easiest thing would be to go into the pantry and wait for help to arrive. The twenty-minutes notice I'd given Vicky should be up by now.

But in case he did decide to get it over with and kill us, I had to keep him talking until help could arrive. "Your aunt didn't like banks, did she? She thought everyone was out to cheat her. But she had a substantial income, and she had to put her money somewhere. I'm guessing in the walls?"

"Under the floorboards, actually. She confided in me once that she kept her money in a safe place. Not only would the banks cheat her, she didn't trust computers or the internet. She only trusted what she could hold in her hands. Like cold hard cash. She said when the world financial system collapsed, she'd be okay because she had cash on hand." He shrugged. "Why she thought that would be worth anything without the government and central banks holding up the value of otherwise useless scraps of paper, I didn't bother to argue with her. One day, she said to me, it would all be mine." His face twisted and his eyes hardened. "It was all a lie. Instead, she gave the house to Raquel's family without telling them about the money. She was addled by the end. Might have even forgotten about it. But I never forgot what should have been mine. Enough talking. Time for me to be on my way. Put your phone on the table and then get in there."

"I really, truly cannot," Mrs. D'Angelo said. She was not pretending. Her voice shook, her hands trembled, and she had to lean against the kitchen island to keep her knees from giving way.

Graham's eyes flicked from me to her.

"She was locked up in there for two days," I said. "No food, no water. No one checking on her. It was a terrifying experience."

"I do not care. Phone. Now."

I took it out of my pocket. The screen told me I had a notification from Vicky.

"Put it on the table and don't try to use it, or I will use this." Graham brandished the hammer.

I took one step forward, laid down my phone, and stepped back. The screen went dark.

"Now you," he ordered.

The panic on Mrs. D'Angelo's face only increased, if that was possible. Which was worse for her? I wondered. Being locked in the pantry—again—or losing touch with her lifeline? But she didn't argue, and she took the phone out of her coat pocket and placed it next to mine.

"See how easy that was," Graham said. "You keep doing what I tell you, and we'll be fine here."

"You didn't know someone was locked in the pantry, did you?" I said. "When you killed Raquel?"

"Raquel. All these years and the stupid girl hadn't changed a bit. As self-centered and selfish as ever. I asked her, politely, to let me use the house for a day or two. It was my aunt's house too. She said no. She said she had business to conduct here. I could only imagine what sort of business she was up to." He was getting jumpy now, shifting the hammer from one hand to another, his left eye twitching.

"You were wrong about that," I said. "Instead, she and her friend were literally printing money."

He laughed, the sound sharp and bitter. "Yeah. Coulda knocked me down with a feather when I heard that on the radio. I shoved her down the stairs and didn't even go down there to check. I should have. Instead, I left all that fake money for the cops."

"Why did—?"

"Enough talk." He lifted the hammer high above Mrs. D'Angelo's shoulder, but he kept his eyes on me. "Move, both of you, now. Walk on your own two feet, or you'll make me have to drag you in. And that's easier to do if you're dead."

Not the Christmas Eve I had planned, but I decided to do as he said. I had little choice. "It's okay, Mabel," I said. "I'll be with you."

"Merry . . . no." Her voice was very soft, the tremor obvious.

I stood near the pantry, facing toward the sliding doors and the deck beyond. Graham and Mrs. D'Angelo faced me. Behind them, outside, something moved quickly and silently across the deck. I tried to keep my face impassive. The lamp over the sink was on, the crack in the blinds letting out light. To anyone standing outside in the dark, we'd be as lit up as my mother had been when she performed as the Ghost of Christmas Past in the musical version of *A Christmas Carol* last year. I desperately tried to think of something to keep Graham talking. "Jean-Claude's disappeared, did you know that? I expect he'll be back, and he'll come looking for you. Not only did you kill his lover and business partner, you caused his operation to be shut down."

"I don't even know who that is, but let him come. I'll be long gone. I'm finally going to be getting as far away from Muddle Harbor and Rudolph as it's possible to get. At last. I've wasted a lot of years waiting for my chance."

Graham had not locked the sliding door behind us. I saw it move, ever so slightly.

Keep talking, keep talking. Keep him looking at you, not at the door.

"You really are a fool, if you think that," I said. "You won't get as far as the town line before the cops are on you. And with what? A bag full of old bills? You can't buy an airline ticket with cash, did you know that?" I didn't know if that was true or not, but I took a guess Graham didn't either. He was no criminal mastermind, just a man who'd been disappointed in his teenage expectations and had nursed a grievance ever since. The door edged open a few more inches.

His lips tightened. As did his grip on the hammer. "You don't know what I can do. Guess it's time I showed you."

"Hey, Graham! Catch." Vicky Casey flew into the kitchen, her arms laden with weapons. She yelled and began throwing . . . snowballs?

Graham whirled around. Instinctively, like any kid on a winter playground, he lifted his arms and crossed his hands over his face. He yelped and ducked as hard white lumps peppered him like birdshot. Mrs. D'Angelo screamed and collapsed. I ran forward, tripped over my landlady's legs, and crashed into Graham. He lost his grip on the hammer, and it flew across the room. I gave him a good, hard shove and he went down. I leapt on top of him and lay there winded, gasping for breath, as he yelled and swore and tried to get in position to give me a solid punch.

"Get up. Get up, Merry," Vicky called. "I've got this."

Graham shoved at me. I rolled away and staggered to my feet.

Vicky had scooped up the hammer, and she brandished it high. "Stay where you are!" she ordered.

Graham whimpered and slithered backward on his rear end until he bumped into the cabinets.

I grabbed my phone and pressed the emergency button.

"Done that already," Vicky said calmly. "The dispatcher said help is on the way, but it didn't look as though I should wait for them." Careful to keep her distance, she leaned over and spoke clearly and distinctly to Graham. "They'll be here soon enough, and we don't mind waiting, now do we?"

Chapter
Twenty-Six

S irens came screaming down our street. I told the dispatcher to tell the police to come to the back of the house.

Candy Campbell was through the door first, gun drawn, shouting, "Everyone down!" As Graham was already "down" and I didn't consider myself to be a suspect, I stayed where I was, as did Vicky.

"Welcome," Vicky said. "Obviously not your normal Rudolph Christmas Eve party."

Candy looked around the kitchen. At the remains of shattered, melting snowballs and broken glass littering the floor. At Vicky, fierce and wild-eyed, expression determined, brandishing a hammer as though she were Xena Warrior Princess with her sword, although incongruously wearing her party finery of a dress with a pink tulle skirt. At Mrs. D'Angelo sitting on the floor. At me, also in my party finery, telling my landlady to take big deep breaths, in and out, in and out. At Graham Johannesen, cowering against the wall, whimpering something about him only wanting what was rightfully his.

Then other officers were in the kitchen and a medic was helping Mrs. D'Angelo stay calm. Graham was hauled to his feet, cuffed, cautioned, bundled out, and taken away. He kept his head down, avoiding my eyes, and he didn't say another word.

"I hope you don't have to call Detective Simmonds," I said to Candy when all was under control again. Reasonably under control, at any rate. "It is Christmas Eve, and she has a young child."

"I'll let her know what's happened here, but she probably won't need to talk to the suspect tonight. He doesn't look in all that great shape anyway, so we'll have to call a doctor to come and have a look at him. What happened here?" She studied the rapidly melting snow on the floor. "Looks like you had a snowball fight."

"Very observant of you, Officer," Vicky said. "We did, as it happens. Fortunately, thanks to growing up in a winter climate with countless numbers of cousins, I am adept at the art."

"Huh?"

Vicky linked her fingers together and stretched her arms out in front of her. "The old skills never leave you."

Candy shook her head. I gave her the bare bones of the story while more officers streamed into the house, preparing to do all they had to do to gather evidence and secure the scene. No matter it was Christmas Eve.

"That should be okay for tonight," Candy said when I finished. "The detective will need a full statement from you both, so she'll likely give you a call tomorrow."

"I'd like to have a quick look at one thing first," I said. "Okay if I go into the rest of the house?"

"I don't—"

"Great. Won't be long." I left the kitchen at a rapid pace, and Vicky followed. Two police officers stood in the living room, not quite sure what they were looking at. A pack of exceptionally large moles might have been let loose in here. Another hammer, a crowbar, and an axe leaned against the wall beneath the window. In an old house like this, the original flooring was a gorgeous red maple, wide planked, naturally streaked and scarred. As was the custom in the twentieth century, that lovely old wood had been covered with carpeting. Tonight, the carpeting had been roughly torn and yanked up and the floorboards beneath either pried up or smashed through.

The police stood in a circle, gazing down into one of the holes. A large sports bag, zipper open, was at their feet.

I crossed the floor rapidly but carefully, dodging gaps, and joined them. I felt Vicky behind me.

I looked down. The hole was full of clear plastic bags, the type used to wrap meat for the freezer. Each bag was stuffed with paper. Green and brown paper, each piece cut to the same size.

"Oh my gosh!" Vicky said.

"That's a good way of putting it," one of the cops said. "I wonder how much is in there."

"Do you think it's real?" another asked. "Wasn't this place used for a counterfeiting operation recently?"

"It's real," I said.

"Santa's storeroom," Vicky said. "Hold on. I'll be back in a moment."

She ran past Candy Campbell and Mrs. D'Angelo as they came into the living room. Curious, the medics followed them.

Everyone stared into the hole.

If the Grinch had taken advantage of this moment to drop down chimneys and raid Christmas trees up and down Broad Street, no one would have stopped him.

"That looks like money," someone said. "Cold hard cash."

"That it does," another replied.

"Must be thousands. Tens of thousands."

"How long do you suppose it's been down there?" Candy asked at last.

"Forty years or more," Mrs. D'Angelo said. "It would have stopped being added to ten years ago. The previous homeowner didn't use banks."

"They would have wished they'd used one if this place ever caught fire," a cop said.

"Or if someone ripped up the floorboards," I said.

Vicky came back, swinging my tote bag. "Speaking of Santa, look what he dropped on his way down the chimney of this house. I took the liberty of having a peek, and I believe this one can be opened early." I'd wrapped my dad's gift with little imagination, dropped it into a store-bought gift bag, and tied it with a ribbon. Easy to tell it was a bottle by the size and weight.

Vicky pulled it out and held it up triumphantly. "The good stuff. Excellent choice, Merry." She twisted off the cap and handed the bottle to Mrs. D'Angelo.

"Only to steady my nerves, you understand." My landlady accepted it and took a healthy swig. She swallowed, said, "Very nice," and drank some more. She passed the bottle to me. I'm not a whiskey drinker, but I figured just this once I could give it a try.

271

I have to say, I didn't like it much. Maybe it's better not consumed directly from the bottle.

I handed it to Vicky, and she took it.

The medics and cops watched her enviously.

"I hope you're not driving tonight, Ms. Casey," Candy said. "Or I will have to call my colleagues and request a RIDE check."

"Spoilsport." Vicky took a second swig and put the top back on the bottle. "Better leave some for the gift recipient anyway."

"Get out of here," Candy said, "before I arrest you for interfering in a crime scene."

We turned to go, and Candy said, "Oh, Merry?"

"Yes?"

"Merry Christmas."

I grinned at my old nemesis. "Merry Christmas to you."

Chapter
Twenty-Seven

M rs. D'Angelo insisted she didn't need to go to the hospital, so the medics left without her, and Vicky and I walked her home. I repeated my suggestion she join us this evening, but she said she would be fine. All she wanted was to put her feet up, make a cup of tea, and watch *The Muppet Christmas Carol*. And, if I wouldn't mind, maybe I could leave her a few inches of that lovely whiskey. To help settle her nerves.

I did so, and Vicky and I left for the party.

In the Johannsen house, as it would likely be known for the remainder of time, all the lights were on. Police vehicles were parked every which way out front. It had started to snow again; lovely soft fat flakes caught in the blue and red lights of the cruisers. In houses up and down the street, curtains in front windows were pulled back to show off brilliantly lit Christmas trees. For once not many people came out to see what was going on. In Rudolph, it was Christmas, and nothing could be more important than that.

"What are you going to tell your dad?" Vicky asked me as we walked through the empty streets. Under Candy's watchful eye, Vicky had wisely decided to leave her car where it was for the night.

"I'm hoping nothing. No one will be listening to the radio or checking social media. Hopefully they haven't invited anyone tonight who'll get a breathless call from Mrs. D'Angelo, so with luck, they won't find out about it until tomorrow."

"I meant about his present. He'll think you've drunk half of it yourself."

"Oh. That. Did you get him something?"

"Of course. A book about the world's greatest fishing spots. Lots of pictures."

"Say it's from us both."

"You mean from Mark and me and you?"

"Might look like I forgot, right?"

"Yup."

"I'll give him half a bottle and tell him a very good story comes with it, but he'll have to wait until tomorrow to hear it."

Vicky laughed as we passed the brilliantly lit bandstand. "Nothing like going to bed on Christmas Eve with dreams about what your present is going to be. Is Alan meeting us there?"

"That's another story." I filled her in on the skunk incident, and she laughed again as we turned onto the street I'd grown up on.

No one ever knows how many people are going to show up at my parents' house on Christmas Eve. Tonight, the street was lined with cars, and more filled the driveway. Laughter, music, and light spilled out of the house. The drapes were pulled back to display the huge, elaborately decorated Fraser fir standing in pride of place in the bow window, decorations sparkling, tiny white lights twinkling. The living room was packed with bodies.

"The chances," Vicky said, "of not one person here tonight hearing about what happened have dropped to nil."

I carried my tote bag of gifts, and Vicky had grabbed her offerings out of the trunk of the Miata. As we approached the front path, the door to the house flew open and Russ Durham bolted out, pulling on his coat and hopping up and down, trying to get his foot into his boot, as he sprinted in the opposite direction from us.

"Yup," Vicky said. "They know. Good thing Russ didn't see us coming."

We watched as his car careened down the road, going at a decidedly unsafe speed considering the snowy conditions.

"Before we go in," I said, "and we find ourselves swept up in a wave of questions, can I say thank you?"

"For what?"

"For saving me. For saving us. I can't be sure Graham wasn't going to kill us after all. Mrs. D'Angelo was not going to step into that pantry willingly, and I fear what he would have done then."

She linked her arm through mine. "No need to thank me. That's what BFFs do, right? Besides, I haven't thrown a good snowball in years. It felt soooo good. Reminded me of my glory years on the softball team at Rudolph High. Never mind snowball fights with my cousins on nights exactly like this one."

The snow had stopped, and the clouds cleared. I stopped walking and gazed up at the stars sprinkled across the night sky and breathed in the cold, clean, crisp air. "I can't help feeling slightly sorry for Graham Johannesen."

"I can. No problem at all. Why?"

"He spent years obsessing about that money under the floorboards, scheming of a way to get into the house and have the time to do what he needed to do. Finally, he did get into the house. He killed Raquel. Then he left. Without bothering to go down into the basement to see thousands of dollars neatly stacked in boxes."

"But that was fake money. The stuff he was after was real."

"Real, yes, but most of it is more than twenty years old. As much as forty, Mrs. D'Angelo said. No one takes much cash anymore, and if someone's handed an old bill, they might reject it. Take it all to the bank, and they're going to want to know where it came from. Banks are concerned about money laundering, not bills gathered up from under the floorboards, but the effect would have been the same. Unlikely Graham would have had time to spend his long-awaited inheritance. That money did—does—belong to Beth Torrone. She inherited the house, which I assume means she inherited all the contents as well. Hidden and unhidden."

"Why do you suppose Graham left after killing Raquel without searching for what he was after?"

"I have no idea. From what he said, he didn't go to the house with the intention of killing her but to ask her to let him spend some time alone in it. We don't know what she said to him, but she refused. It was rather a strange request, wasn't it? It's possible she mocked him. She was not a nice person, remember, although I do believe she redeemed herself at the end when she refused to kill Mrs. D'Angelo. If she laughed at Graham, he might have gotten so angry he lashed out. Whether or not he intended to kill her at that moment is for the courts to determine. Likely he realized what he'd done, intentional or not, and fled in sheer panic. Maybe when he confronted her, she told him her partner was due back any minute and he believed her, so he was afraid of being discovered if he started the search. And then, once he was safely home and no one came after him for the killing, he figured he was in the clear and made plans to get access to the house."

* * *

The door to my parents' house was unlocked, and Vicky and I walked in. Boots were piled high in the front hall, and the closet jammed with coats, hats, and scarves. The sound of conversation and laughter was earsplitting, and the scent of various perfumes mingled with scented candles. In the living room, the huge tree was laden with sparking lights and colorful decorations. Some of those decorations had been made by my siblings and me and proudly carried home from school; many were gifts from Mom's vocal students. The tree was topped with a silver star inherited from my paternal grandparents, and gaily wrapped packages were piled beneath. The big brick fireplace contained cheerfully burning logs; a row of freshly cut greenery interwoven with red ribbon draped the mantel, and while candles in silver and crystal candlesticks of varying heights burned on the top.

As expected, the moment Vicky and I stepped into my parents' party, we were barraged with questions.

"No comment," Vicky said as she sailed through the elegantly dressed crowd in search of our hostess. "Police orders."

My dad almost dragged me into the kitchen, not even giving me time to put my gifts under the tree. Provided I could find room. Eve followed us. Mom was occupied with regaling a crowd of onlookers with the story of when she appeared in *Aida* on Christmas Eve in New York City. Early in her career, she was due to sing a minor role but she was the understudy for Amneris, and she was called upon to take the part at the last minute when the singer became ill. I'd heard the story before. More than once.

"They said she had a sore throat, but everyone knew she'd been on an almighty bender the night before because she found out that her lover, who sang Radamès, had been sleeping with a member of the chorus since first rehearsal."

"What on earth have you been up to?" Dad demanded once we were alone in the kitchen. My mother wasn't much of a cook (truth be told, she wasn't any sort of a cook), and my father specialized in hearty meals for a family with four kids, so as usual when they entertained, dinner had been catered and would be served buffet style. The countertops were covered with casserole dishes, bowls of salads, and trays of canapés. I recognized the enormous platters of cookies and squares as coming from Vicky's.

"Did they get the person who killed Raquel?" Eve asked.

"Yes. The police have arrested Graham Johannesen, her cousin."

"Who's he?" Eve said.

"The guy from Muddle Harbor?" Dad said.

"Yes. Look, I'd rather not talk about it. Not tonight. Not much is going to happen until tomorrow, probably the day after tomorrow, and tonight I want to kick back and enjoy the party. Okay?"

Dad wrapped me in a hug. Eve joined in. "Okay," they said.

"Where's Alan?" Eve asked.

"In the bathtub, most likely. And that is another story."

Chapter
Twenty-Eight

The day after Christmas, I was in the shop early, putting up the sale signs and checking that selected items were priced accordingly.

As expected, I'd spent most of the Christmas Eve party fielding questions about what happened at the Johannesen house. From what I overheard, Mrs. D'Angelo had gone "incommunicado" and was not answering her phone. So suspicious was that, I was grilled as to whether or not she'd been arrested as the mastermind of the counterfeiting organization.

As I headed for the buffet table for another helping (ever mindful to keep room for a piece of shortbread or a mince tart, maybe both), I overheard one elderly woman say to an equally elderly man, "Donalda Reynolds, who lives almost next door, says the attic was stacked to the roof with gold bullion."

"Heavens!" her friend replied. "I can't believe it."

"You shouldn't," I said.

They both turned to me, eyes alight with anticipation. "What do you know, Merry? You were there, isn't that right?"

"All will be revealed in the fullness of time," I said. "Russ Durham should have the story out shortly."

"But the paper doesn't come out for another two days!" the man said.

"My grandson, Edward, that's Rosealee's boy, such a lovely young man, did I tell you he plays fullback for Rudolph High?"

"Several times. What about him?"

"He'll help me get on the Twitter tomorrow, and we can see what the true story is."

I chuckled and hurried on my way. Jim Morrow, husband of mayor Sue-Ellen, was moving in on the last slice of chicken pot pie, and I was determined to get there before him.

Christmas Day had been as lovely as I'd hoped, despite the malodorous odor emanating from Ranger every time he moved (and considering Ranger is a young Jack Russell, he moves a lot). Also despite the slightly less malodorous odor clinging to Alan. He'd scrubbed and lathered himself so thoroughly he had a lovely pink glow about him and his blond hair resembled a halo.

Mattie had recoiled in horror, first from dog and then from man, but eventually he decided the situation wasn't so bad it should be allowed to interfere with his day, and the two dogs bounded across the yard to play. Well, Ranger bounded. Mattie meandered.

Alan stood a careful arm's length away from me as we watched the dogs. He stretched out his arm and tentatively put a hand on my shoulder. "If I'm too close, tell me."

I pulled him into me. "I'd prefer it you don't have another encounter, but you're not too bad."

"Gee, thanks." He returned the hug and nuzzled my hair.

I prepared brunch while Alan entertained the dogs. He came in, ruddy faced, slightly less pink, rubbing his hands together, and I handed him a mimosa.

"How was the party last night? I still have gifts for your parents, so we should drop around sometime."

"Party was good. Half the town came."

"Par for the course."

"Food was great. They tried that new catering company for the appetizers and main course, and they were pleased with it. Vicky did the desserts. I managed to slip a couple of pieces of shortbread into a paper napkin. They're on the counter."

"Nothing says Christmas like Vicky's shortbread." If he'd been Mattie, he would have drooled in anticipation. Instead Alan simply patted his flat belly.

I handed him a plate of toast. "Aren't you going to ask me about what happened last night? I'm fine, as you can see. I'm dealing with it okay."

He put the toast on the table and swung around to face me. Shortbread temporarily forgotten, his expression had turned serious. "What happened last night? Why would you not be fine?"

"You don't know? I thought you were being considerate of my feelings, realizing I might not want to talk about it."

"I repeat: What happened last night? Something at the party? Are your parents okay?"

"You haven't had the radio on this morning? Or checked online sources?"

"It's Christmas Day, Merry. I slept in, had a shower, called my folks to wish them a good day, then a quick walk with

Ranger—keeping my distance, I might add. In case I hadn't kept enough distance from him, I had yet another shower, and then I heard your car. I intend to spend the entire day with the woman I love. I have no desire to have that spoiled by the news."

I decided to think later about the phrase *the woman I love*. That was typical Alan. He lived in the moment, at the moment. One thing at a time. I said, "Take a seat. Breakfast is ready, and do I have a story for you."

I told the story as we ate. Alan shook his head. "The things you and Vicky get up to. After all that, you're okay?"

"I'm okay. I went to the party and spent so much time trying not to talk about what happened, I was able to put it aside. And now I'm here. I've talked about it, and now I can put it aside once again."

After we'd eaten and tidied up, Alan tossed more birch logs onto the fire, and we cuddled together on the soft leather couch to exchange gifts. Mattie settled at our feet and promptly went to sleep, while Ranger dashed from one window to the other to see if he could spot any birds coming to the feeders or squirrels raiding said feeders.

Alan read the Yuletide Inn gift certificate and said, "My mom will enjoy a night out with me."

I tried not to express my disappointment too visibly, and Alan laughed. "She'd enjoy it, but considering they're in Florida for the winter, I guess I'll have to take you."

"If it's not too much trouble," I said.

"Never, Merry, never." He rummaged around under the tree and came up with a large, extravagantly wrapped package tied with an enormous gold bow. He handed it to me, all grins.

I accepted it and grinned back. The package was so light, I knew it wasn't likely to be a kitchen appliance or a garden gnome. I untied ribbons and removed the paper. I dug though layers upon layers of tissue paper to discover . . . a gift certificate to the restaurant at the Yuletide Inn.

"Great minds," Alan said, "think alike. Although you can take your mom, if you'd rather."

"Maybe not."

"Now, how about a walk in the woods?"

It had been the perfect Christmas Day.

But even the most perfect of holidays ends, and it was back to work the following morning.

Back to work not only for me but also for Detective Diane Simmonds. She phoned me as I was telling Jackie what the day's discount items would be.

"I need you to come in and give me a statement, Merry," Simmonds said.

"Can't you come here?"

"Let's do this properly and formally. I had to talk to Mrs. D'Angelo over the phone, which is never ideal. She's still at her sister's place. I had Vicky Casey in earlier. She was kind enough to bring a basket full of pastries and those wonderful individual breakfast bread puddings for us hard-working cops."

Was that a hint? I wondered what I could offer as a bribe. A tree ornament discounted to $9.99? Should I bring just one bribe for the detective, or did everyone working today need something?

Simmonds chuckled. "She was kind enough after I had a civilian clerk call with the order and pay for it on my dime. If I come to your place, Merry, you'll be distracted. I'd prefer to have the conversation here. Hold on, I'm getting an interesting text. Some stuff was delayed yesterday because of the holiday, but it's all coming together now. Let's delay our chat for a couple of hours, and as an incentive, I might have some information to exchange in return for your statement."

"Okay," I said.

"If you don't hear from me otherwise, be here at noon." She hung up.

"Sorry, Jackie." I emitted a martyred sigh once I'd put away my phone. "I've been summoned to the police station for later today. I argued, but I can't get out of it."

"Didn't sound like much of an argument to me. I read all about it in the online paper. Some guy from Muddle Harbor killed Raquel." Jackie shook her head. "My dad says it just goes to show. You and your dad shouldn't have been so quick to try to make friendly with them."

"That had absolutely nothing to do with us. Raquel died before we went to that meeting."

"Dad says Rudolph folk can never trust a Muddite."

"Remind him Raquel hadn't lived in Rudolph for years."

"Once a Rudolphite, always a Rudolphite, Dad says."

I didn't care for the sound of that. My father was working hard, with nothing but the best of intentions, to smooth things over between the two feuding towns. Did Graham Johannesen's actions threaten to scupper it? "That's what your dad thinks. What do you think, Jackie?"

"My mom says my dad's an old fool. He never did get over placing a distant third in the 4-H club's heaviest-pumpkin contest when he was fourteen. Second place wouldn't have been too bad, but a couple of kids from Muddle Harbor took both first *and* second places. To make things even worse, the first-place winner was a girl. I think my mom's right. We've had our fair share of miscreants from Rudolph, right?"

"Right." I started to head for the door and then hesitated. "How was your . . . uh, Christmas?"

Jackie fingered the necklace at her throat. A short but heavy silver chain, holding a large green stone nestling in the gap at the bottom of her throat. She lifted her right arm and tucked a length of hair behind her ear. The thick silver band on her wrist was inlaid with similar green stones. "It was fine. We went to Uncle Jerry and Aunt Beatrice's for Christmas Eve, which was as awful as it usually is. Christmas Day I went around to my parents' place for brunch and presents. Silly me, I forgot to tell Mom to uninvite Kyle."

"Very forgetful of you."

"As long as he'd gone to all the trouble to buy presents for my folks and then to come to the house, I decided I'd give our relationship another try." She touched the necklace again. "I mean, he did bring them some nice gifts. Plus he had a little something for me. It wouldn't have been in the true spirt of Christmas for me to order him to leave, now, would it, Merry?"

"Most definitely not."

"Not to mention Mom made blueberry pancakes. That's his favorite. Mom asked him if he'd heard that someone had been arrested for the murder of Raquel Torrone. He had. Very sad, he said. He was disappointed Russ hadn't called him to come to the scene and take pictures of all the activity."

* * *

I did not hear from Detective Simmonds to the contrary, so at noon I went to meet with her. The Rudolph police always attempt to do what they can to keep up the Christmas

286

spirit. They try, but a police station isn't known for being a cheerful place. Nevertheless, white fairy lights flickered around doorways and plastic wreaths hung on doors. The fake tree (a sacrilege anywhere else in Rudolph) was dusty and showed evidence that once upon a time a family of mice had gotten into the box, but it was gaily trimmed. Some of the desks were adorned with children's handmade decorations, which look absolutely adorable and always perfect wherever they're displayed.

Diane Simmonds, coffee cup in hand, met me at the door and led me to an interview room. It was the "nice" interview room, but nothing had been done in here to meet the spirit of the season.

I took a seat, refused a glass of water or a coffee, and started by asking her if she'd had a nice Christmas. She had, she told me, quiet and peaceful with just her and her daughter and her mother. A fun afternoon of skating in the park and enjoying the toboggan hill. Social formalities over, I began to talk about the events of Christmas Eve night and my line of thinking that led to Vicky, Mrs. D'Angelo, and me confronting Graham Johannesen. I talked; she listened and took notes.

When I was finished, she said, "Is there ever any point in me reminding you to call me or one of my colleagues when you have a suspect in your sights?"

I winced. "Sometimes events spiral out of my control."

"Sometimes." She sighed. "Never mind that now. Good job, Merry. Graham Johannesen was nowhere on our radar for the killing of Raquel. No reason he should have been, but you figured it out. The money he was after, by the way, has been recovered from its hiding place and is being held in evidence. The Torrones will get it eventually, as the rightful owners of the property on which it was found, but I can't say when that will happen. Johannesen would have had a lot of trouble, probably more trouble than he would have been capable of dealing with, trying to pass so many old bills without being able to prove where he got them. But, as they are now passing through our hands and we know the providence, the banks should accept them from the rightful heirs."

"How much is there?"

"I can't say. If the bills were all ones—a couple of thousand maybe. If higher denominations, thousands, tens of thousands. Maybe in the hundreds of thousands. All I saw was a stack of old money, and you can be sure that was taken into evidence mighty fast by people far above my pay grade."

"Has Graham confessed? To the killing I mean?"

"He admits he was in the house with Raquel on the day she died. He says he told her about their aunt Dorothy's hidden money and he suggested they split it. She told him she needed to talk to her boyfriend first, and so he, Graham, left, expecting to hear from her later. Next thing he heard, she'd died. He was totally shocked, he says."

"Do you believe him?"

"Of course not. I'm confident we'll get him soon enough. First, he'd been in the company of the dead woman shortly before she was murdered and he didn't bother to come forward to tell us about it. We call that concealing evidence. Secondly, there's no doubt he threatened you and Mrs. D'Angelo. About that, he says he was afraid you'd pin the killing on him, so he tried to warn you off."

I snorted.

"Yup. According to you, Mabel D'Angelo, and Vicky Casey, he told you he killed Raquel and shoved her down the stairs."

I nodded.

"Three witnesses who have no reason to conspire against him. We have good physical evidence too. Forensics found several strands of hair on Raquel's clothes, almost certainly deposited when her body was dragged to the cellar and pushed down the stairs. Short, dark hair, which we know does not belong to Jean-Claude Lefevre. Because of past indiscretions on his part, his DNA is on file. Now we have Graham Johannesen, I'm hopeful we can make a match. If he only spoke to her, as he says, his hair would not have gotten on her. Forensics are going over his place with a fine-toothed comb. Literally. I'm expecting they'll find something of hers on his things that shouldn't be there. Blood spatter can be mighty hard to get out of everything, and even if he had the presence of mind to burn the clothes he was wearing at the time, including coat, gloves, et cetera, residue often manages to transfer itself to things such as car seats."

"Thanks for letting me know." I started to stand.

She grinned at me. "Sit down. That's not all. The Quebec police arrested Jean-Claude Lefevre yesterday. Frank Lopez spoke to their detectives this morning. That's why I delayed talking to you, hoping to have something to tell you. And I do. Lefevre is being very talkative; wisely, he's ready and eager to confess to counterfeiting to get himself out of a potential murder charge. He claims he and Raquel argued on the afternoon of Saturday, December sixth. He walked out of the house and drove away. Raquel was alive at the time he left, and he did not return."

"Does the time of her death back his story up?"

"Only to a limited extent. He crossed the border not long after the time the autopsy estimates Raquel died, but that's not exact. He's lucky we—you—caught Graham, or he would be very much in the frame."

"What's his story? About coming to Rudolph in the first place?"

"Jean-Claude and Raquel had been having an on-again, off-again, on-again relationship for years. Not only as lovers but as partners in crime. He admits to finding many of the marks she made online friends with in order to ask them for money. They worked together as thieves—she was an attractive woman, and apparently he's quite the looker and fancies himself very charming."

"Raquel must have thought so," I said.

"Hard to say in that sort of relationship. Likely they were both only in it for what they could get out of the other. As a couple they could get themselves invited to the sort of parties where people sometimes lose track of their valuables."

"That happens?"

"Apparently, it does. Until the next day anyway, when the guests have dispersed and the hangover has subsided and no one can remember who exactly invited whom. Jean-Claude, despite his continuing relationship with Raquel, is married to a woman by the name of Louisa, and they have two children. Louisa Lefevre, usually called Lou, is not unknown to the NYPD. Anyway, the plan was they would move into a nice house in a nice respectable neighborhood and set up the counterfeiting equipment they'd somehow come into possession of. Jean-Claude and Louisa and their two kids would live in the house and he'd print the money. The family would provide a nice respectable cover to what was going on down in the basement. Jean-Claude and Louisa would make the money between running the kids to school and soccer games and the like. For all I know, Louisa intended to join the PTA. Raquel's role was to distribute the product. That was the plan."

"But . . . ?"

"But. Shortly before moving day, Jean-Claude and Louisa had a major fight, and she kicked him out. Swore she never wanted to see him again. Left him high and dry to stick out like a sore thumb on nice, respectable Broad Street. Directly across the street from none other than Mabel D'Angelo, she of the insatiable curiosity."

"It can't be a coincidence Raquel's parents were the owners of that house."

"It is not. Remember Frank Lopez told us Raquel was always dismissive of Rudolph?"

"She called it a backwater."

"Her mistake. They were looking for a place to run the operation, the sort of house where neighbors would be unlikely to drop by with offers to 'help' them settle in." Simmonds made finger quotations around the word. "Big house, big yard. The sort of neighborhood where people keep themselves to themselves."

I thought of Mabel D'Angelo, Donalda Reynolds, and the rest of their "network."

Simmonds read my mind. "Looks like Raquel misjudged. Badly and fatally."

"Seems a tricky idea anyway. Jean-Claude and Louisa have kids. Kids go to school. They make friends. Invite friends home from school. Talk about what their parents get up to."

Simmonds gave me what I could only interpret as a fond smile. "What an innocent you still are, Merry. And I mean that in a good way. Kids in families like Jean-Claude and Louisa's learn very quickly to keep quiet about what happens at home."

I thought about that for a minute,

"Raquel knew Rudolph," Simmonds continued. "She thought she knew it anyway, a run-down backwater where nothing ever happens. For all her scorn for the town over the years, she must have been keeping up with many of the goings-on. She got word that her aunt's old house was for rent, and she and Jean-Claude figured it would be perfect for their purposes. Maybe she thought she'd be getting one over on her parents, running her criminal operation on their own properly. That we'll likely never know."

"But she was in the house when Mrs. D'Angelo came over, bearing her cookies. And then Graham dropped by. Mrs. D'Angelo says the man she heard arguing with Raquel wasn't Graham."

"It wasn't. It was Jean-Claude. When Louisa and the kids didn't move to Rudolph, Raquel must have realized their plan might not work. People would notice a man living alone on that street, in that big house, and so she came to talk to Jean-Claude about her concerns. We're guessing she didn't tell him she was coming and he was out when she arrived. Or she did tell him and he made himself scarce. He says he told her he had worries about how persistent the neighbors were being. Jean-Claude's a city boy through and through. He relied on Raquel to tell him small-town people keep to themselves."

"And we know how well that worked out for them."

"We do. Then, when he arrived back at the house, he found not only Raquel herself but an unknown woman gagged and tied up and stuffed into the pantry."

"Can I take a guess he didn't approve?"

"He did not. Obviously he hasn't come out and said so, but we're confident Jean-Claude initially wanted to get rid of Mabel. By which I mean kill her. To her credit, Raquel refused. That would be the argument Mabel heard going on in the kitchen."

"One question before you continue. Why did Raquel not take Mrs. D'Angelo's cookies and say she was too busy to talk?"

"We'll never know, not for sure. But, at a guess, she simply panicked. According to Mabel herself, Raquel was in the kitchen when Mabel came knocking. A sudden rap on the door would have given her quite a shock, and she reacted as her instinct instructed her to. Jean-Claude had told her the neighbors threatened to become a problem."

"In that, she was right," I said. "If she opened the door and accepted the cookies, Mrs. D'Angelo wouldn't have simply gone away and never bothered herself with them again."

"We suspect Raquel suggested they pay Mabel to turn a blind eye to what was going on. Jean-Claude didn't buy that—he figured she'd go straight to the police the minute she was released. Even if such hadn't been the case, it's unlikely he was willing to give up any portion of the small income they were going to make on that stupid scheme.

Frankly, I doubt they'd have turned enough of a profit to pay the rent on the house, but never mind that now. Jean-Claude realized the venture was over. One way or another. Raquel had kidnapped a woman, and there was no going back from that. Mabel wouldn't be bought, and she certainly wouldn't simply go on her way and live and let live."

"Jean-Claude didn't kill Raquel, and then Mabel."

"No. I like to think that when push came to shove, he truly wasn't the type. Maybe he actually loved Raquel. Doesn't matter. He walked out, leaving Raquel to tidy up evidence of her own folly. He knew as soon as Raquel released Mabel the police would be after him, so he headed to Canada. Probably hoping to hide out for a while."

"Why didn't he take the money they'd made?"

"He left half of it for Raquel. Her share."

"That was thoughtful of him."

Simmonds grinned. "Maybe there is some honor among thieves after all. The Montreal police found the money in the basement of his father's house. By the way, Jean-Claude asked Frank Lopez if he would ask Louisa to visit him. He wants to try to make it up to her and be a family again."

"What a convoluted mess."

"As we often get with small-time, not-very-smart criminals. Too eager to make a fast buck than take the time to think things through."

"Graham Johannesen wasn't a criminal. Of any sort. Until he wanted what he thought should be his money and Raquel stood in his way of getting it."

"He was smart enough to keep his head down and well out of the line of sight of our investigation. But then, when the house was put up for sale, he realized the time had come to act. For all he knew, the new owners might have planned to do renovations and they'd find the money."

"But once again, Mabel D'Angelo was lying in wait. Like a hunter at a blind."

"I really should try and get her put on the payroll," Diane Simmonds said.

Chapter
Twenty-Nine

By the end of the week, the post-Christmas sales rush was almost over. Time to take a breath, put my feet up, and sit back with a cup of tea.

Until February when the Valentine's Day promotion started.

It's not easy finding a way to combine every holiday with Christmas. But in Rudolph, we do our best. I was thinking of doing something to celebrate the centuries-long success-ful marriage of Santa and Mrs. Claus.

I'd enjoyed a reasonably quiet day at the store, spending much of the time in my office checking out catalogs from my favorite suppliers. I had some ideas for things Alan might consider making for next year, following up on the success of his train sets and the Santa's village.

Vicky bustled into the store as Jackie and I were going through the end-of-the-day routine.

"Finished!" she shouted, arms reaching toward the ceiling.

"Finished what?" I asked.

"The book. All done except for proofreading and a few last-minute design elements. My part is over. No more changes to the recipes."

"Are you happy with it?"

"Yes, I think I am. I had to finally admit three fruitcake recipes might have been too much."

"Fruitcake recipes?" Jackie said. "No one eats fruitcake anymore."

Vicky was all argued out, and so all she did was shrug.

"I'm looking forward to getting a copy," Jackie said. "But cookbooks can be expensive. Will you be offering discounts to close friends?"

"No."

"Oh. That's too bad. It's not like I'm ever going to make anything from it, am I? No one bakes for themselves anymore. I'll buy one for my mom. She likes looking at the pictures in cookbooks. Okay, I'm off. See you tomorrow, Merry. Don't forget, I'm scheduled to come in at noon."

"I am unlikely to forget," I said.

Vicky watched Jackie skip merrily out the door. Kyle leaned against a lamppost, waiting for her. She took his hand, and they skipped merrily down the street together, arms swinging.

"I have," Vicky said, "poured my heart and my soul into that book. At times I feared my marriage wouldn't withstand the strain. At times I feared I wouldn't withstand the strain. And, after all that, Jackie wants to give it to her mother because it has nice pictures."

I laughed. "Never mind Jackie. She was never intended to be your target audience. Plenty of people all across the country are keen home bakers, and they particularly love anything to do with Christmas baking. Did you use Mrs. D'Angelo's cookie recipe?"

"I did. In the notes I mentioned her name. I might have called her the "social heart" of Rudolph. Do you think that was a bit too much?"

"She'll be delighted, you know that. But some people—Donalda comes to mind—might take offense if they consider themselves to be the social heart of Rudolph."

"Donalda should have given me a recipe, then, shouldn't she? What are you up to now?"

"No plans. Just going home. Quiet night in. Is Mark working?"

"Yup. Big New Year's Eve dinner, dinners plural, tomorrow at the inn, so he's got a ton of prep to do as well as cook for a full house tonight."

"Pizza and bad movie?"

"Sounds good."

We both turned at the sounds of hammering on the shop door. I opened it to see my sister Eve. If all the electricity in Upstate New York had gone out at that moment, her smile would have been adequate to illuminate the town.

"You look pleased with yourself," I said.

She skipped merrily into the shop. "Let me remind you, I am an actor, Merry. I can disguise my emotions as and when required."

"No you can't," I said. "Let me guess: you've been called for a second audition for the role you thought was canceled."

"Even better!" she squealed. "I've been offered a major part in a Netflix drama. I'm the murder victim, but I'm not killed until the third episode, so I have plenty of time to shine!"

I was horrified. "I hope you didn't get that part because of recent events here in Rudolph."

She put her hands on her hips and glared at me. "What, you think I can't get a part based on my own talent?"

"I didn't say that. I just said—"

She dropped the pose and laughed. "Kidding. Heavens, Merry. No one in Hollywood would have even heard of that nonsense. They don't care one whit what happens in a small town on the other side of the country. I'm ready to celebrate! Who's with me?"

"Congratulations on the part," Vicky said. "But I'm afraid it's going to be a pizza and bad movie night for us."

"I'm always in for a bad movie. Long as I'm not actually in it, if you get my meaning." Eve laughed again. "Although no pizza for me. Two weeks of Dad's cooking plus all the party food you people eat around here and they'll have to roll me into the gym at home. Good thing I wasn't fitted for my costume before the holidays."

"I might be able to find some limp lettuce leaves in the back of the fridge," I said as I went to the office to get Mattie.

The first thing I noticed as our stretch of the street came into sight was a large *SOLD* sticker plastered across the FOR SALE sign on the lawn of the Johannesen house.

"Sold already," Vicky said. "That was quick."

"Sure was. I hope they're nice, pleasant, boring people. No muss. No fuss. No drama."

The front door of my house swung open as we turned into the driveway and Mrs. D'Angelo popped out. Earbuds in ears, phone in pocket.

"Merry! Vicky! Eve! Just the people I was hoping to see. We're getting new neighbors."

"The house sold quickly," I said. "That'll be a relief to the Torrones."

"Professional couple. Two children. Twins, by the look of it, or very close in age. He looks like some sort of a business executive, and I think she's a lawyer."

"How do you know?" Eve foolishly asked before I could stop her.

"They were at the house this morning, when Marlene put the *sold* sticker up. Took pictures posing in front of the house. He wore a suit and tie—a very nice suit it was too—and a good overcoat. She has that long, thin, expensively dressed look about her. She wore a brown cashmere-and-wool-blend coat with a wide belt and high-heeled brown leather boots. Looked expensive. She had gold earrings and carried a briefcase, more leather, even in a family photo. Yes, almost certainly a lawyer. The children are going to be a handful. Red hair and freckles. A boy and a girl. Might be adopted, as neither of the parents has red hair. They're around seven years old."

The torrent of words continued, and then . . . "Incoming!" Mrs. D'Angelo yelled, grabbing for her phone. "Sorry, Merry, Vicky, I've got to take this. Angela lives next door to Marlene Jones, and Marlene's just driven up. She's sure to have an update."

We left her to her responsibilities.

"I'm guessing Mrs. D. didn't decide to change her ways after the experience with Raquel Torrone," Vicky said.

"So it would appear. Let's take bets on what the new couple actually do for a living. I'm guessing he's a restaurant manager."

"Why?"

"Wearing a suit and tie on the last weekend of the year. And she's some sort of model or maybe a TV personality."

"The kids," Vicky said, "are the sweetest little angels, who'd never even think about putting a foot out of order."

"I wonder if they bake."

"What's that got to do with anything?"

"You can invite them to your book launch."

"Even better," Vicky said, "if she's a TV personality."

"Wait! Wait!" Mrs. D'Angelo ran around the house, and we turned to face her.

"False alarm. It wasn't Marlene who drove up, as Angela thought, but her husband. He'd used Marlene's SUV because he had a load of supplies to pick up at the hardware store. They're planning to renovate their downstairs powder room. Marlene's husband intends to do all the work himself, because it's a slow time at the golf course where he's the manager. Angela figures they'll be flooded out in a week and Marlene will have to call a professional. She's put her cousin on standby. Angela's cousin, not Marlene's. He's a licensed plumber."

I unclipped the leash from Mattie's collar, and, uninterested in the renovation travails of Marlene, he wandered away to have a good sniff around the backyard.

"That's all very . . . interesting," I said. "Did you have something else to tell us?"

"Donalda suggested she and I pay a joint visit to them on moving day. She'll bring a casserole, and I'll provide my famous welcome-to-the-neighborhood cookies. Just in case, she says."

"You and Donalda have made up, then," I said.

"Of course. Mustn't let a minor spat come between friends."

"In case of what?" Eve asked.

"In case they turn out to be criminals, Donalda said. Can't take any chances these days. Not necessary, I told her. I knew, right from the very first, something was wrong in that house. Didn't I, Merry?"

"Yes. You did. And you were right."

"No time to stand around chatting. I have to get ready. Before I go, congratulations, Eve. I'm looking forward to seeing your new show. I love a good thriller myself."

My sister stared at her. "How did you—"

"Have to get ready for what?" Vicky asked.

Mrs. D'Angelo batted her eyelashes. "George is taking me out to dinner tonight."

"That's nice. Any place special?"

"We're going to the Yuletide. It'll be our New Year's Eve. Every place in town will be full tomorrow, and they always put the prices up so much, just because they can. Oh, one more thing, they have a dog."

"George has a dog?" Vicky asked.

"Not him. He always did, for many years, but when the last one crossed the Rainbow Bridge, he decided he was getting too old to take on a new puppy. The new people. A cute little fluffy white thing. It jumped out of the car and almost completely disappeared under the snow. All that stood out was its pretty pink bow."

Mattie stopped sniffing an unseen trail. He lifted his big head and woofed.

A new neighbor. With a girl dog, by the sounds of it.

Recipes

Amaretto Fruit Cake

Not your average fruitcake. Vicky makes this cake for people who say they don't like Christmas cake. It's white in color, for one thing, beautiful with the colored cherries, and well flavored with almonds, amaretto, and brandy.

This is not a difficult recipe at all, but it takes two days of prep and needs to be made about a month or more before enjoying.

Makes 11½ cups of batter; 5 pounds of cake

Fruit

6 ounces golden raisins
4 ounces diced candied citron peel
8 ounces candied red cherries
4 ounces candied green cherries
8 ounces candied yellow pineapple
¼ cup brandy
¼ cup amaretto

Cake

½ cup all-purpose flour
4-ounce package whole blanched almonds
½ cup butter, room temperature

½ cup shortening
1 cup granulated sugar
4 eggs, room temperature
1 teaspoon almond flavoring
2½ cups all-purpose flour
¼ cup brandy
¼ cup amaretto
¼ cup milk
2 ounces ground almonds

Day 1: Place raisins, peel, and whole cherries in a large bowl. Cut pineapple into ½-inch pieces and add to mixture. Pour ¼ cup brandy and ¼ cup amaretto over. Mix thoroughly, cover, and leave overnight.

Day 2: Preheat oven to 275 degrees F. Grease a 6½-inch and a 5-inch round fruitcake pan. Line pans with greased brown paper. Sprinkle ½ cup flour over the fruit and mix to coat fruit. Add whole nuts and mix.

Place ½ cup butter and ½ cup shortening in large bowl or electric mixer. Beat until creamy. Gradually beat in sugar, eggs, and flavoring. Add ¾ cup flour and mix well. Beat in brandy and amaretto. Add another ¾ cup flour and mix well. Add milk and remaining flour. Stir in almonds.

Pour over fruit-and-nut mixture and stir with wooden spoon until mixed.

Turn into pans and smooth tops.

Place pan of water on bottom oven rack. Bake cakes two to three hours until done. The smaller pan might be done earlier, so check.

When done, cakes should be white on top and tooth-pick inserted will come out clean.

Turn off oven and allow to cool for 15 minutes.

Remove from oven, peel off paper, and cool thoroughly.

Wrap in brandy-soaked cheesecloth. Wrap in plastic wrap, foil, or covered container.

Make about one month ahead of serving, and keep checking to make sure the cheesecloth stays moist—baste as needed with amaretto.

Tip: If you don't have fruitcake pans, you can use any size regular cake pans that hold 11½ cups batter. Baking times will need to be altered accordingly (check after 1¼ hours).

Molasses Spice Cookies

These cookies couldn't be easier to make. Any child can do it (with adequate supervision). It's the perfect recipe for letting kids help their families prepare for the holidays. They love getting their little fingers all sticky.

For the adult cook, these are perfect when you're short of time but want something delicious and home baked. No rolling or cutting is required. They keep in a covered container for up to a week and freeze well.

Makes 36 cookies.

Ingredients

1 cup butter, room temperature
1 cup sugar
2 tablespoons molasses
2 teaspoons vanilla
2 eggs, room temperature
2 cups all-purpose flour
2 teaspoons salt
2 teaspoons cinnamon
1¾ teaspoon baking soda
2 cups rolled oats
⅔ cup dried cranberries, chopped
⅔ cup chopped walnuts

Instructions

Mix all ingredients in order given.

Drop by the teaspoonful on a greased cookie sheet.

Bake at 350 degrees F for 10 to 12 minutes.

Sausage and Sweet Potato Soup

Vicky serves this for lunch at the bakery, and it makes the perfect dish for those cold winter nights, or if you've come in from a walk in the snowy woods or maybe skiing or skating. Delicious, hot, and filling.

Makes 8 servings

Ingredients

2 tablespoons extra-virgin olive oil
1 pound sausage (I use hot Italian for a bit of extra heat)
2 medium onions, chopped
2 large garlic cloves, minced
2 pounds sweet potatoes, peeled and cut into ¼-inch-thick slices
1 pound white-skinned potatoes, peeled and cut into ¼-inch-thick slices
6 cups chicken broth
1 5-ounce bag fresh spinach
Salt and pepper

Instructions

Heat oil in frying pan over medium-high heat. Add sausage; cook until brown, stirring often, about 8 minutes. Transfer sausage to paper towels to drain.

Add onions and garlic to pan and cook until translucent, stirring often, about 5 minutes.

In a large stockpot, add all potatoes and broth; bring to boil. Add garlic and onions, scaping browned bits off bottom of frying pan.

Reduce heat to medium-low, cover, and simmer until potatoes are soft, stirring occasionally, about 20 minutes.

Using potato masher, mash some of potatoes in pot.

Add sausage. Stir in spinach and simmer just until wilted, about 5 minutes.

Season with salt and pepper.

Acknowledgments

Many years ago I got the recipe for amaretto fruit cake from Pat Ashforth, a good friend of long standing. Pat loves Christmas almost as much as the people of Rudolph do, and her baking is testament to that.

Many thanks, as always, to Sandy Harding, substantive editor extraordinaire. Sandy always makes my work as good as it can be. I'm grateful to the gang at Crooked Lane Books, Matt Martz in particular, for picking up the series so I (and you) can continue to enjoy the antics of Merry, Mattie, and the gang. And to my agent, Kim Lionetti of Bookends.